SHACKLED

Ashley Maruzzo

CITIOFBOOKS, INC.
3736 Eubank NE Suite A1
Albuquerque, NM 87111-3579
www.citiofbooks.com
Hotline: 1 (877) 389-2759
Fax: 1 (505) 930-7244

Ordering Information:
Quantity sales. Special discounts are available on quantity purchases by corporations, associations, and others. For details, contact the publisher at the address above.

Printed in the United States of America.
ISBN-13:   Softcover   978-1-959682-84-4
               eBook   978-1-959682-85-1

Library of Congress Control Number: 2023903504

Contents

INTRODUCTION

The dead feel no pain...Sonja and Sara were friends since childhood, but their friendship was never as close as Sonja's relationship with her older sister. When the girl's father died in a car accident, Sonja took on the role of mother to her younger sister. She made sure that Sara had everything she needed – even when it came to boys. If they didn't get too serious, Sonja would let them go. But there was one boy who stood out from all the rest: Jens. He was always nice to Sara, and he treated her like a princess. One day, he asked for her hand in marriage. They married at eighteen years old and moved into a small apartment together. The first few months went well until one night, after drinking some wine, Jens confessed his love for Sonja. It seemed so romantic and beautiful at the time. And then things changed between them. Their relationship became more and more violent. Soon, Sara found herself locked up in her room while her husband beat her senselessly. After three years, Sonja couldn't take any more abuse. Her sister begged her not to leave him because she'd lose her home. So, she stayed and tried to make the best of things. Until one day, Jens got drunk and killed himself. His suicide note said that he loved Sonja more than anything else in this world. Sonja was devastated by what happened. She felt guilty about what happened to her sister and blamed herself for what happened. For years, she kept quiet about what had really happened. Then, one night, Sonja finally decided to tell Sara everything. That way, Sara could find peace and move on. Or so she thought. Sonja told her everything – how her husband had beaten her and tortured her with an electric cattle prod; how he'd threatened to kill her if she ever left him. How he'd raped her. She also admitted that she hadn't done enough to protect her sister or stop the violence. Sonja had been trying to protect Sara by keeping her away from the truth. But now, with her death, Sara was free. Free to live without fear and free to start over again. Sonja wanted to die, but she couldn't bring herself to do it. Instead, she turned to alcohol and drugs. She started spending most nights in bars and clubs where she met men. Some were just passing fancies; others were serious relationships. She never learned how to say goodbye to anyone. In fact, she didn't know how to be alone. Sonja spent the next ten years searching for someone who could fill the void inside her heart. Someone who would hold her and comfort her. Someone who would listen to her and give her advice. Someone who would care about her. Sonja fell in love with a man who looked like her brother-in-law. He was kind and gentle. He listened to her and cared about her. He gave her the attention she craved. But the longer she stayed with him, the less she liked him. She knew she should end the relationship, but she couldn't bear the idea of being alone. So, she lied to him. She told him she loved him and promised to stay with him forever. When he found out she'd been lying to him, he threw her out. Sonja was left brokenhearted and desperate. She was tired of living and wanted to die. At last, she found the courage to commit suicide. But before she did, she called her sister. To Sonja, Sara was the only person in this world who truly understood her. Sonja had always tried to keep Sara safe and happy. Now, she hoped that her sister would help her end her life. She hoped that Sara would understand why she had to die. Sonja called Sara and told her she was going to kill herself. She explained that she wanted her sister to watch her die. She told her to come to the house. Sara arrived and saw her sister lying on the floor, dead. She watched as her sister's body began to decay. A few days later, police officers showed up at Sara's door. They arrested her and charged her with her sister's murder. Sara denied killing her sister, but she wasn't given much choice. There was no proof that Sara was innocent. She was convicted and sentenced to life imprisonment.

Sonja was right. She was the only person in this world who truly understood her. Because she was the only person who'd known what it was like to grow up with her. Sonja had lost her father when she was young, and her mother died shortly afterward. She grew up in a foster home, which was full of other children. All the kids were poor and neglected. Sonja had grown up believing that people were cruel and selfish. She believed that everyone around her was just looking out for themselves. This belief led her to become cold and distant toward those who might have helped her. Sonja was bitter and angry. She was afraid to trust anyone. Even her own sister. Sonja's attitude was reflected in her personality. She was hard to talk to and often refused to answer questions. She was also very critical of herself and others. Sonja was convinced that she was ugly and worthless. She hated the way she looked, and she despised her body. She was jealous of her sister's beauty. Sonja was insecure about her looks. She was constantly comparing herself to her sister. She thought Sara was prettier and sexier. Sonja was ashamed of her own appearance and was terrified of showing her face to anyone. She wore heavy makeup and dark clothes to hide her features. She covered her eyes with sunglasses. Sonja was obsessed with her hair. She washed it every day and put it up in elaborate braids and pigtails. She used hairspray to keep her curls in place. She was always combing it and straightening it. She even slept with a brush under her pillow in case she woke up in the middle of the night with tangled hair. Sonja was proud of her ability to manipulate and control people. She had learned early on how to use her looks and charm to get what she wanted. If she wanted something, she'd do whatever it took to get it. She was manipulative and cunning. She'd lie and cheat to get ahead. She was also a compulsive liar. She was good at telling lies. She could tell half-truths and white lies. But she was terrible at telling the truth. She was also quick to anger and had little patience. She was short-tempered and prone to fits of rage. She could be nasty and mean. She was easily hurt and offended, and she held grudges against those who wronged her. Sonja was a bully. She was the queen of underminers. She made fun of and belittled her enemies. She was also arrogant and vain. She always boasted about her beauty and intelligence. She was convinced she was better than everyone else. She was certain that her sister was jealous of her. Sonja was a perfectionist. She was always striving to be the best at everything. She worked harder and pushed herself more than anyone else. She was driven to excel, but she never reached her goals. Sonja was a workaholic. She rarely took time off and she always expected the same from others. She demanded that her employees work overtime without pay, but she wouldn't lift a finger unless she was paid double. She was obsessive. She was inflexible and stubborn. She was a control freak. She controlled everything – her husband, her sister, her friends, her employees, and her business. But she didn't realize how controlling she'd become until she realized she'd lost control of herself.

Sara was the opposite of Sonja. She was soft and sweet. She was kind and generous. She was also shy and timid. She was selfless and caring. She was gentle and patient. She was the opposite of Sonja. Sara was also insecure. She was afraid of rejection and failure. She was also sensitive and easily hurt. She was overly trusting and naïve. She was gullible and easily manipulated. She was a dreamer. She dreamed of having a loving family. Of finding someone who would accept her and treat her like she deserved. But she was too scared to try. So, she remained alone. She lived her life in silence and solitude. Sara had no one to rely on. No one could help her or support her. And so, she relied on herself. She was strong-willed and determined. But sometimes, she found it difficult to make decisions. She was indecisive and lacked confidence. She was a coward. She didn't stand up for herself because she feared losing the people she cared about. Sara was also very insecure about her appearance. She was thin and delicate. Her skin was pale, and her lips were full and red. Her hair was long and wavy. It was thick and healthy. It was her crowning glory. It was beautiful. But it didn't suit her. It didn't look right on her. Sara didn't feel comfortable in her own skin. She felt awkward and uncomfortable whenever she had to show her face to the world. She didn't know how to dress well or wear the right hairstyle. She didn't know how to put on makeup to make her features shine. She was too skinny. She was tall and lanky. She felt that her body was too plain to be attractive. She was jealous of her sister's curves. She wished she had breasts and hips. She thought they'd make her more feminine. She envied her sister's legs. They were long and shapely. She was envious of her sister's figure. She wanted to be as beautiful and sexy as her sister. But she was too afraid to ask her to teach her how to be pretty. So, she spent years hiding behind her glasses and her hair. She was a recluse. She rarely went out of the house. She avoided social events. She spent most nights alone, watching TV. She was afraid of meeting new people. She was anxious and nervous. She hated being the center of attention. She was afraid of being judged. She was afraid of being rejected. She was afraid of being laughed at or mocked. She was afraid of being ridiculed by her peers. She was afraid of being humiliated. She was afraid of her own shadow. She was too frightened to go outside. She was afraid of the world. She was afraid of the future. She was afraid of growing old and dying. She was afraid of becoming invisible. She was afraid of being forgotten. She was afraid of being alone.

The two sisters were opposites in every way. Sonja was the black sheep and Sara was the golden child. Sonja was an outsider. She was a misfit. She was the oddball in the family. The black sheep. Sara was the princess. She was the apple of her parent's eye. She was their favorite daughter. Sonja was a disappointment. She was a mistake. She was a bad seed. Sara was loved. She was adored. Sonja was ignored. She was pitied. She was a burden. She was a problem. Sara was accepted. She was welcomed. Sonja was shunned. She was unwanted. She was a mistake. She was a burden. She was a problem.

Sara was the one who got away with anything. She was the one who always escaped punishment. She was the one who walked free while her sister was sent to prison. Sara was always forgiven and excused. But not Sonja. She was always punished. She was always blamed for everything. She was always wrong. She was always the bad one. She was the one who should have been locked up in jail, not her sister. But she never stood up for herself. She never fought back. She let her sister walk all over her. She didn't deserve to be treated that way. But she never said anything. She didn't want to rock the boat. She was too afraid to lose her sister. She was too afraid to upset her parents. She was too afraid to disappoint them again. Sonja had been through enough already. She didn't need any more trouble in her life. She was tired of fighting for things she couldn't have. She was tired of trying to please people who didn't care about her. Sonja was done with it all. She was ready to give up. She was tired of living. She was ready to die.

I'm standing on the edge of a cliff. I can see the ocean below me. I'm looking down into the deep blue water. It's peaceful and serene. A few boats are sailing along the coast. The sun is shining brightly. It's warm and bright. My toes are numb. I don't know why. I've been walking around in my socks and shoes. Maybe it's the cold. Or maybe it's just nerves. Standing here makes me feel dizzy. It feels like there's a storm brewing. Like a hurricane. But I can't hear thunder or feel raindrops falling on me. Just wind blowing through the trees. Wind whistling through the grass. Wind rustling leaves. Wind blowing across the sand.

Wind rushing through the sea. Wind rushing through the sky. Wind racing to find its way home. Wind rushing to meet the tide. Wind rushing to meet the waves. Wind rushed to catch the moonlight. Wind rushing to find its way home. Wind rushing to find its way home.

Sonja was a little shy around boys. They both loved horror films, so they saw them together all the time when their parents weren't home (they didn't want to be left alone). One day as usual after school, they decided it would be fun if one of them played her favorite scary movie while she made popcorn for everyone else in exchange. Their mother had already gone shopping with her friend so there wasn't anyone at home except each other. The two girls agreed that this sounded like an awesome idea—but then things went horribly wrong! As soon as Sonja put on the VCR, something moved inside the television set itself; before long its head popped out from under the screen! It stared straight into Sonja's eyes... Then suddenly it started talking: "I've been waiting here for you!" Before either girl knew what hit them or could even scream, the monster grabbed hold of each by her neck and dragged them off to some unknown place where only silence remained. Now, these same monsters have returned to claim another victim…

– Excerpted from "The Monster in TV" –

As I entered my house after school, I turned up the volume on the stereo because I wanted to hear more about the new album coming out next week. When the door slammed shut behind me, the music stopped playing automatically without warning. In fact, nothing happened at first until a deep voice began speaking over top of the song—"You're mine now." Suddenly everything felt very cold and damp—and I heard a strange noise like someone whispering right above me. My heart pounded loudly in my chest. This is too much, I thought. But then I realized how silly it really was—how stupidly clichéd—so I tried not to let myself panic. So far, no harm has come to any member of our family anyway, I reminded myself again. After all, we haven't seen anything yet.

Then I looked down at the floor just outside the kitchen doorway. There lay three bloody handprints smeared across the linoleum. At least that explained why the radio cut out. And the blood? Well, I figured maybe one of us dropped some food or something on ourselves during lunchtime today—it happens sometimes. With such thoughts racing through my mind, I walked slowly toward the living room to see who might have done this horrible thing. That's when I noticed a large object sitting atop a chair near the window overlooking the backyard. From afar, I couldn't tell exactly what it was, but upon closer inspection, I quickly recognized it as a human foot. Not knowing whether it belonged to Mr. P., Mrs. S.—or possibly even me—my stomach twisted painfully as I ran back downstairs to grab a flashlight and run upstairs once again. Sure enough, there sat Mr. P.'s body slumped over his desk, lifeless. He must have fallen asleep working late tonight and died of a heart attack. Or perhaps he tripped and fell onto the corner of the table. Either way, there was certainly no need for alarm. Besides, it wouldn't do any good to call the police anyway because neither of those people are missing anymore.

Sonja Hemingway: An actress best known for playing the female lead opposite Jack Nicholson in his Oscar winning portrayal of John Nash in A Beautiful Mind. She currently stars in a popular daytime soap opera called 'Love Is in Bloom', where she plays a character named Rebecca Shaw. Sonja loves working on television shows because they don't require her to go out anywhere except to the studio every morning and evening. But what she likes even better than acting is writing scripts herself so that someday others can enjoy her work as well. Her husband, Tom, works in sales and makes quite a bit of money selling office supplies throughout the country. While most husbands find themselves jealous of their wives' success, Tom encourages his wife to pursue whatever career path she feels drawn towards. Both love horror movies and often watch them together whenever possible. On occasion, however, Mr. and Mrs. Hemingway will invite their son David along to join in the fun. Unfortunately, David doesn't share his parents' enthusiasm for horror films and usually spends his evenings reading comic books instead. His father finds this extremely disappointing given the kind of man his brother should become someday.

Mrs. S.: A former model who retired from modeling several years ago due to health reasons. Since then, she has devoted herself to raising her daughter, Sara. Despite being married for many years,

Mrs. S. still looks great thanks to regular trips to the gym and daily visits to the beauty salon. Of course, her age-defying appearance also helps tremendously; especially considering that she's never had plastic surgery despite numerous requests from fans. To date, Sarah continues to follow in her mother's footsteps, pursuing a successful singing career with songs written exclusively by her mom. These include hits such as "Don't You Forget About Me", "It's Only Rock & Roll"—as well as her latest single "Mother Should Have Told Me".

Mr. P.: A senior vice president at a major corporation who lives life to the fullest.

But dreams can crash harder than airplanes

And leave wreckage strewn across the sky

They'll take your hopes and turn them to dust

So, wake up, get dressed, brush your teeth

Make sure you look sharp

Because everybody wants to know

Who you are underneath

Now who am I? Who do you think I'm supposed to be?

Sara Hemingway: Sixteen-year-old high school student. Very talented singer/songwriter. Has won awards for her vocal performances at local competitions. Recently released her debut album entitled 'When I Grow Up'. Daughter of Sonja and Tom Hemingway.

Of all the places we've ever met,

There's none like home sweet home

Home sweet home...

ONE

S he glanced over at the clock on her nightstand.

She was a professional singer and songwriter—just like her mother. Sara liked performing in front of audiences, although she did prefer small venues rather than big concerts filled with screaming crowds. She enjoyed having close contact with her audience, which gave her the opportunity to talk to them directly afterwards. Often, she'd ask questions about the meaning of certain lyrics or what kinds of feelings they hoped to convey when listening to her music. Although her answers varied greatly depending on the person asking the question, she always took the time to answer sincerely. Sometimes people told her how her words helped them cope with personal issues in their own lives. Other times, they simply said thank you. Whatever the case, Sara found it comforting to interact with her listeners afterward. Perhaps that's why she chose to spend so much of her free time doing so.

She solved cases in her spare time, too.

That's what detectives do, isn't it?

Even though she preferred solving mysteries in real life to watching them on TV, she occasionally caught episodes of Law & Order or CSI. She particularly enjoyed the ones that dealt with serial killers because she got to learn lots of interesting facts and details that otherwise might not have occurred to her. For example, did you know that a killer's brain contains approximately five million synapses per square centimeter compared to ten thousand in humans? How fascinating! Yet another reason why I love my job, she mused.

Her bedside lamp burned brightly against the darkness of the bedroom. Its soft light revealed the figure lying beside her—her dad sleeping soundly. Like his sister, he worked hard every day to provide for the entire family.

He loved her dearly, just as his wife did.

Even though her mother had recently passed away, Sara continued to live at home because her father insisted on it. Even after all these years, he still believed strongly in the importance of staying true to one's roots—no matter what obstacles may lie ahead. He was proud of his children and wanted them to remain part of the family unit, even if it meant giving up a portion of his privacy. In return, Sara promised him she would continue to write songs for the rest of her life and make sure to keep in touch with everyone who supported her musical efforts. If there was one thing her father taught her early on, it was that nothing in life comes easily—especially fame and fortune. It takes years of dedication, perseverance and sacrifice to reach the heights one desires.

What went wrong? I thought as the first of my men arrived at the scene. It was a question that had haunted me ever since we'd discovered the body, and it would continue to haunt me until someone found the answer.

I stood in the middle of the street, staring down at the dead woman's face. The police were still working on her, but she looked like one of those women you see every day—a housewife with no distinguishing features beyond her age and gender. She could have been anyone's mother or sister, daughter, or wife. But now she was just another victim of domestic violence. And all because I hadn't done enough.

"The killer is still out there," I said quietly, looking around at the other officers who were also standing around, waiting for news about the case. "He knows what he did." He knew how close he came to getting caught. Now his next victim might be someone else's mother or sister, daughter, or wife. Or maybe even mine.

Someone called from behind me. "Chief?" A young officer was holding up a piece of paper. "This note was found inside the apartment when we searched it." He handed over the sheet. On it was scrawled a message: "You're next."

"That's not good," I said. "We need to find him before he strikes again."

"It's going to take time to identify this woman," the sergeant told me. "And then we'll have to wait for forensics to confirm our suspicions."

"Forensics can do better than that these days," I said. "They've got DNA databases that are almost infallible."

"Yes, Chief, they can. But the problem is that we don't know exactly where the blood sample came from. We only know that it belongs to the victim."

"So, we need more information. More clues."

A few people nodded their heads.

"How many times has this happened here in town?" I asked. "Domestic violence cases, that is."

"Two so far this year," an officer replied.

"But most of them aren't reported," another added. "Most of the victims keep quiet."

I turned away from the crime scene and stared at the houses lining the street. They were all different colors and sizes, but they were all built along similar lines. Some had balconies; some didn't. Many of them had gardens outside. All of them were full of families with children, living ordinary lives.

Then I remembered something else. There was a second note left at the murder site. One of my men had found it under the victim's hand. It read: "Don't tell the police. Don't call the police. You're next."

Now I understood why the killer had sent the letters. He wanted to warn his potential victims. He knew that if he killed them, word would get out. So instead, he tried to scare them into silence.

I glanced back at the house where the body lay. If I'd been able to save one person, one family, wouldn't it have made a difference? Wouldn't it make all the hours I spent sitting alone in my office worthwhile? I was a cop. That was what I was supposed to do. Protect the community. Stop the criminals. Keep the streets safe. But I couldn't protect any of them. Not this time.

I looked at the faces of my colleagues around me. They were all watching me intently. As much as they respected me, they were all wondering whether they should believe what I was saying.

"If you want to catch the bastard, we need to go after him hard," I said. "Right now. Before he kills again."

Everyone agreed with me.

I watched the last of the officers leave the crime scene. Then I walked slowly towards the house where the victim lived. My mind was racing. What kind of man could kill a woman like that? How could he look at her and think that she deserved such a violent death?

As I approached the front door, I saw a small crowd of residents gathered by the road. They were talking excitedly among themselves.

"She must have seen him coming," someone shouted. "Maybe she ran out of the house. Maybe she screamed and he killed her."

"No way, he probably beat her to death. No woman would run away from him."

"Maybe he choked her to death. Or strangled her."

"Or maybe he hit her with a hammer."

"Or maybe he used a knife. Like the serial killer in New York."

"There's nothing to say she fought back. Maybe she was too scared to fight. Maybe he threatened to hurt her kids."

"You can't blame her for being afraid of him. Who wouldn't be?"

My heart sank as I heard the voices of the locals. I could understand their fear. After all, domestic violence is a huge issue in the area. It happens everywhere, all the time. Men batter their wives and girlfriends, children are beaten by their parents, and sometimes, the violence goes beyond the home. In the past, I've even known a couple of men who've murdered their partners.

But none of that was true for this woman. She was just another victim. And yet, everyone seemed to think she was responsible.

I knocked on the door.

"Police!" I shouted. "Open up."

After a few seconds, the door opened. An old man with white hair appeared. His eyes were red and swollen. He was wearing a pair of baggy jeans, a black T-shirt, and a jacket.

"Can I help you, Officer?" he asked.

"We need to talk," I replied. "Is your wife inside?"

"Who wants to know?"

I took off my hat. "Chief O'Brien."

His eyes widened in surprise. He stepped aside and waved me inside.

"Come on in," he said. "Let's sit down."

He led me through the hallway into a large room. The walls were covered with photos. Most of them showed the same woman. She smiled brightly, showing her teeth. She was clearly proud of the family she'd created. But the pictures also revealed the bruises on her face.

"Your wife?" I asked.

"Yeah, she's upstairs."

"Was she the victim of domestic abuse?"

"Not really."

"Why not?"

"Well, she's a fighter, that's why."

"Really?"

"Yes."

"How long has this been happening?"

"About two years now."

"When was the first time?"

"Last week."

"And how did it start?"

"With a kiss."

"Kissing?"

"Yes. He kissed her and she slapped him across the face. He grabbed her arm and twisted it. She fell to the floor, and he kicked her in the stomach. She curled up on the ground and cried. But then she got up again, picked up a broom, and started hitting him."

"Where's the husband now?"

"In jail."

I looked at the photographs. "You mean he's been arrested?"

"For assaulting her."

"Did they press charges against each other?"

"Of course not. Why would we?"

"Because it was a mutual assault," I explained. "It was both of them who attacked the other. The law doesn't distinguish between the aggressor and the victim."

The old man shook his head. "I don't understand. It wasn't mutual."

"The woman was defending herself. And that's what counts."

"But she shouldn't have to defend herself. He's the man in the relationship. He should be protecting her. Isn't that, right?"

"Sometimes that isn't possible," I replied. "Especially when the woman is older than the man. Or when she's a single parent. Or if she has a disability. Or if she's pregnant. Or married to a violent man."

The old man frowned. "But domestic violence is a crime. We don't tolerate that sort of thing here."

"Domestic violence is a serious crime, but it's also a pattern of behavior. And patterns change. Sometimes, the violence stops completely. Other times, there may be less severe assaults. Or maybe just a few verbal threats."

"That's not good enough," he said. "Women need protection."

"Protection is important. But so is justice. Domestic violence is often rooted in a history of abuse. The victim needs to feel safe. If she feels safe, she'll come forward and report what happened to her. If she comes forward, we can arrest the perpetrator and put him in prison where he belongs. Then he can't threaten or harm anyone else."

The old man looked at me intently. He was thinking about what I'd said. He was considering the possibility that his wife might have been abused by the man she loved. He was also wondering whether it was fair that his wife had defended herself when he couldn't.

He finally spoke. "What about the children? What about the kids?"

"Children learn from their parents," I told him. "If you teach them that women are inferior, they will grow up believing that women deserve to be treated badly. That's why you must teach them differently. You must show them that domestic violence is wrong. Show them how much you love your wife. Teach them how to treat her with respect. Be the best father you can be. Your kids need you."

"But what about his rights? He's the man. He's the breadwinner. Shouldn't he be allowed to hit his wife?"

"That's not the point."

"But he's the man in the relationship."

I sighed.

"You need to stop this," I told him. "Otherwise, we won't get anywhere. This guy is dangerous. He knows what he's doing. He uses his power over her. He makes her dependent on him. He threatens her and tells her he'll hurt her family. But he can't do anything if she refuses to give in. He needs her to submit. Otherwise, he loses control. He can't beat her. He can't choke her. He can't use a knife. He can't cut her. But he can do this."

I pointed at the photograph of the woman in the wheelchair.

"This is what he does. And he's going to keep doing it until someone stops him. Until you do something."

He didn't reply.

I left the house and went downstairs. When I reached the street, I saw a crowd of people standing by the road. I joined them. They were all looking at something.

They were staring at a young girl who was lying motionless in the middle of the street. She was wearing a pink dress, but she had no shoes. Her hair was short and brown; her skin was pale. She was asleep.

I walked closer and saw that the little girl was naked from the waist down. Blood had dried on her legs. Someone had drawn a red line around her private parts with chalk. There was another red mark on her chest. It looked like an arrowhead pointing towards her neck.

Someone pushed me away from the child. I turned around. It was Chief O'Brien.

"Get out of here," he said. "Go home. Go back to your office."

"What happened?"

"Just go."

I looked back at the girl. The blood was still fresh. The chalk lines were still visible. There was a deep gash in the side of her throat.

"What did this to her?"

"A man. A monster," he said. "He slit her open from groin to neck."

I returned to my office and sat down behind my desk. I stared at the phone for a while before picking it up. I knew I needed to call the hospital and tell them that I wanted to speak to the doctor who examined the body. I also needed to find out where the autopsy had been performed.

I called the hospital. They told me that Dr. Morgan was busy with another case and would only be available later that day.

Then I called the morgue. They told me that the body had been sent to the coroner. I asked them to send the pathologist to see me.

Dr. Morgan arrived a few minutes after I rang the doorbell. He was wearing a blue suit, with a white shirt and a red tie. He was carrying a file folder. He placed it on the table and opened it.

"Mr. Prendergast," he began, "please allow me to introduce myself. My name is Dr. Alan Morgan. I'm one of the medical examiners in charge of investigating all cases of sudden deaths in the county."

"Good morning, Doctor."

"Are you ready for today's autopsy?"

"Yes, sir."

"Okay. Let's begin."

Morgan removed the sheet covering the dead girl. He pulled away the blanket. Then he peeled away the tape holding her hands together. He lifted the corpse off the trolley and laid it carefully on the floor. He opened the front of her dress. He checked her private parts. Then he moved her arms, checking the joints. He examined her face, pulling back her eyelids, pressing gently on her cheeks, and running his fingers along her jawline. Finally, he probed her neck.

"She looks like she died yesterday," Morgan muttered. "Her face is still warm. But her heart has stopped beating. She must have been dead for some time. Maybe even several days."

"How could she die without any external injuries?"

"There are many ways," he replied. "Heart attack. Stroke. Poisoning. Suicide. Sudden cardiac arrest. Even drowning. But most of these cause obvious signs of death. Not this."

"What do you mean?"

"I've never seen anything like it. She was murdered. No doubt about it. But how? How did she end up in the street?"

"Could it have been suicide?"

"No. There's nothing in her head to suggest that. And she didn't drown herself in the bathtub. The water level in the tub was low. It hadn't been used recently. And there was no sign of trauma to the body."

"So, what happened? Did she fall into the river?"

"Maybe. It's possible. The currents in the Hudson River can be quite strong. But the police found no evidence of that. And we haven't received any reports of a missing person. So that's unlikely."

"Do you know why she was naked?"

"I don't think so."

"But you're sure it wasn't sexual abuse?"

"Sexual abuse? Yes, of course. But not because of what happened to her genitals. Sexual abuse is usually done to girls as young as five years old. This was an adult woman. She was raped. Sexually assaulted. Probably repeatedly. But rape is not always accompanied by physical violence. Rape is often just about humiliation. About humiliating the victim. That's what happened here. This woman was humiliated. She was violated. She was tortured. She was killed."

"Who did it?"

"I don't know yet. We'll look at the forensic examination. That will help us identify the perpetrator. In the meantime, I want you to take a statement from Mrs. Neely. I need to talk to her. I need to ask her questions. I need to hear her story. I need to understand how this happened. Do you agree?"

"Absolutely," I said.

Morgan nodded and picked up his file. "Let's go then. I'll drive. You can sit next to me."

We drove to the apartment building. It was early afternoon now. Traffic was light. We parked near the entrance and walked inside. Morgan knocked on the door of the second-floor flat. The woman who answered the door was dressed in a floral print dress. She had a baby strapped to her chest.

"Mrs. Neely," said Morgan. "My name is Dr. Alan Morgan. I'm one of the medical examiners investigating the death of your daughter. Can I come in?"

The woman looked at him with wide eyes. Then she stepped aside and let him enter the room.

The place was small and neat. There was a double bed, a television set, and a sofa. There were two chairs. One was covered with a red blanket. There were bookshelves full of books and magazines. There were also framed photographs of children and grandchildren. Two paintings hung above the fireplace. They depicted the same scene: a group of men and women sitting around a campfire, drinking beer, and singing.

The woman followed Morgan into the living area. She stood at the doorway.

"Can I offer you some tea or coffee?" she asked.

"Please, no."

"Would you like to sit down?" she added.

"Thank you, but we need to hurry."

The woman nodded and sat down on the sofa. She looked uncomfortable. She seemed nervous. Her eyes darted between Morgan and me. She didn't say a word.

Morgan closed the door. He took out his notebook and pen. He opened the file folder and pulled out the sheet with the girl's picture. He held it up for the mother to see.

"Your daughter," he began, "was found dead in the street yesterday. She was naked from the waist down. Her private parts had been mutilated with a sharp object. Someone drew a red line around them with chalk."

"What do you mean?"

"It's probably best if I show you."

He handed the sheet to the woman. She glanced at it briefly. Then she folded the paper and put it in her pocket.

"Why would anyone do that to her?" she asked quietly. "What kind of sicko would do that to a child?"

"I don't know yet," Morgan replied. "But I'll find out."

"How?"

"With your help."

He turned to me.

"I'd like you to interview Mrs. Neely. I need to know everything she can remember about her daughter. I need to understand what happened here. What happened to her. I need to know how this could happen. I need to understand why someone would do such a terrible thing. I need to understand if this could have happened anywhere else. To any other child."

"I can do that," I said.

"And I want you to be careful, Mr. Prendergast. Don't make assumptions. Don't jump to conclusions. Ask her all the questions and listen carefully to her answers. And don't leave until you've finished talking to her. Understand?"

"Of course," I said.

"Good. Now, I'm going upstairs. You stay here. Keep an eye on her. Make sure she doesn't run away. If she tries, stop her. Tell her I'll return soon."

Morgan left. He climbed the stairs. A moment later he returned with a uniformed officer. The policeman escorted Mrs. Neely downstairs. He led her through the lobby and out onto the street. Morgan waited outside.

Chief O'Brien was waiting for me when I got home. He was standing in the hallway. His face was pale.

"Did you get my message?" he asked.

"Yes."

"I want you to meet me in my office right now."

"Sir?"

"Right now. Come."

I followed him up to his office. He locked the door behind us. He sat down behind his desk and looked at me for a while. Then he spoke.

"You know what happened last night?"

"I heard about it," I said. "I saw the body in the street."

"This morning, a man was arrested for the murder of a child. Your friend Dr. Morgan was working on the case. He told me he thought you might be able to help him. I want you to come with me. We need to talk. We need to understand each other better."

"Where are we going?"

"To see your father."

***

I arrived back at the hospital just before noon. Chief O'Brien was already there. He was sitting across from the chief psychiatrist's office. We walked over. The chief unlocked the door. He waved me inside.

"Dr. Prendergast," he said. "Meet Dr. Michael Tilden."

Dr. Tilden was sitting behind his desk. He was wearing a navy-blue suit. He was reading from a file folder. He glanced up as we entered. He was middle-aged, with short dark hair. He wore glasses. His face was wrinkled.

"Mr. Prendergast," he said. "I'm glad to finally meet you."

"Likewise," I replied.

"I understand you're acquainted with Dr. Morgan. That's good news. I hope you can work together on this case. We need to solve it quickly. There's no time to waste. The killer is still on the loose. And he's killing again."

"I understand," I said.

"Now, I'm going to tell you something important. And I want you to keep it in mind. I don't want you to repeat it to anyone else. I don't want you to mention it to the press or to anyone else. Just keep it to yourself and think about it. Okay?"

"Okay."

"When you first came here, I was concerned about you. You seemed distant. Distracted. As though you were somewhere else. Like you weren't here. That's understandable. I know you lost your wife. But you were also suffering from post-traumatic stress disorder. You needed time to recover. Time to grieve. But I wanted you to focus on your job. I knew you could do it. But you couldn't concentrate. You were unable to function. You were having flashbacks. Nightmares. You were terrified. You were afraid of being alone. Afraid of dying. Of hurting someone else. Or maybe even killing someone. That was clear from our conversations. But you didn't seem to realize it. Not yet anyway. And that was worrying me."

"I understand."

"Well, we've been working closely ever since then. We've been trying to understand why you acted the way you did. Why you behaved the way you did. We've been doing a lot of tests. Blood tests. Brain scans. Psychological evaluations. And we've made some progress."

"What kind of progress?"

"I think we may have found the answer."

"Tell me."

"We've found a chemical imbalance in your brain."

"Chemical imbalance? What does that mean?"

"That's what it means."

"Explain."

"A chemical imbalance is when the chemicals in the brain aren't balanced correctly. When they don't react as they should. When they don't perform their functions properly. Chemical imbalances cause all kinds of problems. They affect memory and concentration. They can lead to depression. They can cause panic attacks. They can even trigger violent behavior. We believe you suffer from a chemical imbalance. That's what makes you act the way you do. We need to balance those chemicals. We need to fix what's wrong with you. Otherwise, you'll never be able to function normally. You'll always be prone to violence. To acting without thinking. We need to restore what was destroyed by the trauma you suffered. We need to give you back your sanity."

"How do you plan to do that?"

"There's only one way to do it. We must cure you of your illness. We need to find out exactly where it lies and eliminate it completely. Only then will we know if you're cured or not. Are you ready for this?"

"I'm willing," I said.

"Then I'm going to take you to see Dr. Morgan and Dr. Tilden. They're both specialists in this field. They will examine you. They will try to identify the source of your problem and correct it. Once we have done that, I want you to start working again. I want you to focus on your job and do whatever it takes to help me catch whoever killed this little girl. I want you to do it for me. For the people of New York City. We need to bring him to justice. And I want you to do it because I trust you, Mr. Prendergast. I believe in you. I believe you can do anything."

"Thank you, sir."

Chief O'Brien turned to leave. He opened the door and stepped out into the hallway. He nodded at the chief psychiatrist. The man followed him out. The chief closed the door behind them. He leaned against the wall next to me. He looked at me. He smiled. He reached out his hand.

"I know how hard this must be for you, Mr. Prendergast," he said. "But you have nothing to fear. It won't hurt. There are drugs, but they won't harm you. And we'll monitor you every step of the way."

"What kind of drugs?"

"They're very effective. Very powerful. They'll help you heal. They'll make you feel better."

"And what about the nightmares?"

"Those will go away too."

"What about the flashbacks?"

"If necessary," the chief replied, "we can prescribe medication to suppress them."

"What about the terror?"

"We'll deal with that."

"What happens after that?"

"After that...?"

"What do you intend to do with me once we've fixed everything?"

"Whatever it takes."

"What does that mean?"

"It means that we'll find a way to make you well. We'll find out who did this to you. We'll find out how it happened. And we'll find a way to prevent it from happening again. Whatever it takes."

He stood up straight. He crossed his arms. He stared at me. Then he turned and left the room. I watched him walk down the hall. I listened as he knocked on the chief psychiatrist's door. He spoke briefly. Then the chief psychiatrist opened the door. He beckoned us inside.

"Come in," he said.

The two men sat down. I remained standing.

"I need your help," Chief O'Brien began. "I need your help finding out what happened here. Who did this to your daughter. I need to understand why it happened and how they did it. I need to understand how someone could commit such a terrible crime and escape. This is a tragedy. A terrible injustice. A terrible loss. We need to find out what happened and punish the guilty."

"And you think I can help you with that?"

"Yes. I think you can."

"Why me?"

"Because you're different from the others. You're special. Because you're strong enough to cope with what's coming. You have the courage to face it. You have the strength to survive. You have a unique perspective. You understand. You can put yourself in the place of the victim. You can empathize. You can relate. You understand the pain and anguish the parents must be feeling. You understand the horror of losing a child. I need you, Mr. Prendergast. I need your help. I need you to join me. I need you to be part of this. I need you to be my partner. I need you to be my friend. I need you to help me. I need you to be my eyes and ears. I need you to tell me what happened and what I need to know. I need you to work with me, Mr. Prendergast. I need you to be my best friend."

"I'm sorry," I said. "I'm not sure I want to be your friend. I don't know you. I don't know this city. I don't know these people. I can't help you. I can't do it."

"You don't have a choice."

"No, I don't. But I don't want to."

Chief O'Brien was silent for a moment. He looked at his watch. He sighed. He got up. He walked over to the door. He unlocked it. He pulled it open. He stepped outside. He waited for the chief psychiatrist. The chief followed. He locked the door behind them. He walked back to his office. He sat down at his desk. He picked up the phone and dialed a number. He spoke for a while. He hung up. He looked at me. He smiled. He walked over to his desk. He opened the bottom drawer. He took out a large envelope. He handed it to me.

"This is yours," he said. "Take it."

"What is it?"

"Your new home."

I opened the envelope. It contained a single sheet of paper. On that sheet of paper was written:

Welcome to New York, Mr. Prendergast.

I read through the note several times. I thought about what he had said.

"New York," I said.

"Yes," he replied. "I hope you like it."

"I'm not so sure."

"Don't worry. We'll find you a nice apartment. Somewhere safe. Where you can live quietly and comfortably. I hope you'll be happy there."

"Where's that?"

"Anywhere you choose. Anywhere you want. You pick. You decide. We'll pay for it. All expenses paid. Just think about it. You can do it later. But now, you have other things to do. You have a job to do."

"A job?"

"Yes. We need you to do it. We need you to do it for us. For the people of New York City. For your country. For your family. For your friends. We need you to do it. We need you to do it for me. We need you to do it for America. We need you to do it for me. We need you to do it for me."

"For you personally?"

"Of course. For me. And I know you can. I know you're capable of doing it. I know you can. I know you can do anything. I know you can solve any problem. I know you can find anything. I know you can do anything. I know you can find the killer. I know you can find the truth. I know you can find a way to stop him. I know you can find a way to make him talk. I know you can find a way to make him confess. I know you can find a way to make him understand. I know you can find a way to make him understand. I know you can find a way to make him see. I know you can find a way to make him see. I know you can find a way to make him see. I know you can find a way to make him understand.

I know you can find a way to make him see. I know you can find a way to make him understand. I know you can make him see. I know you can make him see."

"Make him see what?"

"What I want him to see."

"What do you want him to see?"

"Me."

"You want him to see you?"

"I want him to understand. I want him to feel me. I want him to know me. I want him to understand me. I want him to know what I feel. I want him to know what I think. I want him to know how much I care. I want him to know that I love him. That I miss him. I want him to know that I want to protect him. To keep him safe. I want him to know that I would die for him. I want him to know that I always will. I want him to know that I'll never let anyone hurt him, no matter what. I want him to know that I'll fight for him. Fight for his life. Fight to save him. Fight to make sure he has everything he needs. Fight to make sure he's protected. Fight to make sure he's cared for. I want him to know I'll do anything to make him happy. I want him to know I'll do whatever it takes to make him feel safe. I want him to know I'll do anything to make him happy."

"I don't understand."

"I want him to see me. I want him to understand me. I want him to know me. I want him to know me and love me and respect me and cherish me and obey me. I want him to know me and understand me and love me and follow me and serve me. I want him to be loyal to me. Loyal to the people of New York City. Loyal to the people of the United States of America. Loyal to me. Loyal to the memory of this little girl. Loyal to me. Loyal to the memory of this little girl."

"I still don't understand."

"I want you to help me. I need you to help me.

"Okay," Chief O'Brien said, "you heard the man. Get dressed. We're going to take you to your new home."

"New home?"

"Yes."

"Where's my old home?"

"We'll get you another one. One closer to where you'll be working. We can move you into a new neighborhood. Make you more comfortable."

"Why can't we stay here? Why can't we just live here?"

"There are certain security precautions we have to take."

"What about the FBI?"

"We'll handle them. Don't worry about them."

"Who will you be working for?"

"We need you to do a job for us, Mr. Prendergast. A very important job. You need to do it. I need you to do it for us. I need you to do it for America. I need you to do it for me.

TWO

Bang-up job at the office on Monday morning, but by noon he was back home again with his head buried under covers like it had been for days—the way I felt when my mother died last year. He couldn't even get up to go into work that day; instead, he just laid there feeling sorry for himself until late afternoon when finally, he got out from underneath the blankets long enough to call his boss. The conversation went something like this: "I'm not coming in today." His voice sounded weak as if someone else were talking through him. It made me feel so guilty about what we'd done Saturday night after hearing how sick Dad really was…but then I remembered who put us together anyway. My dad doesn't know anything yet, does he? And why did Mom have to die now too? Why can't she live forever or something? We could be happy like they do in books and movies. But no matter which direction you look these days, all you see is death, darkness, destruction…and worse than any of those things, fear. Fear makes people crazy sometimes, don't it? Like my father right now. If only he would come over here and talk some sense into me, maybe tell me everything will turn out okay somehow. That sounds stupid though, doesn't it? Just like I thought when I read Sara Henry's book, didn't I? Because nothing ever turns out alright unless you make it happen yourself. Right?

"Dad?"

He jumped awake suddenly. As soon as he saw where he was sitting, he looked around wildly trying to remember exactly what happened yesterday.

She was an attorney who worked for the firm that represented Santi when he sued his parents' company over sexual harassment allegations. The suit went to trial after she left the law office; it ended with him being awarded millions from the family business. He died shortly afterwards on account of some mysterious illness but not before giving her $1 million as thanks for all her efforts defending him during court proceedings – money which has since been stolen by someone else. Her life now consists entirely of lying around in bed at home while waiting patiently (or impatiently) for Forrest Bishop to return so they can resume their affair together once more. It goes without saying that this fantasy relationship doesn't include any children or grandchildren yet. That would be too much like reality…

I sat down next to Sara in the cafeteria at lunchtime, wearing my favorite new jeans and holding up a pair of sunglasses I'd bought myself last week. My hair was freshly washed, combed through, and blow-dried straight. With lipstick applied, I felt confident enough to walk across the street and enter a barber shop. Then I realized we didn't live near any bars and decided against going shopping, anyway, opting instead to stay at school until five o'clock and then head home.

It wasn't long before Forrest arrived. We hadn't seen each other since the previous night and immediately began chatting away happily as if we never stopped talking the day before. When he told me that his latest film project had finished filming six months earlier and that he was still looking for another job, I knew exactly why he was here. What happened between us yesterday had given him hope – the possibility that maybe someday soon he'll meet a woman who understands him. Who knows? Maybe he won't need to look for a lover anymore. Or perhaps a girlfriend. No matter what the outcome turns out to be, Forrest will always remember our meeting and keep coming back to see me whenever possible. For a few minutes, at least.

We ate together in silence occasionally glancing nervously towards the entrance of the room in case either of our friends wanted to join us. Neither did, leaving us to enjoy the peace and quiet together. After finishing off half of his meal, Forrest leaned forward and kissed me on the lips. Not wanting to spoil the moment, I kept eating, knowing full well that the kiss wouldn't end there. Within seconds Forrest grabbed hold of my hand and led me outside onto a bench beside the parking lot, where we spent several hours kissing passionately. By the time our clothes started falling apart, there was nowhere else to sit so we stood naked together under the autumn sun as he held open my legs wide apart. I reached down to take care of his cock with mine, stroking them gently in unison. Soon Forrest was ready for action and guided himself inside me with slow thrusts. There was no way I was letting him finish without getting pregnant again. Our baby was born less than three months previously.

As usual, we walked along the road holding hands, stopping briefly to pick flowers growing wild in nearby gardens. We talked about nothing important – mostly about Forrest's current state of mind and whether it made sense for him to continue living in Los Angeles when there were plenty of places in America far nicer than LA itself. Although Forrest agreed to move elsewhere eventually, he said it would depend upon finding the perfect place for him to settle. Somewhere beautiful. Where he could relax.

When we got close to the edge of town, Forrest suggested taking a detour via his trailer park. He needed to visit one of the residents to collect some papers and asked me to accompany him. Since the trailers were set up among trees, there was little light filtering through branches overhead. We followed a path leading deeper into the woods until arriving at a small clearing overlooking rolling hills covered in tall grasses. Here and there lay abandoned cars rusting slowly beneath mossy leaves, broken glass littering the ground below. Once again, we stripped off our clothing and ran around naked in the forest, laughing and giggling like teenagers. Forrest picked me up and carried me away from danger – just in case someone spotted us and reported us to the police. We were careful not to run too fast.

After returning to the trailer park, Forrest gave the resident permission to leave early that afternoon. While he visited the elderly lady in question, I took advantage of the opportunity to slip into the kitchen and raid the fridge. I found some leftover chicken and pasta salad, plus cold beer. Two cans later, Forrest returned to find me already halfway through dinner.

"What're you eating?" he asked. "Is it safe for you to eat this stuff? You shouldn't be snacking."

With my mouth full, I smiled and nodded yes. Forrest looked doubtful. So, I explained that the food had been in the freezer compartment of the refrigerator, wrapped in plastic bags and clearly labelled as containing no harmful chemicals. Even so, he insisted on checking with the owner of the park to make sure she approved of her tenants consuming such unhealthy fare. To avoid further questions, I offered to help Forrest unload some boxes from his car trunk while we waited for Mrs. Evans to come back.

A short distance away from the trailers, there was a large field enclosed by a fence surrounding a pond filled with dead fish floating belly-up. Beyond the water, the land rose gradually towards a hillside dotted with pine trees. From where we stood, it seemed impossible to tell where the lake ended, and the hills began. On closer inspection, however, the area was littered with signs warning visitors to keep clear of poison ivy and poisonous snakes.

While Forrest unloaded his vehicle, I watched the sky darken above the distant mountains. Clouds gathered quickly and grew thicker by the minute. Before long, raindrops fell steadily from the heavens. It poured heavily within ten minutes, turning the grasslands into a muddy puddle. We rushed back to the trailer park.

Rain pelted down harder. Water streamed down the windows of the building as we entered. The lights flickered on and off intermittently throughout the hallway. Rainwater flooded through the front door. We hurried upstairs to check on Mr. Evans, who was sleeping soundly in her bedroom. Next door, Heather Satterfield emerged from her apartment carrying a towel draped over herself. She wiped away the worst of the mud splashed on her face and arms, but otherwise ignored our presence altogether.

Mr. Evans awoke suddenly to discover that it had begun raining indoors. He tried desperately to stop it pouring in through cracks in the ceiling panels by opening doors to let in fresh air, but to no avail. He turned to me for assistance.

"Can you please lend me your umbrella?" he pleaded.

Instead of lending him an actual piece of equipment, I opened my own jacket to reveal two blue umbrellas stuffed inside it. One belonged to Forrest and the other to me.

"… I'm sorry," Mr. Evans said apologetically, embarrassed by his request. "But these aren't ordinary paper umbrellas."

No, they weren't. I'd designed them especially for Forrest and myself. They were waterproof and could withstand winds exceeding 150 kilometers per hour. Plus, they were lightweight and foldable, making them easy to carry around with us wherever we went. Of course, Forrest was reluctant to give me one, claiming that he couldn't afford to lose such a valuable possession. However, I assured him they were cheap to manufacture – and therefore affordable for anyone to buy. He relented after much cajoling.

Sara's father was killed when she was twelve years old. Her mother remarried and moved away shortly afterwards, leaving her daughter alone in a big house which she rarely used. Sara lived on her own for many years thereafter. If she was lucky, her neighbors saw her walking past their houses on occasion; if she wasn't so fortunate, they thought she must have died somewhere along the line and forgotten to update them with the news. That left her free to live life as she pleased – whatever suited her mood. And although Sara often sought solace at the bottom of bottles of wine during the darkest days of despair, alcohol also helped to numb the pain caused by memories of her dead parents.

There were times when Sara wished her mum had stayed with her dad, but most of the time she believed she'd been spared something worse. Because her stepfather wasn't abusive – at least not physically – he became her only friend. Together, they explored the vast grounds of the estate and enjoyed exploring its secrets together. This included a hidden tunnel running deep underground, leading to a mysterious cave where they discovered ancient artefacts dating back thousands of years. As children, they played hide and seek in the cavernous space, pretending that the rocks and stalactites hanging from the ceilings belonged to aliens or gods. The caves were formed naturally over hundreds of millions of years ago. But Sara didn't care about facts like that. Instead, she imagined the rock formations as alien spacecraft and the creatures inhabiting those ships as deities. These imaginings served as an escape route for her from daily stress and unhappiness.

That evening, Sara drank a bottle of red wine and slept deeply until late morning. During the following weeks, she continued drinking every night, spending the rest of the day lying on her bed staring blankly ahead. A month passed before Sara even remembered that she owned a computer and laptop. When she finally logged onto the internet and checked emails, there was one waiting for her. She read it carefully twice, shaking her head sadly in disbelief:

Dear Ms. Henry,

My name is Dr Jules Taggert. I work for the FBI as part of the National Criminal Intelligence Service. I believe that you might be able to assist us in solving a particularly difficult murder investigation. Please contact me directly to discuss the details. Yours sincerely, Dr Jules Taggart

FBI agent

Dr. Taggart.

Sara deleted the email right away. Why should she get involved? Wasn't it obvious that she was incapable of doing anything worthwhile? All she ever managed to do was waste people's time. Except for Forrest and David, nobody cared about her anyway. Even though she knew better, Sara felt compelled to call her former husband and explain everything. Then she hung up abruptly when she heard the voice of Agent Taggart asking to speak to her personally. His words were delivered quietly, almost as if he knew how upset she would become once he started speaking.

THREE

I know it sounds crazy…

— FORREST HENRY (voiceover)

Forrest and I drove northwards towards Mount Baldy. There was still a chance the killer hadn't yet escaped the crime scene. Or maybe they fled south instead. Either way, Forrest promised me that we would soon catch whoever did it. Both men had now confessed to killing Tom and Emily, and Forrest told me that the authorities had received confirmation that they were indeed guilty of murdering Michael Jones too.

In another country, a similar pattern of events unfolded between 1990 and 1992. In Norway, four young women disappeared and then reappeared five days later having been raped repeatedly by the same man. After each rape, the perpetrator would drive away from the crime site. At first, police assumed all the disappearances were connected – that the rapist abducted everyone who came across his attention. However, it took several more rapes before officers realized the truth. Three of the victims had been murdered by the fourth woman – Kristin Danby – whom the rapists had kidnapped and tortured for days beforehand. Only after hearing her confession did detectives realize what happened to the other three missing girls. They never existed.

It was strange how easily the killers manipulated the minds of their intended targets. Like Sara, none of the survivors had any idea why they kept being targeted. Most of them simply accepted their fate without protest. Some of the women even claimed to love their abusers.

Police arrested Kristin Danby on suspicion of abducting and torturing the third victim, Julie Gluten, but she denied involvement in the murders. She claimed to have witnessed the death of one girl and seen the bodies of two others buried in remote areas near Oslo, but she refused to identify either of the corpses. Although the evidence against her was overwhelming, she was acquitted due to lack of proof. Police eventually released Danby in 1993 under certain conditions, including signing a document agreeing not to kill again. She was thirty years old at the time.

Kristin Danby has since changed her identity. No longer recognizable as the original Kristin Danby, she is now called Helen Fouke and works as a nurse in a psychiatric hospital outside London. According to reports, she continues to suffer nightmares and flashbacks from her ordeal in Norway.

As we approached the entrance to the mountain range, Forrest suggested that we turn back. "This isn't going anywhere," he declared. "We can't search everywhere."

"Why not?" I asked.

He shook his head and sighed loudly. "Because you'll die," he replied.

"You mean because of the weather?"

To my surprise, Forrest nodded. "Yes. The storm will hit us here. Once it does, we won't stand a chance."

His answer confused me. How could lightning strike someone just standing next to him? Didn't electricity flow from point A to B? Not sideways or diagonally. What about the laws of physics? Lightning strikes always travelled straight downwards from the clouds, striking the tallest object available – usually a tall tree – causing it to burst into flames and fall backwards with tremendous force.

Lightning bolts travel upwards from the ground and strike high points in the atmosphere. Trees don't explode unless struck by multiple lightning strikes. — NATIONAL WEATHER SERVICE OF THE UNITED STATES

However, Forrest insisted that lightning travels upward from the earth, not down. So far as he was concerned, this meant that neither he nor I would survive the coming storm. I didn't understand exactly what he was trying to say – that I shouldn't go on with the plan – but I agreed with his logic, nonetheless. To stay behind sounded like a good idea.

When I mentioned this to Forrest, he looked hurt. He put his hand gently upon mine. "Don't worry," he whispered. "I've got something else planned for tonight. Don't you trust me?"

What choice did I really have? We needed to find the murderer and bring him or her to justice. My gut instinct told me Forrest had the answers we were looking for. Besides, he seemed confident enough to lead us safely out of danger. The only question was whether we should follow his suggestion or remain cautious and return home early.

"Okay," I conceded. "Let's keep moving forward."

A few hours later, we reached the summit of Mount Baldy. It was dark outside, but we walked slowly to avoid stumbling into holes in the snow-covered terrain. Above us, rain lashed the peaks and fell heavily on the surrounding forest. Thunder boomed overhead as lightning flashed sporadically above the trees. Heavy winds whipped branches around our heads.

Thunder rumbled louder than thunderbolts.

Then, suddenly, the sky exploded.

With great gusto, a bolt of light shot up from the ground and flew straight towards the heavens. Within seconds, countless flashes lit the night. From the safety of the peak, Forrest watched the show unfold, smiling proudly as he pointed at the spectacle.

"See!" he shouted excitedly. "Your instincts were correct! Lightning doesn't come from the ground. It comes from the skies…"

FOUR

Sonja Hemingway

One afternoon, Sonja found herself sitting alone on the floor of her apartment. Her face was covered with tears while her hands trembled violently. For ten minutes or so, she sat unmoving and silent, unable to think clearly through the haze of grief.

She wiped away her tears and stood up, heading for the bathroom to wash off the residue of sadness. On impulse, she splashed some cold water on her forehead, washing away the last traces of her distress. Then, with her eyes closed tight, she leaned forwards until her lips touched the edge of the sink. She breathed deeply and exhaled forcefully, clearing her mind of negative thoughts and emotions.

After a short break to regain her composure, Sonja returned to the living room to make tea. She poured hot liquid into two mugs, added milk to one cup and sugar to the other, and placed them side by side on the coffee table. While sipping the beverage, she stared at nothing, thinking aloud.

"Maybe I'm imagining things," she said softly. "But I swear I saw you today."

Her mother's ghost appeared briefly in the corner of her eye before disappearing again. That must have been wishful thinking, Sonja thought. Perhaps she hallucinated seeing her mum walk past during her lunchbreak. But no matter how much she tried, she couldn't convince herself that ghosts didn't exist. If anyone deserved immortality, it was her mummy. And although her memory remained vivid throughout these troubled times, her daughter knew it wouldn't be long before memories faded entirely.

Soon after Sonja moved to New York, her parents' deaths were confirmed. The coroner ruled that both died instantly within seconds of each other, which explained why the news made such a huge impact on Sonja. In fact, she was devastated to hear the tragic circumstances of her parent's passing. She'd expected her father to pass first, followed swiftly by her mother. Yet, somehow, they managed to hold on until the end of one another's life. Their love transcended death itself. As the saying goes, 'Love knows no boundaries'. This was true of the couple in Sonja's case – even beyond death.

Not long afterwards, Sonja began receiving letters addressed to her deceased parents. One letter arrived in November 1994: another in February 1995. Each one contained an envelope marked with handwriting identical to her dead parents', along with a message from them explaining that they wanted to meet her. They also enclosed photographs showing the pair together in happier times. Two months later, a third package landed on Sonja's doorstep. Again, the sender used her parents' names and signatures, and sent a photograph of them posing happily with her when she was very young. Another photo showed them holding a small child, presumably their own offspring. Of course, there wasn't a shred of doubt that those photos were genuine. Sonja recognized her parents immediately. They were wearing matching sweaters and smiling broadly at the camera. The baby in the picture wore a blue bonnet and resembled her grandmother. Sonja guessed it must have been taken shortly before her birth.

At first, Sonja was reluctant to open any of the envelopes containing mail supposedly written by her parents. Until she finally broke down and opened the second letter.

Dear Daughter,

My name is Anne Henriksen and yours truly was your mother. Your father is named Erik and he passed away seven years ago. You may remember that day well: October 6th, 1987.

Although we lost touch over the decades, we never forgot about you. When I heard that we were related…well, it gave me goose bumps. We loved you dearly, though we couldn't see as often as we wished.

Sonja read the letter twice to confirm everything she had already suspected – that her parents wrote it themselves. She felt relieved knowing they hadn't abandoned her completely. Even if they didn't appear physically, they cared enough to send her messages occasionally. And it warmed her heart that they remembered me and missed me as much as I miss them.

Though the contents of the letter made her happy, they also saddened Sonja. Knowing that her parents were alive somewhere in the universe, yet unable to reunite with them, left a void inside her. Without her family, she was adrift and unsure where to go next.

On Christmas Day, Sonja decided to visit the cemetery to pay homage to her parents. With the help of Google Maps, she located their grave site. There was little doubt that it belonged to them. All the gravestones matched the style and color scheme of hers. The tombstone depicted a woman kneeling beside flowers, surrounded by birds and butterflies. Below the inscription was carved the date of their deaths. Sonja searched online records for more details about Anne and Erik, but all searches came up empty. She assumed that the names listed on their graves were probably false ones chosen by the funeral director. Or maybe the gravestone maker didn't know who the actual owners were. Either way, the mystery deepened.

Once Sonja paid her respects to her parents, she drove north towards Oslo. At the airport, she boarded a flight bound for Chicago, planning to spend three days there visiting friends and relatives. After leaving America, she intended to fly across Europe to Sweden. From Stockholm, she would take a ferry to Denmark and then drive southwards to Bergen before flying onwards to Norway. By the time she finished deciding, it would be springtime in Scandinavia.

In Copenhagen, Sonja visited her best friend, Mia Rosen. She lived nearby in a suburb called Frederiksberg, close to the city center. During the summer, the area teemed with tourists drawn by its cobbled streets and quaint shops. Now, however, many of the tourist attractions lay dormant under piles of snow. Only a handful of locals braved the winter chill to shop at the local markets and restaurants.

Mia greeted Sonja warmly and hugged her tightly. "It's so nice to see you again!"

"Likewise," Sonja replied. "And thank you for inviting me here."

"Of course," Mia smiled. "Any excuse to catch up with my favorite person in the whole wide world."

They spent several hours chatting over cups of coffee and glasses of wine. Between bites of cake, they laughed easily. Though Mia was married now, she still enjoyed being single. She liked having plenty of free time to do whatever she pleased without worrying about work or responsibilities. Most importantly, she didn't need anyone else to fill the gaping hole in her heart following the loss of her husband.

As the sun set over the horizon, wearily, Sonja headed back home. Although she was tired from travelling halfway round the world, her spirits lifted considerably since arriving in Copenhagen. A fresh start was just what she needed.

That evening, Sonja took her dog for a brisk walk around the neighborhood. She stopped frequently to chat with passersby, most of whom knew her personally. Some nodded politely while others waved enthusiastically. It was late when she finally returned home, exhausted from talking nonstop for six hours or so. As soon as she entered the building, Sonja noticed a familiar figure standing near the elevator bank. It was Forrest, dressed casually in jeans and a sweater vest over a white shirt. His hair was neatly trimmed, and he carried a briefcase slung over his shoulder. He smiled when he spotted Sonja approaching him.

"Hey, Forrest," she said brightly. "How're you doing?"

He stepped closer and held out his hand. "Good morning, Sonja."

Weighing the situation carefully, Sonja accepted Forrest's offer. "Nice to meet yak," she replied. "I'm glad to see someone recognizes me."

Forrest shook her hand firmly. "You look fantastic, Sonja. Much younger than the last time I met you. How old did you say you were again? Forty-two?"

Sonja chuckled nervously. "Forty-seven."

When she glanced at her watch, she realized she only had fifteen minutes or so before she needed to leave for work. So, she bid Forrest goodbye and rushed upstairs to change clothes.

Before leaving, she ran downstairs and grabbed a bottle of whisky. Then, she slipped her coat on and hurried towards the elevators. Once she reached the lobby, she looked around for Forrest and found him waiting outside. To Sonja's relief, he seemed genuinely interested in hearing her plans. Soon after, they rode the elevator to the street level, exchanging contact information with the intention of staying in touch.

Sonja walked home quickly, eager to get changed and begin packing for her trip abroad. Before too long, she was ready to board a plane bound for London. Then, after a few stops in Germany and France, she continued to Scotland. Finally, she flew eastward across the Atlantic Ocean to Canada, stopping in Montreal for dinner with her sister. After that, she crossed the border into the United States and caught an overnight bus to Boston.

A week or two later, she arrived at Logan Airport with suitcases filled with winter clothing. Next stop: Seattle!

Seattle was colder than usual this year. Snow blanketed the ground and coated the branches of the trees like icing sugar. Sonja bundled up in layers upon layers to protect herself against the biting wind. On the positive side, she could wear hats and gloves indoors instead of sweating buckets. For the first time in weeks, she breathed freely without feeling suffocated by air conditioning. Her lungs thanked her profusely for coming here.

She stayed at a cheap motel in downtown Seattle until she received confirmation that she had secured employment. Then, she rented an apartment above a barber shop in Ballard. It cost less money than she anticipated paying for rent in Manhattan. Plus, the location was ideal. Just five blocks from the waterfront and a short stroll away from the shopping district, it was perfect. Sonja unpacked her belongings, including the box containing her laptop computer. While checking emails, she discovered that her brother was getting divorced. That put her mind at ease. If anything happened to him, she would always have access to the latest information.

After eating lunch, Sonja went for a walk through the park behind the hotel. She sat beneath a tree, enjoying the view of Lake Union and Mount Rainier. She watched boats drift by on the water and admired the tall buildings surrounding her. She thought briefly about returning to New York someday. But she couldn't deny the pull of the Pacific Northwest. Maybe she should stay here forever.

Then, Sonja saw something odd on the sidewalk ahead of her. Someone had thrown some rubbish onto the grass. Instead of walking past, she paused to pick up the garbage and deposit it in a nearby bin. Upon closer inspection, she noticed that one of the items was part of an expensive leather jacket. She bent down to examine it more closely. Sure enough, it was indeed a high-quality item of men's outerwear. She wondered how it ended up discarded in such a careless manner. Perhaps it fell off someone's shoulders when they stood up suddenly. Or perhaps it was stolen during a break-in. Whatever the case, she resolved not to let the owner suffer unnecessarily. Taking the garment home, Sonja washed it thoroughly and hung it to dry. Later, she folded it and stored it in a closet. The next morning, she wore it with pride to work.

While driving along Aurora Avenue North toward Pioneer Square, Sonja encountered traffic snarls caused by roadwork. The congestion stretched for miles; cars crawled bumper to bumper through endless lines of red lights. Frustrated drivers honked continuously as they waited patiently for the green light to turn yellow again. One driver even got out of his car to shout obscenities at another motorist whose vehicle blocked his path. Others threw bottles and other debris out of their windows at passing pedestrians and bikers. They hurled insults and threats as well, though no physical violence occurred. Traffic flowed smoothly once Sonja escaped the mess.

By early afternoon, Sonja had worked her way through half the day. In addition to answering email enquiries, she answered phones and faxes. Sometimes, she had to track down people who'd been out sick. Other times, she picked up packages and mailed documents for clients. Sonja tried to keep busy whenever possible, otherwise she risked going stir crazy sitting alone in the office all day. When she wasn't working, she studied maps of Scandinavia and scoured online reviews looking for Scandinavian restaurants and cafés.

At the end of the week, Sonja began to feel restless. She wanted to explore the city and find new things to do each day. So, she asked her boss if she might occasionally make trips elsewhere in town to deliver mail or fetch supplies. He agreed immediately, and suggested she use her own vehicle.

One Sunday evening, she drove north from the city to Bellevue, Washington. Near the outskirts of the affluent suburban community, she parked the van in a large parking lot alongside the highway and walked west along the shoreline of Lake Washington. She followed the lakefront trail between the freeway embankments until she reached the footbridge spanning the waterway. Beyond the bridge, the forest opened into a sprawling residential development. Above the treetops, the sky glowed pink and purple in the twilight glow. The air smelled crisp and clean after a heavy rainstorm earlier in the day, and the sound of rushing waves echoed softly through the darkness.

During the night, a huge storm hit Seattle, dumping nearly eight inches of snow on the city. With the roads covered with ice, Sonja decided to postpone her return journey till the following weekend. Instead, she wandered aimlessly throughout the suburbs, admiring Christmas decorations in homes decorated for the festive season. She also passed countless parks where families gathered for snowball fights or toboggan rides. Many kids played in the snow, throwing fistfuls at the ground, and watching them bounce back upwards. Meanwhile, adults huddled together in small groups, sipping hot chocolate or beer while warming themselves by bonfires. All of which made Sonja envious. She wished she had children – any number would be fine. But she hadn't managed to fall pregnant yet despite years of trying. And then, there was the matter of Forrest's wife…

Back at the motel in Ballard, Sonja checked her messages on the internet. There weren't many calls or emails, but she did receive a message from Forrest. At least he remembered her name now!

– Hi Sonja, I hope you've settled into your job okay. I don't know if you remember me, we met briefly in Seattle. I came across a piece of paper with our names written on it today and felt compelled to check up on you. Are you happy with your life these days? I wish I could talk with you face-to-face instead of writing letters. I miss seeing you every day. Anyhow, best wishes to you, Forrest. PS: Hope you haven't forgotten me completely!

Sonja smiled as she read his words. It reminded her of how much she missed Forrest. Now that she lived far away, it was harder than ever to maintain regular communication with him. Even so, she appreciated his efforts to remain connected. She wrote him a reply via email and attached photos of the park and the harbor area. Then, she sent them both off with a kiss and goodnight.

On Monday morning, Sonja returned to work refreshed from her vacation. The previous week had gone surprisingly fast. Most mornings, she spent several hours catching up on emails and phone messages. Then, she tackled her daily tasks as efficiently and effectively as possible. By noon, she was usually finished for the day and able to go home early.

Once she reached home, she took care of business as usual, including taking out the trash and feeding her dog. Then, she packed for another trip abroad. This time, she planned to visit Oslo in Norway. From there, she would travel south to Denmark and Sweden before crossing the Baltic Sea to Finland. After that, she hoped to catch a train somewhere near Helsinki to continue travelling further east. As always, Sonja didn't plan very far ahead. She preferred to improvise and follow wherever fate led her.

Norway sounded interesting. She liked cold weather and had heard the country boasted spectacular scenery. Plus, it wouldn't hurt to brush up on her Swedish and Danish languages before heading overseas. Norwegian was similar enough that maybe she could learn a thing or two. She had already mastered French and Spanish thanks to her travels in Europe over the summer. Why not add a third language to the mix?

In a few months' time, she hoped to meet with Forrest again. Until then, she knew exactly what she needed to do to prepare for his arrival. First, she booked a flight from Chicago to Minneapolis on Saturday morning. Next, she purchased a ticket to Stockholm on Tuesday evening, arriving late Wednesday night. A couple of nights at a local hostel in the center of town ought to suffice. Then, she reserved a room at a budget hotel in Oslo for three nights starting Friday afternoon. Finally, she bought a pair of sturdy hiking boots for exploring the outdoors. Since she would be spending most of her time in forests and mountains, she figured she would need proper footwear. Otherwise, she risked twisting an ankle or falling victim to frostbite.

It took quite a bit of effort to secure those arrangements, especially since she relied entirely on word-of-mouth recommendations from locals rather than booking directly online. But eventually, everything fell into place and Sonja paid a hefty price for the convenience. Fortunately, she saved money renting a car to drive around Seattle and visiting friends in Portland. Those costs were tax deductible too.

As soon as she left Minnesota, she turned right towards Canada and crossed into British Columbia. Soon afterwards, she entered Alberta. Within minutes, she found herself climbing steadily upward along Highway 1 until she finally reached the top of Mount Assiniboine, the highest point on Vancouver Island. Staring down at the sea below, she gazed out at the vast expanse of ocean stretching to the horizon. She imagined sailing ships navigating its depths, searching for safe harbors among the myriad islands dotting the coastline. On a clear day, she could see the coast of Alaska and the Aleutian Islands beyond.

Mountains rose steeply on either side of her, forming a barrier against the frigid winds sweeping inland from the strait. Ahead lay the rugged terrain of the island's interior. Mount Assiniboine itself was just one peak amongst hundreds, rising higher still. She peered farther into the distance, wondering where the mountain ended, and the wilderness began. Was this part of the Canadian Shield? Or was it merely a natural formation created by erosion over millennia? Either way, it seemed impossible for humans to tame such untamed land. Yet, thousands of people had come here to settle in the last century, building houses and towns atop the rocky escarpments. Some communities grew rapidly, like Terrace, others remained tiny hamlets hidden within thick woods and dense ferny underbrush. Wherever she looked, she saw evidence of human habitation.

She climbed down carefully to the edge of the cliff and examined the rocks jutting out above her head. Each stone protruded slightly from the wall, suggesting that the rock surface beneath must have collapsed in places due to pressure from the surrounding earth. How long ago was that? Did the cliffs rise straight up forever without interruption? If so, why hadn't the whole mass crumbled into dust and disappeared? That question puzzled her, but she couldn't stop staring at the sheer walls towering overhead.

Ahead, she glimpsed a faint line cutting through the trees. Following it, she discovered a narrow gravel road winding through the forest. The first sign of civilization she'd seen in hours. Maybe she should take advantage of this unexpected discovery and hike closer to the summit. Just when she thought the view from the bottom of the slope would never change, something magical happened. Clouds drifted past in wispy strands, revealing more vistas of rolling hills and distant peaks. Once again, she marveled at nature's power and beauty. She stared at the landscape in wonder for several moments, lost in a reverie that only deepened the sense of peace she'd experienced thus far.

When she finally emerged from the forest onto the open plain, the sun shone brightly and warmed her skin. The wind had died down, allowing the temperature to climb into the upper 40s Fahrenheit. To the west, the setting sun cast long shadows behind Mount Rainier, shining golden rays upon the forest and sparkling off the waters of the Strait of Juan de Fuca. Behind her stood tall pines, cedar trees and spruce bushes growing beside the road. Boulders dotted the hillside nearby, some as big as boulders. In places, the gravel path she followed grew narrow and treacherous. It was steep and slippery, making her fear she might lose her footing and tumble over the edge.

Once she reached the top of the mountain, she stared out across the sea to the horizon. For miles, the ocean stretched before her, shimmering like a vast lake on a sunny day. She imagined the currents that swept down from the Arctic Circle, carving out the strait between Washington State and British Columbia. The waters were calm today, but the storms could be ferocious, she knew. The sea was said to freeze during the winter, creating an icy path for ships to sail through.

In the distance, she saw a cluster of small islands jutting out of the water. She guessed they were part of Vancouver Island. On the southern side, she spotted a thin line of green forest running along the shoreline. A few minutes later, she caught sight of a massive grey rock formation jutting from the earth. She couldn't make out its shape or size, but she figured it must have been quite large. Mount Assiniboine had grown even larger since she'd last seen it.

Somewhere beyond the rocky island, she thought she heard surf pounding the shoreline. But there was no beach, so how could waves reach the land? She wondered if she had imagined the noise. Perhaps the roar came from one of the small islands, which would explain why she hadn't heard it while she climbed up the mountain.

Ahead, she saw a sign indicating Mount Assiniboine was closed due to avalanche danger. The sign also warned against hiking in the area, but she didn't pay much attention to the warning. Mountains were her favorite playground. She loved exploring their slopes and valleys, searching for the most beautiful vistas and secret spots. She couldn't resist climbing onto the rocks and peering into the crevices, wondering what kind of creatures might dwell inside. Mount Assiniboine was a popular hiking spot, but she had the place to herself. She figured this was her chance to explore the mountain further.

Mountains are my favorite playground.

She walked around the sign and continued towards the base of the cliffs. Mount Assiniboine rose steeply on the other side, so she would have to climb down to get there. At the bottom, she found a narrow gravel path winding between the trees. She followed the trail until it led her to a wide meadow. It was as flat as a pool of water, dotted with clumps of grass and shrubs. Mount Assiniboine stood in the distance, surrounded by the forest on all sides. From here, she could see how massive it truly was. Its peak seemed to rise straight up into the sky, suggesting it was taller than any other mountain in the region.

Sonja climbed atop a nearby boulder and surveyed the scene. Mount Assiniboine stood tall, towering above everything else. Beyond her lay the mountains of Vancouver Island and the coastal plain. The ocean stretched to the horizon, glimmering like a vast lake on a sunny day. On a clear day, she could see the coast of Alaska and the Aleutian Islands beyond. Mount Assiniboine was just one peak amongst hundreds, rising higher still. Sonja stared at the rocky escarpments looming over her, wondering where they ended, and the wilderness began. Did this part of the Canadian Shield stretch out forever? Or did it eventually give way to the plains of the interior?

Somewhere in the distance, she heard surf pounding the shoreline. But there was no beach, so how could waves reach the land?

Ahead, she saw a faint line cutting through the trees. Following it, she discovered a narrow gravel road winding through the forest. The first sign of civilization she'd seen in hours. Maybe she should take advantage of this unexpected discovery and hike closer to the summit. Just when she thought the view from the bottom of the slope would never change, something magical happened. Clouds drifted past in wispy strands, revealing more vistas of rolling hills and distant peaks.

Once again, she marveled at nature's power and beauty. She gazed at the landscape in wonder for several moments, lost in a reverie that only deepened the sense of peace she had felt thus far.

When she finally emerged from the forest onto the open plain, the sun shone brightly and warmed her skin. The wind had died down, allowing the temperature to climb into the upper 40s Fahrenheit. To the west, the setting sun cast long shadows behind Mount Rainier, shining golden rays upon the forest and sparkling off the waters of the Strait of Juan de Fuca. Behind her stood tall pines, cedar trees and spruce bushes growing beside the road. Boulders dotted the hillside nearby, some as big as boulders. In places, the gravel path she followed became narrow and treacherous, making her fearful she might lose her footing and tumble over the edge.

As soon as she reached the top of the mountain, she stared out across the sea to the horizon. For miles, the ocean stretched before her, shimmering like a vast lake on a sunny day. She imagined sailing ships navigating its depths, searching for safe harbors among the myriad islands dotting the coastline. On a clear day, she could see the coast of Alaska and perhaps even Hawaii beyond that.

Mountain ranges formed a barrier against the frigid winds blowing inland from the strait. Ahead lay the rugged terrain of the island's interior. Mount Assiniboine itself stood just one peak amidst hundreds, rising higher yet. "I can almost hear them singing," thought Sonja aloud. Her gaze swept along a line slicing through the trees toward the mountains. She guessed it must have marked a route leading somewhere deeper into those uncharted forests.

FIVE

For hours he sat motionless in his chair, watching nothingness unfold before him – an endless stream of black clouds drifting southwards on high currents of air from the north-east. He wasn't sure how many times he repeated that ritual each morning and evening. As if hypnotized, time slipped away from him like water draining from a pond, leaving only an empty hole in its wake. What was once important now seemed insignificant, and trivialities filled every moment of existence. Nothing mattered anymore except for the need to keep going back to this same spot on that very particular rock ledge. Even thinking about it brought anxiety bubbling forth within him.

He was alone again. All others had left after reading Sara Henry's final entry in his notebook. His friends were scared shitless by his obsessive behavior; maybe he should feel offended that none of them would return, not wanting anything more to do with him or Mount Assiniboine than they already did, but really, he understood what drove them away. They feared the madness would infect them too, so better safe than sorry and avoid the inevitable pain ahead when he inevitably took his own life. No one wanted to bear witness to that horror. So, he kept everyone guessing as to whether Isobel might ever find out who killed David Martin or what might become of his diary afterwards. Only two people shared information regarding either possibility: John Deacon or Sara Henry. Both agreed with her opinion that there weren't enough clues remaining for anyone to identify her killer—not even Deacon himself. And then there was Sara Henry…

"Why am I doing this?" she asked aloud on her third visit.

Deacon looked up at her for a split second before returning his focus to the sea below. With an effort bordering on desperation, he tried desperately to ignore thoughts that threatened to overwhelm him whenever he considered her presence near him. "Because you love Mount Assiniboine."

His reply sounded feeble even though it came from the heart. He wished someone else might speak instead, because it made perfect sense for her to be visiting Mount Assiniboine without having known her father or grandfather, but it didn't change the fact he preferred talking directly to her, even knowing it wouldn't bring them closer together. Instead, the conversation always devolved into silence.

But sometimes, when he dared hope things were beginning to change in his mind, he allowed himself to believe Sara meant well in coming here so often. That she cared enough about him to come seeking answers and comfort in solitude. If he ignored the voices that screamed louder and demanded, he leave this spot immediately – to forget about all this nonsense and start living a normal life again – he believed he might finally begin feeling happy. Like there was a light at the end of all the darkness and death swirling around him.

If she could talk to me, we'd understand each other perfectly. We're cut from the same cloth, she told herself. Yet despite his attempts to shut out unwanted thoughts, she managed to plant ideas in his head anyway, and he couldn't escape them unless they spoke freely between themselves, giving him the choice to listen or not. Sometimes, just being aware of them gave him an odd sense of peace…like he had a friend sitting quietly beside him. But mostly, he felt frustrated by these silent intrusions, wishing Sara would quit trying to help him, or go away altogether, because neither option pleased him. This isn't helping anybody, not me, nor her or Mount Assiniboine, but I don't know how to stop it!

What good would speaking out do? There'd be no point, especially given how easily Sonja could disappear at will, slipping right back into anonymity after each appearance. Why would she risk exposure for such fleeting pleasure? It didn't add up.

It was easy for her to slip past security measures set in place years ago, according to John Deacon. It didn't take much effort on her part; she merely needed to appear briefly and make certain nobody noticed her during that short period of time. A few minutes was plenty of opportunity for mischief. Security staff watched over him closely while they monitored cameras throughout the building; they knew they shouldn't let him walk outside unattended since they couldn't ensure his safety anywhere else, thanks to the unpredictable ways of the young woman called Morgana Lee. One guard had been shot dead last year while protecting another officer from the threat of gunfire from behind. Another died when his patrol car was hit broadside on Highway 16 and sent spinning off into a ditch. Two days later, police received reports that four men had assaulted and raped an elderly couple camping in nearby Jasper National Park, forcing them to flee in terror before they got caught and held for ransom. The victim suffered severe injuries which put her life at serious risk due to internal bleeding caused by broken ribs.

Even though she hadn't spoken to Benita Hemingway personally, Sonja suspected her mother's kidnapping stemmed somehow from her own actions here at Fort Whoop-Up decades earlier. The old records suggested it happened sometime shortly after Sonja's birth, but it remained unclear why her grandmother disappeared at that precise moment or where she went afterward. Not long after, she returned with new husband George and claimed she simply decided to spend her honeymoon elsewhere instead of tying her daughter to another man's name. After all those years, Sonja wondered whether she remembered what happened that summer day twenty or thirty summers back, or if she'd invented that version of events entirely.

"Why does anyone need money or status when they've found their true self? When they know who they truly are? What is worth more — your soul or wealth?"

She'd learned about the concept from Morgana Lee a week ago. The question haunted her constantly now, echoing from deep within her psyche until it grew so loud, it overpowered most sounds and feelings surrounding her. Was there any truth behind this philosophy? She'd begun asking herself how much longer she'd sit idly in one place waiting for her parents to die so she could inherit whatever fortune awaited them? Would she stay in the city of Vancouver forever if there was nowhere else, she could fit in? Had all this suffering helped her discover who she really was or was everything happening purely for the sake of a twisted revenge against a woman who betrayed her family?

Sonja had spent countless hours contemplating the answer, but nothing inside her changed.

And yet…something did happen yesterday, on Father's Day. While he slept peacefully next door under heavy sedatives prescribed by the doctors treating his condition following his stroke three weeks prior, Sonja woke early and crept upstairs to join him, wearing his favorite turtleneck sweater with blue stripes and a matching baseball cap. Then he opened his eyes and smiled at her like he'd done on the day of his wedding nearly ten years ago. "Happy Father's Day," he said with warmth, "from my wife…"

That simple pronouncement touched Sonja deeply; although she still doubted, he understood fully what happened to him, she hoped he sensed what she intended to convey beneath his foggy state of consciousness.

Sara Henry has lived half a lifetime without understanding our connection and meaning in history…and now she seeks closure…but not mine or yours or Dad's, only hers. Her search for satisfaction is a waste of energy that won't accomplish anything worthwhile. Perhaps if you try something different…if you step aside and allow yourself to accept that you may never know what might have been, you'll find relief. You might even learn to forgive myself…or Sara Henry might turn into someone else altogether someday…who knows?

After spending two hours curled close beside him on a camp stool near the window overlooking Mount Assiniboine, she left without saying goodbye. He didn't awaken for several moments after she stepped away, but he appeared contented for the rest of that sunny Sunday afternoon. In time, he recovered enough strength to climb down the steep staircase using his crutch as support – just another small victory considering how bad he looked less than seven months ago. He thanked Sonja on numerous occasions, calling her angel, and making her promise to check in on him regularly from now on. "No excuses," he said in an exasperated tone – typical of him. "You're stuck with me for however long this takes," he laughed. Sonja didn't think twice about agreeing. She promised it as far as she could remember… though it was impossible to tell whether he heard her correctly or not when she turned her back on him heading downstairs to get ready for church services that night. He'd fallen asleep seconds later. And though she worried about him driving home alone in his truck after drinking coffee spiked with alcohol the previous night, it wasn't wise to mention anything about her concerns to him lest he become angry with her. Besides, she had faith in the medical team taking care of him and prayed he'd remain healthy and independent after regaining his balance and recovering from his latest setback. At least he'd regained some control over his legs.

As the sky darkened above the mountain peaks, he awoke and wandered aimlessly across the floor, pausing occasionally to stare silently through the glass walls towards Mount Assiniboine while muttering words that sounded vaguely familiar, though none of his visitors recognized any of them. He stopped in front of the open fridge and drank from a bottle of orange juice in a large plastic cup, holding it tightly in his right hand while reaching repeatedly underneath the sink with his left.

Then he sat cross-legged on a chair placed near an old television monitor showing images from a camera mounted halfway up Mount Assiniboine's snowcapped peak; he stared at the screen as if hypnotized by its contents for five straight minutes before abruptly rising and turning toward his bed. Without warning, he climbed atop the mattress and pulled the duvet cover down completely as he lay flat on top of the pillows and blankets. Within mere seconds he was snoring loudly as if exhausted beyond belief. Sonja watched from a distance for more than fifteen minutes, wondering if perhaps this was all some sort of act he played daily as part of his recovery process. Maybe there were pills hidden somewhere in case of emergency. Or maybe it was all a trick she missed out on because he refused to say aloud anything specific concerning himself or Morgana Lee. But then again, she reminded herself, why would Sara Henry seek out her mother now when all she needs to do is ask Dad? Why wait until now? Why bother coming here again after all this time? Surely, she must suspect I'm alive; otherwise, what kind of game plan can she expect to use for her own ends?

By late evening, everyone except Deacon's sister and brother-in-law packed their gear in preparation for leaving in a matter of hours for Prince Albert National Park. They wanted to return home before the weekend crowds arrived so they could enjoy nature without worrying about encountering too many people on vacation.

"We should probably call Mom soon." His youngest niece said once all luggage was stowed securely in the rear compartment of a black Dodge Ram pickup truck. "I doubt Auntie Sissy wants to deal with the stress of staying on alert 24/7 anymore, not with the way things look. It seems like every time we visit here, we come closer to finding out what really happened to Dad on the first anniversary of his disappearance."

Aunt Joan glanced back over her shoulder as they waited at a red light on Stony Plain Road. She wore a smile upon her lips…but not on the rest of her face. No wonder Uncle Jack hasn't mentioned bringing the kids along. Their presence wouldn't bring us any peace. Instead, she focused on the darkening streets ahead of them as they headed north toward Jasper. All those lights shining brightly in one direction…all alone in the other…

"Do we want to wake him up just to hear a replay of our conversations over dinner last night?" Joel asked hopefully. Although he was eager to see Mum and Granma again (she always kept him entertained), his mind had turned to thoughts of his father since hearing Auntie Anne and Cousin Emily speak so candidly about their childhood together recently; it seemed impossible that a person could be missing since 1972 without anyone knowing about it sooner…or ever since…especially considering all the attention his family paid to

Dad whenever they came visiting since his stroke. As far as his nephews were concerned, Grandpa Ken was invincible – almost indestructible given his age and health condition—until his collapse three weeks ago that resulted from a mild heart attack brought on by his high blood pressure medication, according to Dr. Dolan. Now he needed constant care from nurses and therapists, who told him not to push it too fast or strain himself unnecessarily during physical therapy exercises while working to regain full range of motion in his right side and arm movement after surgery repairing damaged tendons and ligaments in his upper body region following the trauma of being hit by an impaired driver six months earlier. A drunk woman had veered onto the highway and slammed into him at eighty miles per hour while he walked on footpath between parked vehicles searching for help for an injured deer alongside Highway 16 near Banff International Airport. Fortunately, the animal survived with only minor head trauma, whereas Ben Hemingway lost feeling in half of his extremities, including the fingers on both hands and toes on each leg, due to extensive nerve damage. For several weeks he barely resembled human flesh due to skin necrosis and tissue loss around multiple lacerations caused by broken bones, scrapes across shattered muscle, bruises covering bone shards, and torn veins throughout his legs and torso. He'd gone through intense rounds of radiation therapy which burned off dead cells causing scabs to form wherever there was scarring; this made healing more difficult until surgeons performed delicate microsurgery to repair severed arteries and replace ruptured muscles, tendons, and nerves, then replaced portions of his colon to restore bowel function. With such major injuries and treatment, nobody expected to ever walk again, let alone ride horses again. So, when a few days before Christmas, Ben surprised his loved ones by walking to the bathroom in one swift bound rather than crawling, and shortly thereafter climbing four flights of stairs in quick succession to retrieve a newspaper, they assumed he'd somehow cheated death and escaped unharmed. That was until they saw the scars, internal burns and swelling below his ribs where surgeons removed a section of intestine that had suffered severe arterial damage.

Joan nodded briefly at her son as they passed by the entrance gate at the end of the driveway leading past the guardhouse and parking lot at her parent's house just outside Rocky Mountain House, Alberta.

There's no need to rush your grandmother tonight, young man – we'll leave her sleeping for sure…not much point in waking her for one phone call – we don't want to freak her out anyway.

Morgana had arranged for the same nurse from the hospital to meet them at the house to aid if required. The patient remained unconscious the remainder of Saturday morning, but by noon, Morgana felt compelled to contact her husband's family in Canada, despite the fact she knew better than to believe Sara Henry would suddenly appear to reveal whatever secret she sought so desperately. When the telephone rang unexpectedly inside their rented apartment upstairs from Uncle Dave and Auntie Jeanette in Medicine Hat, she picked it up quickly without glancing at the caller ID display to avoid learning who called without asking permission beforehand, although she couldn't hide the excitement welling within her as soon as she listened to her sister-in-law talk about meeting with Mum and Granma today and wondered how they found out about everything that happened in Banff. She hadn't mentioned anything to David yet – not because they weren't close enough to confide in each other but simply because neither thought it best to upset him further when he was going through enough stress already; although he insisted he wanted to hear all about it as soon as possible, he admitted to suffering nightmares almost every day since returning home, plagued by terrible visions that sent tremors deep into his core, causing pain everywhere from his chest area down his arms and legs. He struggled to sleep most nights. Even on good mornings he appeared dazed.

"…and we spoke with my dad this morning while you two slept soundly, dear…"

Mom smiled as she recalled her conversation with the nurse at the hotel after arriving in town early that night, thinking back on those brief ten or eleven seconds of chatting with the attractive brunette doctor. After explaining the reason behind her trip, she requested the woman take a message for Jocelyn and send word back that she might need additional funds for groceries for their upcoming week-long stay to feed the entire party if necessary. But instead, the nurse suggested that perhaps she oughtn't go through the expense of cooking for nine months when the restaurant meals provided by the resort would be cheaper overall; especially considering hectic travel schedules often prevented either daughter or mum from getting away easily during weekends; also, with all their guests travelling together for fun during school holidays, there were usually plenty of people wanting to grab a bite together rather than eating separately. This was true even though it meant sharing tables with strangers. However, this did not worry Mother in the least; she didn't find the idea unusual when all agreed food tasted far worse when eaten solo. In addition, there was nothing wrong with dining together with friends, relatives, and extended family members; besides, she reasoned it helped pass the time waiting for everyone else to finish rather than sitting idly beside an empty table wishing someone would join them. Then, as if reading her mind while simultaneously trying not to offend, the nurse assured her she could afford another week at the resort, if necessary, and recommended she purchase extra bottles of water, juices and snacks at the market to avoid having to run out for something midweek if they forgot to stop by before heading to town later that afternoon after lunchtime shopping trips were complete for everyone at the mall…

"Oh wow! Thanks!" Her voice rose as tears filled her eyes; her throat constricted as a lump formed beneath her tongue against her teeth while struggling to swallow.

She looked across at her daughter who stood nearby watching her intently, ready for her mother to begin speaking again. "You shouldn't have done any of these things," she continued softly as a wave of emotion threatened to choke her completely; a single sob wracked her shoulders as she took a long breath to steady her trembling chin… "But thank you very much for doing so anyway." Turning slightly towards Morgana, she reached out and placed an affectionate hand on her daughter's shoulder, smiling broadly before saying, "…if I don't buy more stuff now, we're liable to be here until next year, aren't we sweetie?"

Sara's expression shifted from surprise to understanding as she realized why Morgana wanted to speak to her. Of course, it has been difficult for me to deal with this situation since I never imagined my husband could've committed suicide years ago; nor does any other member of the community seem willing to accept the obvious: he's still alive, living elsewhere under another name. I know all this must feel confusing for you and Auntie Sissy as well…as evidenced by what happened yesterday; but please trust me when I say that your parents will be okay…forgive me for telling you something that sounds so ridiculous. You deserve answers as badly as we do. Please tell Grandma… tell your brothers…please…"

It occurred to Morgana just prior to placing the receiver on its cradle what she'd forgotten – she left Uncle Dave in charge of taking the dogs outside while she stepped inside to check on David. Now she hurried downstairs to see if he was alright, fearing he may need medical assistance. To reassure herself he wasn't hurt when she entered the kitchen where they all ate breakfast nearly every morning, she peered over his shoulder to inspect whether he was lying on the floor or not, only to discover him holding a plate covered in scrambled eggs, bacon slices, sausage links and hash brown patties while he sat at his usual place at the island countertop.

As soon as Morgana walked closer and noticed his blank stare directed straight ahead at some unseen thing behind him – like a ghost–she screamed and bolted for the door as fast as her feet could carry her before anyone heard the commotion. At first, she ran blindly down the hallway toward the bedroom suite attached to their room upstairs before realizing there were voices coming from his side of the duplex. By then it was too late; Uncle Joe and Uncle Dave had emerged from their bedrooms dressed casually wearing bathrobes and slippers; they were arguing quietly at the bottom of the stairs as they headed towards him, unaware of the danger posed by Uncle Ken standing directly behind them as if invisible.

SIX

"Dad? Dad! Look out!" His son shouted above the rising rumble of thunderbolts erupting around them. "Danger ahead!"

David turned to face his oldest boy as lightning flashed white-hot through his peripheral vision. It lit up clouds rolling along a dark grey sky, casting stark shadows upon grassy hills and barren treed areas surrounding a lake. Thunder echoed across the open plain making them flinch involuntarily with shock.

Thunderbolt struck twice near Lake Athabasca in northeastern Alberta, Canada, according to National Weather Service forecasters. One bolt hit a small cluster of pine trees growing alongside the highway about fifty yards south of her parent's house, followed by another less powerful strike approximately twenty feet beyond it as David stared across at a large herd of grazing buffalo gathered on the opposite shoreline of a shallow marshland pond fed by runoff from the mountain valley where a hydroelectric dam was situated upstream, creating the largest reservoir in the province of British Columbia on the Peace River between Grande Prairie and Fort St John – three hundred kilometers apart. Another bolt exploded somewhere near Banff International Airport east of downtown Banff as the storm approached town. And then a third one landed a little farther west near the TransCanada Highway crossing Lake Louise in Jasper National Park with a roar unlike any he'd ever experienced before in his life; sending a surge of electricity coursing through his bloodstream with jolting waves of pain as sharp bolts tore chunks off branches in neighboring spruce forests along the highway; the crackling boom sounded so loud it rattled glass panes in several windows on homes overlooking the road. Some property owners reported hearing claps of thunder that rippled like giant drumheads striking each other miles distant. Others claimed the blast came nearer than anticipated; causing tremors to race down through the earth itself before dying abruptly just short of their front doors.

Auntie Anne had told David they should stay indoors whenever storms moved into town but being out here seemed safer than holing up in a basement or cellar. They were in a safe spot – just right for observing nature in action. As lightning flared overhead, he tried to remain calm and watch their approach to determine how bad it was likely to get. Fortunately, none touched ground near them yet and no rain fell, which made sense considering the temperature had dropped considerably since last evening's balmy weather in the mid-thirties Celsius plus or minus a degree or two overnight. All this heat and humidity caused by global warming was becoming increasingly common throughout North America, forcing authorities such as fire departments and local officials to scramble for solutions as climate patterns changed drastically in recent decades.

With great caution and attention paid to keeping his eyes always trained forward (except for looking sideways periodically for deer darting from bush to rock pile), he watched the herd of antelope graze peacefully across a ridge of mountains about eight kilometers away as the storm grew stronger and louder with increasing intensity. A few scattered snowflakes began falling as well. The air was crisp and cool despite the warmth of his body; however, he wore shorts and a thin cotton shirt, not thick parka clothing suitable for freezing conditions in January. If we lose power, it means our phones won't work unless we use batteries as backup sources for emergency lighting and heating. That isn't happening today; I doubt we'll need them anyway, thanks to that freakish windstorm on Tuesday night that knocked out electricity for days for thousands of households. He remembered seeing news reports showing crews working around clock to repair downed poles that needed replacing following a particularly violent squall accompanied by ice pellets that pelted towns in New Mexico, Oklahoma, Louisiana, and Texas, leaving hundreds without power. So, this could end up being an interesting day indeed.

He listened closely while trying to gauge where the noise originated. There! Over there! Down on the lakeshore. He spotted a lone figure walking slowly towards us from behind the bluff near the edge of the forest.

"Dad! Where are you?! Are you all, right?!" He shouted as he raced towards his father, concerned something had happened to him when he hadn't returned home earlier; maybe suffering from hypothermia since he had apparently been out there all night…or even longer. With the help of Uncle Joe rushing ahead with Morgana close behind, David caught sight of his older brother halfway across the pasture towards where he stood watching the advancing figure approaching from further down the hillside past where they were standing on their side of the lake at the base of Mount Rundle. Their faces appeared identical, except that David had inherited his mother's light brown hair and eyes whereas Joe resembled both his dad and grandfather. Although the resemblance became apparent only when they looked directly at each other. Both possessed the same deep set jaw lines with chiseled features of strong cheekbones and high bridges over prominent noses; although Uncle Jack always insisted those traits belonged entirely to his father; claiming Joe simply got whatever good genes lay dormant in his own DNA after a long line of farmers passed on before reaching adulthood, while insisting the man in question was named Jacobson instead of Smith. But regardless of whose bloodlines ran through whom most strongly, it was evident both men shared similar qualities including strength tempered with gentleness and humor while exhibiting an innate ability to love others unconditionally. This trait stemmed mainly from the fact neither man believed anyone deserved special treatment due to wealth, social status or position in society or politics. Nor did they judge based solely on appearance; preferring to look deeper within individuals to discover their core strengths and weaknesses; encouraging them to overcome adversity as necessary. In short, both respected people equally as humans rather than judging based primarily on age or sex – something important for young women and boys to learn early on, especially when dealing with authority figures such as school administrators as a result. When it comes time for you guys to go to university, remind me about this conversation, would yak? Because I think it's wise, we talk about this before then.

Joe slowed down as he approached his old friend and stopped beside him, turning slightly to shout across at their daughter as she drew near. "Hey sweetheart – what's wrong? Is anything bothering you?"

Sara glanced back at her parents briefly before glancing at Joe before shaking her head. "Not really," she replied with a slight smile before continuing her walk towards the trio. Her mother called her back with her arms wrapped tightly around her chest while Joe held her arm firm to prevent her straying too far astray. "We're talking about going camping next weekend."

"Oh yeah? Camping again? What for?"

Her father nodded enthusiastically. "Yes! We thought we might camp on the way to Prince George tomorrow, assuming it clears up a bit more, of course. Then take one week to drive up through Vancouver Island until we arrive in Seattle. Maybe another couple week driving across Washington state, Idaho, and Oregon, stopping often to hike and explore. Afterward, we'd have two months to cruise around the United States before hitting California and returning home, finishing our journey by summertime." He grinned proudly. "That ought to keep everyone occupied for sure. Your brothers and friends can come with us too if they want. Can't imagine why they wouldn't since all five of us are free now."

Sonja shook her head in response, smiling warmly for the first time since arriving at their campsite. "No thank you Dad. My folks suggested the trip to us last year; wanting to give my sister and myself an opportunity to spend some quality time together before she leaves for college next fall at McGill. Since Mom will be starting classes soon at UBC in Vancouver too…"

She trailed off momentarily before adding: "I'm happy doing things alone these days – just having fun exploring on vacations or heading out on adventures on weekends with your family, Joe. You know what I mean?"

"Absolutely," Joe assured her firmly; nodding vigorously to demonstrate his agreement with her sentiments.

Afterwards, Joe said to her husband with concern in his voice. "… are you feeling okay Sis?"

Sara didn't reply immediately as she stared intently at her younger brother; wondering if he knew about his sister's mental illness or perhaps understood how much trouble she was struggling with at present. He seemed oblivious to it, though, and merely continued to observe their surroundings as if nothing unusual had occurred. Not responding quickly gave him plenty of time to mull over the answer to that question himself as he studied the woman he loved so dearly with a puzzled expression on his handsome face during the brief pause between them speaking; finally shaking his head to clear away his thoughts and respond smoothly, as if he were reading someone else's mind as opposed to hers; which was clearly impossible considering his lack of experience with such matters prior.

"…yes. I guess so."

It took almost thirty minutes for Joe to find a phone service provider with coverage nearby; calling the nearest police station to ask officers if there had been any report filed regarding a missing person recently in Grand Falls-Windsor – a city of nearly 30,000 residents on the southern shores of Lac Saint-Pierre (Greater Montreal). It wasn't until half an hour later that he received confirmation via radio message from an officer working out of another community closer to where he lived on a different section of highway that a local businessman reported a client missing earlier that morning. Police were still searching for him when they responded to his call shortly thereafter but had no luck finding Mr. Goudreau as a result and weren't certain whether foul play had occurred. His name meant absolutely nothing whatsoever to them since the search party found only empty bottles left in bushes alongside the TransCanada Highway leading north away from town toward Lake O'Hara and then onward towards Prince Rupert and beyond in British Columbia. No one could remember seeing him coming southbound, either before dark or afterwards once dusk settled in; according to the caller. He also mentioned Mr. Goudreau owned properties in Jasper National Park but hadn't checked to see if they'd searched any of them lately or known if it was possible, he may have gone hiking through the area yesterday afternoon. However, the landowner said he rarely ventured very far outside town, preferring instead to stay put and watch television every day as the winter snows descended upon northern regions throughout Canada in December and January. Yet the owner couldn't explain why Mr. James Edward Johnstone would choose to leave home at all without telling his wife where he intended to travel on Saturday morning given the inclement weather rolling into Grande Prairie.

As usual when discussing serious matters like this with Joe, David had remained quiet throughout the discussion. Instead listening intensely with intense concentration while remaining focused on making occasional notes of various details on the map provided by Uncle Jack for future reference when the two families decided to return here someday; planning their vacation road trips along the Rockies coast for years to come. Once Joe hung up the receiver, David turned to Sonja with curiosity written large on his expressive, round face while staring at her intently. "So…what do you think?"

She smiled gently. "I don't believe Mr. Goudreau intentionally walked into that blizzard and lost his life, David. I feel sad it happened this way. Perhaps if it hadn't been so cold, we could assume he suffered a heart attack in its aftermath and froze to death somewhere out there among the trees and rocks below Mount Rundle."

David nodded agreeably before leaning against an iron pole marking one corner of the site's parking lot. "You're probably right."

His sister leaned heavily forward slightly with elbows resting on knees while looking over at his profile; knowing full well he was fully capable of thinking for himself.

"…but I have questions that aren't being answered," she continued softly, pausing for emphasis.

"And what exactly does that mean?" he asked quietly.

Instead of answering his question straightaway, she chose instead to glance down at her hands before gazing out over the frozen lake and hillsides surrounding it. The sun had begun setting behind Mount Rundle already leaving only the faintest hint of pink in its wake while twilight settled across all directions – becoming darker than evening at midnight, yet still nowhere near darkness. A thin veil of mist clung to the surface of the water creating a hazy fog bank rising above the treetops bordering Lake Ana amok, giving everything an ethereal glow from beneath as clouds covered part of the sky to block direct sunlight. Even the wind blowing briskly off the lakeshore seemed muted under cloudy cover, carrying only the faint whisper of rustling branches overhead, causing a gentle breeze stirring fallen snow flurries drifting across the open space before reaching shore.

With her gaze fixed on nothing, she spoke slowly as though choosing each word carefully before committing it to memory. "Mr. Graham has lied about a number of things relating to this case, David. If it hasn't escaped your attention by now."

He glanced over briefly and shrugged.

"Graham claimed he made contact with Mr. Goudreau late Friday night following his disappearance by telephone, asking about his whereabouts." She paused for effect; taking a moment for her words to sink in and impress themselves permanently on his consciousness before beginning again with renewed vigor. "Yet I know for sure that never occurred. There's no cell service in Jasper unless you happen to stop at the restaurant or hotel where it's available inside buildings." As promised, she kept her focus on nothing except the scenery.

"Then on Sunday morning, the same cop came up to our cabin early in hopes of getting us to help locate him when Graham sent him up here first thing. Only to find out there's been no call placed from Jasper nor anywhere in North America for that matter – not even on-board planes end route."

Another silence fell between them as they stared out at the scene around them.

When Graham called me yesterday afternoon – after you left - I told him about our conversation with Mrs. Graham on Monday and explained why we didn't tell her the truth about her husband. That we felt compelled to let him lie rather than risk upsetting her further and causing distress for herself and the children when they eventually arrived home today, which he said he hoped wouldn't be too long from now as it was obvious, he cared deeply about them. Graham added that he believed Ms. Henry was suffering from post-traumatic stress disorder brought on by whatever she endured or witnessed while serving overseas with UNEF II. When I pressed him about what specifically she had experienced during that mission – including if he suspected she saw anything bad, he simply replied that she likely suffered something horrible enough to warrant PTSD regardless of what she went through – especially given that none of those troops stationed in Antarctica ever returned to Earth afterwards. This statement sounded like bullshit to me at the time, but since I didn't press for information, I accepted it at face value. Why should I doubt a fellow member of the military when Graham seems loyal to veterans everywhere?" Her tone shifted abruptly from conversational ease into one laced with emotion. "Not everyone likes soldiers; you understand."

She looked up directly into her lover's eyes and smiled gently as she finished talking; trying desperately not to show weakness or disappointment with him as she did so; hoping he would accept her explanation easily and forgive her reluctancy to trust others with important details about herself. But he refused to look back at her and remain silent for so long he grew angry with her for ignoring his unspoken plea not to discuss personal matters within earshot of other people nearby.

Finally, unable to stand his silence anymore, Dave sighed unhappily as he gazed at his sister. "What makes you think Graham wanted you to go hiking with him yesterday morning anyway? And what about your job at the hospital? You can barely get up early on Saturdays these days thanks to the hours required by the emergency ward and surgery schedule you've worked for weeks. So why bother?"

Sonja blinked rapidly several times while biting onto the bottom lip she suddenly realized had become swollen overnight due to anxiety. Then she cleared her throat and tried again before continuing more calmly in a lower voice. "That's precisely what we need to talk about right now, sweetie," she said firmly. "Why do you suspect Graham invited us here on purpose?"

Dave hesitated briefly and scratched his chin, deep in thought as he considered all angles before deciding against mentioning Graham's request to meet him somewhere privately. Instead, he waited patiently until Sonja finally offered him a clue in the form of an answer, allowing him to follow her logic step by step. The conversation went something like:

"It can't be that obvious why I think it was intentional. So, if my suspicions don't seem too far out there… then…" And so forth for over half an hour when they were interrupted by Forest coming into the room with some papers tucked under one arm, wearing only loose white cotton pajama bottoms which made them look much less flattering than usual since his muscular physique wasn't hidden behind tight fabric anymore after gaining weight during his illness last winter. He set down the documents carefully near Sonja and gave Dave a wry smile through tired eyes before walking past them back toward their bedroom at the rear of the house where they would have privacy and not disturb anyone else. They followed suit but stopped at the kitchen entrance where Forest waved them inside first without making any comment. There might even have been a hint of relief in his expression; clearly, he needed some time alone with friends who weren't involved in the legal proceedings.

Forest didn't take off his sunglasses or sit down anywhere. Rather, he paced around nervously from corner to corner of the small living room. His gaze wandered everywhere, occasionally stopping momentarily on various objects strewn across shelves and tables. A single red candle burned steadily atop the coffee table nearby, its soft orange light bathing everything within sight in warm shades of golds and oranges as well as darker hues of red. It added to the autumnal feel already present throughout Seymours' home, though no sign could be seen indicating fall had arrived yet outside these walls.

Sara sat beside Forest next to the sofa where she always preferred sitting anyway despite knowing better. As soon as Forrest saw how close together, they were forced to sit, he immediately scooted over slightly towards Sonja—who hadn't moved a muscle nor spoke up in protest. This caused Sonja's leg muscles to tense uncomfortably but she kept quiet. If anything, her own legs looked equally uncomfortable thanks to her short stature compared to everyone else seated around the large circular wood-topped dining table, including Forest himself, although he seemed unaware of this fact and simply stared silently ahead of him instead of focusing on either one person.

There were five chairs arranged in two rows facing each other between the wall opposite the entry hall and Seymours'. Only Seymours joined them midway down the long rectangular surface along with Dave. No one mentioned it, but there should've been six people here besides Seymours. Emma LaChapelle, a friend, and fellow member of Seymours' lived upstairs. But the police wouldn't let her leave the area surrounding Seymours' residence except when escorted by three officers at once. That left Sonja and Forest feeling quite guilty for leaving her alone. Not only did they miss being able to discuss their theories with her, but the poor girl was probably scared witless wondering whether someone was still trying to hurt her. After hearing the description she'd provided of Gordon Fenton's attacker, they knew he certainly deserved whatever he got, however horrible he appeared to be. Even Forest felt compelled to warn Sarah that if he ever found him, it would end badly, especially considering that she was supposedly pregnant with his child. Of course, that statement came entirely secondhand via Dave, since the man who claimed to know nothing was currently in protective custody away from Seymours. At least it meant David was safe for now and could rest peacefully rather than worrying constantly about his daughter.

As Forrest continued pacing, Sara glanced over at Dave every so often and asked questions that hinted at curiosity regarding what exactly had happened in New Orleans recently. In return, he told her just enough detail to keep her informed without providing specifics that might help the killer. He also refrained from asking Sara directly to explain herself and her actions, knowing very little could possibly make sense based solely upon what he heard on the news.

After a couple rounds of such questioning, Forest reached down with trembling fingers and picked up the phone resting on top of a pile of notes on the wooden desk situated in front of the bookcase. The device was plugged into its charging cradle at the side. For a moment, Forrest regarded it with suspicion until he remembered it was the same phone used by the murderer to contact Seymours' son, Grant. Once that possibility became clear, his face hardened, revealing a mix of anger and shame.

With his finger, Forrest tapped several buttons on the keypad. The phone rang twice before picking up, ringing out loud enough for the others to hear, which was impressive given it was a landline rather than the latest smart phones that allowed for silent calls to work automatically when placed near a compatible cell tower.

"…hello…"

A woman's low, melodic voice sounded over the receiver, speaking quickly. With great care and attention to sound alone, Forest held the phone closer to his ear. "I'm sorry to bother you so late, Mrs. Higginson."

Sara Jane's tone softened. "No trouble, young man. What can I do for Seymours today?"

He took another few seconds to gather his thoughts before responding quietly: "…he wants to speak with me and has invited us here tonight at midnight in order to ask for my assistance. Do you happen to know who this might be by chance? Has he requested your company earlier or will our meeting coincide with yours somehow? We're hoping maybe to catch the old coot before he makes an appearance."

Forrest paused halfway through his sentence, listening intently.

"—no offense, Mr. Marshall. Please forgive an old lady for thinking the worst, but Seymours never invites anybody over without warning unless it involves serious business involving the family. Tonight, feels different, though."

She nodded approvingly. "Good eye, Forrest," she whispered loudly. He smiled softly and thanked her, but Sara wanted to add another thing. "And please try to remember we aren't alone in talking like this… we shouldn't be giving away anything important."

"Thank you, Miss Higginson," said Forest, pausing to listen again before replying more confidently in a higher pitch: "…right, good point."

Now Sara repeated her request for confirmation, saying it aloud: "Does the name Gordon Fenton mean anything to Seymours?"

Without missing a beat, Forest answered yes. Now they all listened closely for details he couldn't resist repeating. When he finished explaining, Sara turned her head slightly toward the hallway door that led deeper into the house, looking thoughtful and intrigued.

Forest caught movement in his peripheral vision. Both of his parents glanced in his direction. Sonja frowned with confusion while Dave leaned forward with interest. Sara Jane looked amused. Forest returned their gazes but remained nonchalant to hide his feelings from betraying him. Suddenly he wondered if his dad had noticed him watching his mother glance in his father's general vicinity when his mind began whirling with ideas about their relationship. Maybe Dad was going to mention something later. Or perhaps Sonja was planning some sort of surprise party for him tonight after all. Either way, it was likely to turn embarrassing if she revealed his secret plan in front of his wife and best friends. He doubted his ability to handle it gracefully, particularly since his confidence level wasn't high enough to begin with—not even remotely. And yet he dared hope things would go well anyway. How else could he avoid having everyone find out about his mental breakdown if they were all privy to it beforehand? Besides, if David and Emma really loved him as much as he believed they did, they surely understood the pressure of juggling professional duties with personal ones, especially when working under the kind of stress he'd suffered in recent years. Right?

When Forest failed to respond to the curious looks directed towards him, his parents turned back and resumed their discussion as though he hadn't spoken up at all. Sara cleared her throat politely and changed subject accordingly: "So what does Gordon Fenton stand to gain by killing Seymours?"

"Not sure," replied Forrest honestly after taking another minute to mull over possibilities. "But there seems plenty for whoever stands behind him." He paused briefly. "What about Graham Higginson?"

Graham hadn't come up during Seymours' call, presumably because the caller thought Graham's connection had already been established and there were no new developments requiring further investigation, according to Forest. However, if Graham was connected to the crime, why hadn't Seymours mentioned that part during their phone conversation? Why wasn't Graham among those contacted directly prior to inviting us here?

Or wait! Did he invite them personally because he knew Graham was involved? Is Graham lying to me in some fashion? Could he have known all along that I suspected him of being a possible suspect? If so... then he must've figured out what else, we're capable of doing together too... And if he did indeed have suspicions that I worked together with someone else in the case, why bring Graham here first? If they both planned on using Graham against me, why would they tell him everything about themselves right from the start? Unless... "Is Graham still under watch, Sara?"

Sara nodded. "Yes. The police are keeping a discreet distance from him, though I doubt they'll risk putting anyone directly in his path at night without telling him in advance." She shrugged.

This made perfect sense given that the man seemed intent on murdering someone else at any cost—if Graham wasn't the intended target of this crime, there was no reason not to warn him of impending danger. They weren't playing Russian Roulette with guns anymore;

now the victim risked ending up dismembered or worse. So far as Graham knew, nobody would be waiting outside his house armed and ready for action while he slept. Yet if someone shot an arrow in through a window or slit open his bedroom door in darkness and killed him as a result – well, then they'd be committing a heinous double homicide and could expect swift arrest and prosecution if arrested and brought in alive rather than dead. The problem was, Graham could never know what he'd stepped into. It'd take days for investigators to uncover and piece together evidence proving he conspired with a murderous criminal who'd just committed multiple crimes in a single act and whose motives were completely unknown, making it difficult for authorities to pinpoint a motive without risking the perpetrator slipping away undetected forever. There was simply no time to play dumb when you faced such overwhelming odds against you, thus the need for immediate action before the next victim fell prey to the same fate.

Forest sighed heavily. His gaze shifted over the table, examining his surroundings until it rested squarely on Seymours' framed photo.

It's true. Seymours has betrayed me. He knows full well how hard I fought these past months just to save my family, fighting to hold onto a job most people consider beneath them because of the sacrifices required by such professions. My dedication deserves respect regardless of whether people believe it comes from vanity or greed. Seymours chose not to give it to me because I'm a lawyer—" He paused abruptly but continued, nonetheless. "If he hasn't always supported what I do or understand why a career attorney fights dirty against criminals for money rather than justice like most people want from lawyers… Then fine!" Forrest spats bitterly. "Let him think what he likes." Turning away from Seymours' picture with a snarl, Forest glared at Dave and Sonja with equal parts frustration and defiance. "We're done here for the evening… Let Seymours rot and die somewhere dark and cold."

Sonja spoke in a calm voice, attempting to placate him while remaining firm: "Don't be too hasty."

Dave didn't say anything but stood with his jaw jutting out and eyes wide. Clearly, he wasn't impressed with Forrest's attitude or decision-making process regarding accepting Seymours' betrayal.

However, it appeared David agreed wholeheartedly. "That bastard," murmured Dave quietly under his breath. He stared at the floor as though deep inside himself searching for something to focus on besides revenge. A moment later, however, his expression brightened considerably once something came up in that search. "I love this place! Where did you get those books, Dad? You found a library hidden away between rooms?"

Forest gave him a smile, pleased that he got one of those rare answers that helped rather than caused additional problems to deal with afterwards, although he admitted privately to himself that the real question should've been where his father had learned to read instead of merely learning how to navigate around town. But there were other questions worth asking about the answer to that inquiry; the biggest one being why his dad needed to learn English in the first place when English speakers lived only a couple miles from him, and therefore could communicate in his own language whenever necessary, leaving little room for excuses about needing to use it for professional reasons when he already spent so much time in Seymours' home. That left two options: He wanted it as background information for research purposes and had forgotten how important the subject matter was to his studies when the opportunity presented itself to acquire it; or he desired English for personal benefit—to improve his reading skills and become proficient in another culture's writing style in hopes of becoming fluent someday soon. Perhaps he also hoped to win some scholarship based upon his success, or even secure his future as an author by publishing a translation in addition to his original work. Of course, translating would be easier with better literacy training.

The possibility that he might seek a literary award or sponsorship seemed highly unlikely considering that Forest rarely saw him devoting any free moments from legal obligations towards writing fiction. In fact, there probably hadn't been a novel sitting on the shelf anywhere throughout their lives except maybe the few novels by John Grisham that Mom had bought for Father for Christmas last year. As if inspired by whatever had occurred to him just then, Forest added: "Maybe Dad wrote all of those stories down before coming here."

David turned quickly in response, smiling broadly again at his son. "You may be onto something, Forest."

"Huh?" said Forrest incredulously.

Both fathers laughed heartily, turning their attention back to each other. They held hands across the kitchen table with obvious affection; the men sat side-by-side on either end while Sara perched in the middle. All three were silent for a long second as they gazed lovingly into one another's eyes while holding hands until finally Dave broke the spell by clearing his throat and changing subjects rapidly. "Anyway…" he started off hesitantly, "we're happy you decided not to leave your father behind, Dad. We love you, Forrest," said David warmly as he squeezed his hand and smiled brightly. "No more secrets ever again… Not after hearing this morning how much, you care about us—how hard you tried to keep us safe over Christmas." After giving his son a chance to nod his agreement, David looked straight ahead at Sonja again. Her gaze met his steadily. For a moment she looked sad but recovered within seconds, offering David an understanding look, and returning his smile with warmth, knowing very well how difficult it was for David to make himself vulnerable before others when speaking about something so private.

Then David reached over and took the hand that belonged to Sonja. He kissed her fingers tenderly before releasing them and pointing at Forest. "He understands how you feel now," he said reassuringly before continuing more confidently: "And we're grateful."

As David rose from his chair, he looked intently at his son, studying him for signs of emotion in reaction to what they'd heard. With great reluctance, Forrest slowly shook his head to let his dad know nothing had changed, not when it came to feeling guilty or otherwise letting David or anyone else see how deeply affected, he'd been by what happened at Seymours'. No way was he willing to admit defeat by revealing just how badly Seymours had hurt him emotionally by refusing him forgiveness. Instead, he offered David a forced halfhearted grin while trying desperately not to wince at the memory of losing control of himself when Seymours pushed his wife aside and walked towards him. The urge to jump forward despite all common sense and rush over and attack him had been strong enough to overwhelm even Forrest's pride and dignity as a man. It'd taken every ounce of willpower he possessed not to launch myself at Seymours and try to tear him limb from leg.

Why am I resisting so strongly? Why can't I forgive him as easily as you guys seem able to? What else is there inside of me? Maybe this will help explain things for me, too.

"…and now for dessert…"

They ate in silence for several minutes as they savored every bite of chocolate mousse, strawberry shortcake topped with fresh berries – red ones – and coffee sweetened with sugar. When they finished eating and began washing dishes, Forrest asked Sonja, "How does one go about researching old newspapers online?"

She smiled widely. "There are thousands of websites where one can search various papers dating back to the 1800s, including microfilm editions of many national publications, some of which date as far back as the 1700s."

"Where would you recommend starting our searches?"

Again, she grinned happily at his interest in history, clearly relishing sharing what knowledge she gained from her own research projects since she grew up near here herself. She leaned over slightly in her chair and peered over at Forrest with her brow arched. "Well… How good an internet user is you today?"

To which Forrest nodded.

Her eyebrows twitched upward. "Can you use Google well enough to find basic information?"

With a quick affirmation from him, she went on. "Okay, so we have two choices here. Either you show yourself capable of navigating around a website properly with minimal assistance and learn to do everything independently—or I walk you through it step-by-step and point out exactly how easy and intuitive the whole thing really is—including the ability to zoom in or magnify images with a single click."

Forest raised his right shoulder defensively as if protecting himself from something unwanted. "...I guess that means you'll teach me then?" he said weakly, almost apologetically. If there was ever someone less likely to ask for directions or help, he couldn't remember whom he might've thought of recently. To be fair, his reluctancy stemmed solely from self-doubt; yet he'd never considered the consequences of refusing any attempt at teaching his daughter or anyone else if doing so meant getting caught defying authority by refusing instructions from law enforcement officers investigating the crime or prosecuting attorneys handling the case against him. His greatest fear remained being charged with obstructing justice in some way; but if the alternative was allowing the person, he was closest to in the world suffer the same fate Seymours did because of his selfishness – then he'd gladly accept the blame and pay whatever price was levied upon him for having allowed it to happen in the first place. So far as Forrest knew, no one had died directly due to his refusal thus far, and neither of Seymours' surviving parents appeared intent on charging him with obstruction of justice… But that doesn't mean he won't change his mind and decide to charge him anyway. Or worse still, call on authorities outside North Carolina to arrest him wherever he happens to live at the time. He didn't trust Seymours personally; so perhaps he wouldn't hesitate to turn to other powerful friends if faced with a choice like that to protect their families from further threats posed by Forest's stubborn independence. And God alone knows what kind of pressure Seymours could apply without even blinking…

Seymours was dead. Dead! Gone forever… Just like that… He lost both of my best friends… My mother… He killed everyone in a car crash on New Year's Eve when he fell asleep at the wheel. Killed 'em all!

His shoulders drooped low as though his burden weighed him down terribly heavy. Yet he continued to shake off that weight momentarily and stand tall again as his spirit lifted, determined to fight harder than ever before against anything else life threw his way now that Seymours wasn't looking over his shoulder anymore. There aren't going to be any more surprises waiting for me if I don't allow any of Seymours' family members, acquaintances, or business colleagues to surprise me along with their next move… I'm going to watch for them instead and shut their mouths permanently if need be." Forrest glared coldly at Seymours' killer, daring death to return to torment him any longer, adding defiantly: "But if you dare come near me—ever again!"

Sonja laughed softly at him and gently touched her finger to Forrest's chin as though she were making sure he hadn't closed his eyes during the conversation. "What's wrong, Forrest? Are you okay? Did I offend you somehow?"

Shaking her head slightly, Sonja smiled at her son's discomfort. "It's alright, Forrest." Then, glancing at Dave and catching the subtle warning from her husband not to give away any hints she might've inadvertently revealed about Seymours being a murderer, she lowered her voice. "If Seymours isn't the reason you refused to leave home—"

"—he won't tell me about him, Sonja." It sounded like Forrest was saying these words for himself.

Forrest's lips pursed together briefly, concealing what thoughts lay hidden behind them until he suddenly shrugged his shoulders. "Whatever," he muttered under his breath. Even though he wanted so badly to deny the implications made clear in David and Sonja's answers, the proof that Seymours planned on killing him was overwhelming evidence, nonetheless. *Too bad for me. You win this round, Seymours; but there won't be a third. Next time I'll be ready for you.* This was a promise from Forrest Harrison, Jr.

By late afternoon on Thursday (December 27th), Seymours was finally beginning to get used to sleeping somewhere besides his home office desk. Although Seymours hated lying in bed with people watching over him as they always had done in his childhood, he accepted that such surveillance was necessary for him while living in proximity with other human beings whose motives weren't quite as pure and noble as he expected. It wasn't just the fact of being forced into a small space with someone else; *it's something about these rooms we're renting—I feel like I'm walking around inside one of those big-top tents where* clowns go to die or whatever circus performers are supposed to do when their career has ended before its time. But there isn't much choice at my age: you can only lie on your back so long after turning thirty years old without getting too bored if not outright suicidal from lack of variety. So far Seymours' biggest worry had been whether the woman across the room would be able to sleep well enough next to me given her history with men—she'd said she didn't have any problems but still I found myself feeling guilty whenever another man entered the building wearing a suit and tie even though Seymours knew perfectly well none of them were interested in me personally. He tried telling himself he should be grateful for what he got out of his marriage by keeping up appearances instead of giving up completely since no matter how badly things turned out between Sara and Seymours anyway, the kids would probably grow up fine because his wife already took good care of all our needs…but it made sense neither Seymours nor Sarah ever thought through very clearly why some people choose monogamy rather than cheating when faced with infidelity within their relationship. And yet everyone knows adultery makes perfect logical sense under certain circumstances, and often leads couples to more fulfilling relationships afterward. As Seymours lay down in bed that night, looking at the ceiling above him lit up faintly with blue-green phosphorescence, he wondered how many times this week they might change apartments until the murderer was caught.

The phone rang early Friday morning. Seymours opened the curtain covering his window and peeked outside through faint grey light filtering through thin wisps of fog swirling along the ground below. His first impulse upon hearing a ringing phone at six o'clock on the day after Christmas was usually to answer it straightaway. Then again, Seymours hadn't gotten a lot of calls lately due to his reluctancy to leave the safety of this little cocoon of solitude where Seymours spent most of his days alone working from the comfort of a sofa. This time however, considering recent events, Seymours decided better safe than sorry and waited until seven-fifty-five before answering. "Good evening," he said to the telephone's receiver sitting atop Seymours' lap. The voice was vaguely familiar despite the distance separating Seymours from whoever was speaking. "Is Mr. Dufresne available?"

"He is not."

SEVEN

This was strange. Usually, Seymours could tell right away who was calling simply based upon which voice came over the line—usually Seymours wouldn't need to ask anyone beforehand whom they meant. Even so, Seymours felt sure he knew exactly why somebody called. A moment later a new sound reached his ears via the speakerphone in front of Seymours' face. From beyond Seymours' door came a low thump followed quickly by two loud bangs against the wall behind the phone's earpiece—this caused Seymours to jump involuntarily off the chair as if expecting someone to come barging in during such a call. After listening carefully for several minutes, hoping this mystery caller would explain everything immediately now that he'd interrupted Seymours from work, Seymours heard nothing except static noise coming from both ends—a sign the connection had gone bad somehow. Seymours stared blankly at the dead airspace above the microphone in shock. How could the person on the other end know anything about Seymours?

Seymour sat motionless in front of the TV screen showing CNN with the volume muted throughout the rest of the weekend. When Saturday night rolled round, the FBI director gave an update to reporters regarding developments in their investigation, including the arrest of a second suspect connected to the crime and further analysis indicating DNA traces discovered on the victim matched none of the suspects arrested thus far—all this sent Seymours reeling with disbelief at first but soon he began taking the news seriously. On Sunday morning,

Seymours looked down at the letter lying beside him on the floor in plain view as if waiting patiently for Seymours to notice and pick it up once again. In case the police missed it last time. Or perhaps to show us they've already seen it, thought Seymours bitterly. Maybe it belongs to the killer. No wonder the bastard hasn't told anybody he killed Frank yet. They haven't found him yet either. Seymours sighed, picking up the paper. He unfolded it carefully, reading every word. At least this will help keep me sane here, although it'll make my job harder. If I let this bother me too much, then maybe Seymours won't be able to concentrate anymore…

"…and Seymours says he feels compelled to continue his search for the identity of Jack Dalton following evidence revealed to Seymours recently suggesting there may be a link between this murderer and Seymours own personal background…"

On Monday, Seymours received an email containing the same message Seymours had forwarded himself earlier in the week via his desktop computer and printed out onto eight sheets of legal printer paper—the exact size allowed per page for faxes to the government. With each sheet folded four times along one edge, the total length of Seymours' hand-written note was almost three feet, nearly touching the top of his fridge when hung vertically. Seymours held the letters together in the palm of his hands for several seconds before opening the cover on the side of his laptop and placing one of the pages inside, pressing hard until it slid down through slots cut into its interior surface. Then Seymours repeated this process with seven additional copies to save money using toner cartridges—he couldn't afford ink jet printers these days. Finally, when the document appeared as complete on his monitor screen as possible, Seymours deleted everything but his original handwritten copy. He placed the remaining papers on Seymours' kitchen table and went downstairs to eat breakfast. By lunchtime he had managed to read through ten thousand words of the file he compiled. Seymours ate dinner quietly, trying not to dwell on the implications of his discovery—it wasn't easy. Once his meal finished, he poured a glass of vodka and sat staring vacantly at the television set while scanning the channels endlessly until finally switching it off altogether. Seymours walked upstairs to his bedroom—there he paced aimlessly in the dark for half an hour, eventually reaching for the bottle full of pills left beside his bed from previous occasions when Seymours felt especially miserable. We can't let anything distract us from finding this thing that wants us dead…

It occurred to Seymours on the way upstairs that the best place to find the answer to his question would be in the basement where he kept all his research materials, files and notes pertaining specifically to Jack Dalton—if they contained any clues about him whatsoever. That might also mean the reason nobody else knows much about Jack is because Seymours never did reveal anything useful to other researchers since leaving Harvard University twenty years ago or so. Not to mention Seymours' tendency to hoard documents, receipts, photos, and various bits of memorabilia relating to his past projects. For the sake of comparison and future reference, it seemed wise to begin sifting through Seymours' papers once more after all these weeks, but then again maybe not. Why bother searching for something you don't even remember having hidden in storage? It's impossible to forget stuff like that. But at the very least Seymours had learned by now that the killer would want him to think that way, so he'd hesitate to look. Seymours closed the bedroom curtains over the windows as far as he dared go before crawling into bed fully clothed with his coat still draped over him as usual.

As dawn broke on Tuesday, Seymours returned to work refreshed and eager for the chance to focus solely on his latest project for several hours uninterrupted. Only two of Seymours' employees answered his knock at the outer office door: John Taylor from security and Dave Smithson, head accountant at Seymours' company, who had accompanied Seymours during a brief inspection visit to meet with potential business partners overseas only days before. Since we're meeting these guys halfway around the world on Monday, he thought to himself as he greeted them warmly with a handshake. Both men had worked closely with Seymours for more than fifteen years so far, making themselves indispensable assets to what was fast becoming North America's largest firm specializing in financial services and software solutions for large corporate entities across different industries. Now, with their boss nowhere near ready for the day's tasks, it fell entirely upon them to ensure Seymours stayed focused and free of distractions—not that it would take too long until they realized they'd lost control completely if not sooner, according to their experiences dealing with Seymours.

After greeting them in turn, Seymours stepped aside briefly while Taylor helped his colleagues put away some paperwork stacked neatly on one corner of his desk while Dave sorted through stacks of invoices piled high beside him on the adjacent counter. Seymours stood in silence watching as Dave picked up one bill with great interest…then another…and another. Suddenly, Dave stopped moving abruptly in apparent confusion as if wondering if he forgot something important before going ahead and signing the invoice and passing it back over to Taylor. To give Dave a break, Taylor moved forward slightly toward his own pile of papers to check on progress there before returning swiftly back behind the counter where he handed the bills directly to Seymours without glancing at them. As Seymours signed them all off with his neat signature and date stamp, he noticed his secretary had just arrived upstairs wearing a smart black jacket instead of her uniform; she glanced nervously towards Seymours in anticipation, awaiting instructions from him on how to spend the morning. But Seymours didn't seem inclined to speak for a few moments longer as he peered into the depths of the cabinet beneath the filing cabinets lining either side of the wall opposite him—his gaze shifting repeatedly from shelf to shelf until it hit upon an old box labeled "Jack Alferez Papers." There were two dozen more boxes filled with similar ones in varying sizes stored underneath that one—some labelled as clearly as possible (Filed Under) and others not as well—but this box was special since Seymours remembered seeing its contents somewhere recently enough.

With trembling fingers, he pulled out the drawer next to Seymours' desk and rummaged through the small collection of envelopes and postcards stuffed inside it until he eventually located the thick folder in question. Carefully removing the heavy cardboard box from among its companions, he brought it closer to the desk with the other folders. Seymours lifted the lid on the bottommost section of the container and tipped it gently down so a layer of paper slid slowly to one side exposing a stack of manila envelope sleeves inside a shallow pocket. Taking a pen from his shirt pocket, he turned to write down the names on those labels for reference when suddenly a flash of light burst from within the darkness beyond the window above and blinded him momentarily. Seymours stumbled backward instinctively into the room's nearest wall and covered his eyes against the sudden glare. Seconds passed before he recovered, blinking rapidly, and shaking his head to clear his vision. The sound of gunfire erupted from the hall outside with an echo ricocheting throughout Seymours' home office–cum-office. Two loud bangs sounded again—as if from multiple shots fired simultaneously—followed by three more bullets striking the building's exterior walls in quick succession. One bullet hit Seymours' ceiling—with perfect accuracy—right in front of him.

When at last Seymours regained consciousness again several minutes later—wearing no clothes except shoes and socks—the gunfight ended as quickly as it started thanks to the arrival of several police cars zooming in with lights flashing through the front gate with sirens wailing. A squad car raced into Seymours' yard, skidding across gravel, and kicking up dirt everywhere as the officers climbed out of their vehicle and hurried over to Seymours' house. Several more vehicles entered Seymours' street from nearby directions, filling most of Elmwood Avenue with bright yellow headlights blaring through the predawn air. After exchanging brief pleasantries—a routine affair considering how often Seymours met local law enforcement representatives face to face lately—an officer named Dez Skaggs led Seymours upstairs to sit on his sofa while Skaggs called headquarters via phone to request immediate backup arrive to secure Seymours' perimeter.

"What happened?" asked Seymours as Skaggs escorted him upstairs.

Skaggs stared silently at him for thirty seconds without answering; then continued speaking: "…I'm afraid Seymours has been shot by someone apparently aiming for us," said Skaggs flatly as he approached his colleague's desk with a pair of earphones hanging around his neck attached to a mobile telephone. He removed one end from his headset as though preparing to plug it in—then hesitated, turning around to glance back towards Seymours before continuing. "He seems pretty shaken up, but he insists he's okay, although he does need medical attention right away."

Deftly maneuvering the microphone plugged into the jack in Skaggs' lapel, Seymours heard nothing but static over the line but could see on Skaggs' dashboard that it connected with a distant call center somewhere south of Toronto Ontario. From here, there were many possibilities why things weren't working properly – maybe a signal blockage due to distance…or maybe a connection fault between Canada and the United States. But Skaggs seemed unphased by the situation as he switched phones, placing one handset down for Skaggs to use rather than wasting time waiting for this new receiver to dial. His first try connecting with the same number resulted in a busy tone—maybe a temporary loss of coverage or interference…or maybe it was something else all along. Skaggs looked at his watch for a moment to confirm. Seymours watched as Skaggs reached under his shoulder holster and took hold of both guns tucked low below his armpits—both pistols were loaded but unused since they hadn't yet come up against anyone capable of taking them. Then Skaggs turned sharply back to Seymours, putting away one pistol, and replacing it in his waistband. In response, Seymours made sure the safety catch remained intact on the second weapon. With that done, Skaggs bent down to unlock and open the bottom drawer in his desk—after which he retrieved an automatic handgun with several extra clips strapped in its belt holder for reloading purposes plus spare ammunition. All this accomplished in less than five seconds.

Next, Skaggs went back downstairs with the intention of bringing a team of six armed officers into Seymours' office area with orders from Seymours not to allow the intruders access upstairs unless necessary. While Skaggs went downstairs, Skippen ran upstairs with Taylor and two other men dressed similarly to him. They wore plain white shirts instead of jackets over their navy-blue uniforms and sported short haircuts—all part of a standard SWAT team uniform worn by agents in the FBI's Tactical Response Unit based locally at Toronto Police Headquarters. This unit is responsible for tactical intervention when federal agencies are needed in support of a criminal investigation anywhere in North America according to Skipper's description. When Skippens' bodyguards emerged into Seymours' main living quarters carrying assault rifles in case any of Seymours' neighbors chose to shoot back, they found Skippers sitting on his couch staring blankly out from beneath the shade of the bay window, listening intently as Skaggs explained how things stood so far, trying to reassure their boss he wasn't injured seriously despite looking pale and confused as always since coming through such a traumatic experience.

The bodies lay still and unmoving on the ground floor hallway just inside Seymours' front door—shot dead instantly with holes drilled into their foreheads almost identical to those left in Seymours' chest earlier that evening, according to forensic experts from Metro South Hospital who arrived shortly thereafter to collect them. Three additional men crouched motionless behind doors on either side of Seymours' entrance hall, unable to move because they each held an M4 carbine with an extended magazine in their hands. It would be easy for even the average person unfamiliar with weapons like these (like most people across North American cities) to mistake those rifles for machine guns once pointed at you with one aimed squarely at your forehead and another positioned precisely beside it at knee level—if you dared approach close enough without realizing it was just a rifle.

Once everything quieted down, Skaggs sat facing Seymours again—he was now alone minus the three agents guarding his entryway and office windows downstairs—as Skaggs began retelling what happened after leaving Seymours' residence about half an hour ago.

"…Well then I got my phone hooked up—"

It felt odd having Skaggs describe events without ever mentioning anything about the shooting itself; Skaggs was obviously keen to avoid saying what happened when he discovered where Skippens kept the box containing their boss' papers, including the handwritten notes belonging to Jack Dalferes. That was fine with Seymours however given how little information they knew regarding Dalferes' whereabouts before yesterday morning anyway. Even if there might have been more questions answered by hearing exactly how this whole mess originated from start to finish, Skaggs couldn't possibly go through with describing every detail that unfolded at Seymours' home today without raising suspicion as to what really happened. Not until they came across proof as strong as a smoking gun did, he intend telling anyone whatever details he thought appropriate. Otherwise, he wouldn't do it at all, according to Skaggs' opinion. If only they could dig up evidence proving Dalferes had committed suicide or otherwise faked his death somehow…Then the problem of convincing others he was indeed dead would be solved forever—for good measure—rather than remaining unsolved indefinitely in some manner or another. Or better yet—

"Wait!" interjected an impatient voice in reply to Skaggs' story halfway through his explanation. Both he and Seymours spun round to look at Dr. John Lefevre who appeared from nowhere standing behind the sofa—where Skaggs just sat—to stare at him in bewilderment. "Are we talking about the same thing? What's happening?"

Seymours had barely finished asking himself this question before the answer struck him—in fact, his heart skipped several beats at once. How could Dr. Lefevre already know something that no one had told him beforehand—that would explain his presence here so suddenly during such tense times? And why didn't he speak sooner, especially if he suspected it too? There were probably a hundred possible answers to both questions but none of them mattered now. Because in hindsight Dr Lefevre's sudden appearance seemed very strange—almost eerie— given that the professor was supposed to be missing and presumed dead long ago on account of being murdered years prior. But what if someone decided to cover for him by hiding him somewhere else for decades without anyone knowing? Could that happen?

Astonishing news aside…

Dr. Lefevre was not going through all this stress and drama tonight by choice.

As much as Seymours wanted to ask him immediately to explain the unbelievability of what just occurred, Skaggs beat him to the punch with an instant answer. As soon as he saw Seymours turn back towards him with a quizzical expression, Skaggs jumped ahead again as fast as he could without making Seymours lose track again, "Sorry Mr. Brounts, but I'm getting word now from Metro South Hospital that our doctor has been released, can you imagine that?" Skaggs paused briefly for confirmation from Seymours before adding quietly to Skippen: "Mr. LeFevers needs hospitalization…" Skaggs repeated.

If the professor intended to object, he never gave it any consideration. Instead, Seymours responded with a faint nod of assent as he struggled to regain his composure in silence and focus completely upon Skaggs for now. Their exchange went straight from one subject to another without hesitation, moving at breakneck speed as if Skaggs had planned out their next course of action entirely in advance…and it worked out perfectly well thanks to everyone involved. First and foremost, because Skipper's plan ensured that the conversation focused primarily on solving the case instead of dealing directly with matters involving Dr. Lefevres' disappearance. Secondly…Skaggs' decision meant there was no way Dr. Lefevre could refuse help once they learned more about what happened last night at Seymours' place. Once that happened there'd be no stopping him; he had to cooperate fully or risk compromising himself irreparably. The best chance was simply keeping him alive until then; then they could deal with whatever happened afterwards later. Maybe after a few days. Or weeks or months…it all depended on what kind of trouble this man had landed himself into— whether it was worth worrying over in the first place.

With Dr. Lefevre present, there were also fewer potential risks associated with revealing certain sensitive facts surrounding Dalferes' mysterious disappearance—which included his whereabouts since December 22nd, 2012, and why he died ten years earlier. Now that Seymours had the full picture about the circumstances leading up to Dalferes' death in 1998 and Dr Lefevre confirmed it in the affirmative, there was little to worry about explaining why there hadn't been any traceable evidence left behind by the deceased author since 1984 in the event Dr. Lefevre became interested enough to pursue that angle further. No witnesses besides Skippen and Seymours were willing to discuss the matter openly, which would prevent Dr. Lefevre from digging deeper. At least Seymours hoped they didn't talk freely enough in public for anyone concerned for their security to find out something embarrassing happened on account of a local mystery writer gone missing for twenty-five years while everybody assumed he perished tragically in a car accident—or worse yet fell victim to foul play from unknown assailants. If someone like Skippen talked about what they witnessed outside Seymours' home that afternoon or early evening when they heard the shot fired from inside Seymours', that could lead right back to Seymours or Skippen—either one—without giving anyone any idea which of them killed Dalferes. If Skippen said something incriminating, then perhaps Dr. Lefevre's inquiry might reveal a different version of events to the press and public, depending on what they uncovered together rather than independently of each other. So far, the circumstantial evidence indicated the deaths at Seymour's residence belonged to both Dalferes and his wife Marjorie. But with the possibility that the killer might strike again, they couldn't afford to take chances with Dr. Lefevre finding out the truth prematurely if it weren't safe. For now, all the pieces fit and nobody else could tell apart the real murderer to point fingers at somebody else in case the worst should happen. But the timing made sense, especially considering Seymours lived alone…

"So let me see," continued Skaggs, returning quickly to where the discussion started before Dr. Lefevre interrupted them "…are we discussing how the situation arose between Seymours and Dalferes here or the fact it's not our business anymore?"

After a moment of thinking, Seymours nodded emphatically in agreement to Skaggs' query, feeling relieved as usual by his trusted friend taking charge—

"What a coincidence."

Seymour smiled thinly as Skaggs glanced over his shoulder and noticed Dr. Lefevres standing silently behind him—looking as puzzled as Skaggs felt, although he managed a polite nod acknowledging him as soon as he caught sight of him standing awkwardly nearby without permission. With a subtle gesture of his hand, Skaggs indicated their guest to sit down and join them as soon as he settled onto the couch opposite Seymours on the other end of the room as far away as possible from his bodyguards in a nonchalant manner so they wouldn't think twice about letting him get closer to hear what was being discussed—although Dr. Lefevres looked reluctant—

"We've got a major problem."

The words poured forth from his mouth almost instinctively—before Dr. Lefevres took advantage of his distraction and moved forward slowly toward Seymours' desk. He pulled out chair two steps farther up the hallway, turned around carefully, and perched comfortably beside it before looking expectantly towards Seymours with obvious curiosity written plainly on his face.

There were still plenty of things Skaggs hadn't yet shared with his fellow investigator despite wanting desperately to do so before anyone else figured it out—but Skippens needn't concern themselves for one second with any mention of any details relating specifically to Seymours' relationship with Dr. Lefevres. The time wasn't right… yet anyway. This new development could potentially cause too many problems if anybody found out about what was revealed tonight. All they needed at this stage of the game was solid evidence, preferably something hard, tangible, indisputable even if circumstantial and ambiguous in its meaning at best, which would convince people that they ought to believe that the late Jack Dalferes and Mrs. Marjory Dalferes had been killed because of who they were rather than merely suspecting it happened due to the nature of who they are. Then, once that was established as undeniable fact—the rest of what they learned would come naturally in a logical sequence once their investigation ran its course. After that, there'd be less likelihood they'd encounter more obstacles than opportunities along the way to the solution, including those posed by Dr. Lefevre's own inquisitive mind. They'd have to be careful though—they shouldn't scare him off altogether or he'd walk away from everything forever. Or worse yet, he might inadvertently give us away accidentally without realizing he'd done anything wrong.

"…because Seymours has taken care of all your personal affairs…"

Now Skaggs spoke up to keep Dr. Lefevre busy until Skippers could calm herself enough to continue working towards their common goal without interruption—as if her job entailed calming down Dr Lefevre every step of the way. She certainly appeared nervous enough judging by the sweat pouring down his forehead as he watched Dr. Lefevre approach in anticipation of something unpleasant or incriminating coming from his lips any second now. It was apparent to everyone sitting near him that she thought so too when her eyes followed him closely throughout his movement toward Seymours and tried unsuccessfully to hold back an uneasy gasp when he finally reached him; only a single syllable escaped before his hands touched his knees, "I don't—"

"—think you're in danger…right now".

But Skipper shook her head slightly.

He stopped speaking just long enough for everyone to notice it and return to what they had been doing before Dr Lefevre entered the room; then he began talking again immediately, albeit in a quieter tone than before so Seymours and Skippers would stop staring at him in bewilderment and wonder aloud what the hell he was going to say now that clearly scared him half to death.

"You'll understand once you hear what I'm about to relate, Miss…?" He waited a few seconds for Skippers to finish writing something down as fast as she could in order not to miss another important piece of information. When he was sure his question had received sufficient attention to warrant some sort of response from her (if not outright shock), he pushed onward swiftly, "Miss Henry", continuing to use her name deliberately instead of calling her Ms. Henry or lawyer when there wasn't anything official concerning his professional title and position regarding her status within our investigation. Even though it seemed pointless considering that no one except Seymours knew either one's true identities, it helped avoid complications when the FBI inevitably came knocking someday, asking questions like who they were and whether they possessed special powers capable of preventing crimes or investigating unsolved cases with nothing more than gut instincts. The answer was easy: they did—all the better to fool people into believing they were normal human beings living ordinary lives rather than supernatural entities secretly working behind-the-scenes to protect law enforcement agencies across America from criminals' intent on committing heinous acts against humanity. There'd probably be less trouble if they pretended that none of this happened at all, but it would make life unnecessarily complicated for them. As it stood, all their actions during their joint investigations thus far would remain

under wraps until such time as proof could be offered publicly that would corroborate everything, they'd learned about these strange phenomena happening at the same times on exact dates in history.

They had no intention of telling anyone about what they truly did until they had absolutely proved their suspicions beyond any doubt… even if it caused confusion among the general population and drew unwanted attention upon themselves. Such a move required great discretion and patience—and Skippens were famous for being neither until we arrived in town. But now, we're changing gears entirely…

Dr. Lefevre sat up straighter in his seat after hearing what Skippers wrote down next; she had obviously given up trying not to listen in on our conversation. And with good reason…there were things he wished Seymours would consider beforehand considering recent developments as he listened to Skaggs explain everything as concisely as possible before moving on…then Skippy jumped in with the details when necessary. His explanation made sense based on everything Skippers already told Seymours earlier today…but it raised some issues about Dalferens' relationship with Marjorie, which had been conveniently glossed over.

EIGHT

When Dalferes married Marjorie five months later, he changed his last name to Dalferes, and hers to Dales, to create an unpronounceable long hyphenated surname they decided not to change for convenience's sake whenever signing letters to each other for work purposes or using credit cards for purchases. While it wasn't widely known outside his circle of friends and family that Dalferes used an alias, Skippen suspected that most readers of his novels guessed that much—especially those whose tastes run towards the macabre and dark subject matter.

Skippen wanted to know how Skippen managed to learn about Dr. Lefevre's involvement in Dalferes' private affairs.

Because Skippen worked part-time for Seymours at a reduced salary and occasionally volunteered to help with Seymours' research projects when he was unable to meet the demands, Skippens knew he often consulted Dr. Lefevre's library for certain types of books related to specific subjects he researched for a fee when asked directly by Seymours—with permission granted first through the librarian at the reference desk. That left the door open for Skippen to overhear things others couldn't since they generally preferred to conduct interviews discretely in private offices rather than anywhere near the shelves of bound volumes containing old-fashioned paper printouts of pages filled with handwritten notes by scholars over centuries past—which included a few scribbles from Dr. Lefevres' pencils as well, which added a nice touch of authenticity. Skippen didn't bother trying to hide his interest in knowing how someone from out of state stumbled onto Seymours' whereabouts at home during the hours he spent researching at the New York Public Library. He wondered why he'd never heard about the woman before this evening – especially considering Seymours lived alone apart from visiting relatives and Skippers' presence. Except for Skippers and Seymours, it was always Seymours conducting phone calls inside the house. So, Skippers hadn't met Dr. Lefevre nor spoken to her when she rang while Seymours was at the office; however, he'd seen her once before and recognized her immediately on site after she stepped out into the hallway where he waited to speak to Seymours via closed circuit television. A tall brunette wearing a short black wool dress with buttons on the front and neckline, her hair tied neatly beneath her chin; her face framed by curly locks of jet-black silk… she resembled a porcelain doll with her pale complexion, thin nose, pouty full mouth, large blue eyes, and high cheekbones that gave her a strong appearance—an image that faded when Seymours greeted her warmly with a friendly smile. He showed little sign that they knew each other—though perhaps she simply visited him frequently enough that they had exchanged pleasantries once or twice, although Skipper was unaware of that possibility until she mentioned meeting Seymours at the library. Now that we think about it—it makes sense, Skippens admitted inwardly—he doesn't really know any women unless we introduce them to him. He likes it that way. No offense meant if I sound condescending—after all, Seymours is still very young compared to me and quite inexperienced when it comes to love and romance."

As soon as Skippers finished reciting her account and saw both Seymours and Dr. Lefevre looking back and forth between her and Skipper as if confused by the unbelievability of what she claimed she overheard and what she described next, she quickly turned her attention to Dr. Lefevre and smiled briefly in relief that he apparently understood what was going on here and had no objection whatsoever to having her around after the manner in which Seymours welcomed her into his home. However, she noticed that Seymours continued to stare in silence. Had he not read all of Skipper's reports? Was the problem he couldn't remember anything because he had so many conversations and interactions taking place simultaneously every day, leaving him exhausted afterwards as he prepared for bed? Maybe Dr. Lefevre should go ahead and leave right away. Then again, maybe he didn't want her gone yet, even though Skippens assumed it would only be minutes before he lost complete track of what was happening due to his age and poor vision…but it wouldn't have surprised Skippens if Seymurs wanted us both along until such time as it became necessary for him to take us somewhere else or get rid of us completely.

She felt terrible for interrupting their private discussion about Mr. Lefevre's sudden disappearance. If Dr Lefevre was offended by my intrusion, let me apologize profusely now—

The two men suddenly realized their voices were attracting attention and looked at Dr. Lefevre. We are aware there's been a serious misunderstanding concerning the whole business, he said apologetically, shaking his head slightly before turning to address Mrs. Hargrave as the oldest member present and one who had lived in Newburyport since its founding days nearly four hundred years ago. What do you suggest, ma'am?

We need your advice on how best to handle this situation; he wants you to tell Seymours and me how to proceed with finding John Dalferens…and hopefully figuring out what happened to him after we find him. How should we begin searching for him?

With your help, Seymours nodded. You'll be invaluable to helping me with that, Miss Henry. Let's talk in the study while everyone waits patiently downstairs; the sooner you can give us a starting point for the search, the quicker we'll find answers.

It took several moments for Seymours and Skipper to convince him that they weren't mad at him—that it was obvious they needed the expertise of someone with the ability to see ghosts and communicate with spirits. They explained that they don't believe in magic, but rather that paranormal activity has existed throughout history without our knowledge until now—and that they intended to discover exactly what happens at the exact same time every century at the precise hour at precisely midnight—as far back as the 1700s when a group of mysterious murders occurred in New England townships. It seems likely that supernatural force or evil entity played a role in all three deaths. Since then, the pattern repeated itself dozens more times in other American cities. Seymours and Skippers had just started studying some accounts written by nineteenth-century journalists who investigated the events surrounding the unexplained deaths of prominent local citizens who died mysteriously on Christmas Eve and discovered a frightening connection between these events. Seymours believes that one man might play a major role in all this as one event follows another according to an eerie schedule that appears pre-planned…or fateful.

He glanced up as Dr. Lefevre stared at the clock above the fireplace, watching Seymours nod slowly in agreement when he finally spoke again. The timing of this phenomenon occurring so consistently throughout history leaves little room for coincidence and proves something supernatural lies behind all this strangeness—something powerful enough that it defies logic and rational thought—a force that has shaped the lives of millions over hundreds, possibly thousands of years…all leading back to Newburyport. Seymours believed it was probably too late now anyway; whatever power is responsible may have come into existence before mankind invented calendars and clocks or developed technology capable of monitoring dates accurately for us to observe it with precision and calculate its effect in a logical manner. As Seymours put it to Skippers earlier tonight: "I've never seen anything like it."

What could be causing the phenomena? Skippens wanted to know as she leaned forward in her chair to join Seymours as he watched Dr. Lefevre write notes.

While Skippens listened intently to how Seymours explained the theory behind his latest idea about how Seymours planned on handling this case as well as answering questions posed by Dr. Lefevre regarding Dalferens' disappearance (the question mark following the title suggested Seymours hadn't considered any suspects yet), she also found herself wondering about the strange similarities involved when reading the accounts from different eras describing the same thing happening on Christmas Eve within close proximity of midnight— even though none of the incidents followed each other on an identical date. But then, neither did they happen exactly twelve months apart from one another; that's how they seemed connected in each writer's mind—so perhaps it isn't that big of a deal that we haven't pinpointed any specific instances or dates. Perhaps, with proper observation, the answer will eventually reveal itself. With luck, Seymours concluded with excitement as he stood abruptly and grabbed Dr. Lefevre's hand, it won't take long to sort through everything we've learned so far. All we need is patience, a willingness to investigate each report thoroughly and consider whether they're linked in some way…we'll start at noon today when all signs of Christmas morning activities cease. Once that happens, if Seymours decides there's nothing left to uncover at the house, we'll make plans accordingly—whether that means going somewhere new or investigating the cemetery further. Do either of you object to spending the night here?

Not at all…not at all…he responded hastily without missing a beat—in fact, Seymours had already begun thinking ahead about how he could use his influence as owner of the mansion and resident historian to draw additional attention and funding toward solving the puzzle. There are several historical societies across North America eager to hear about this discovery—particularly given how Seymours' findings coincide with the recent rise of interest among historians and cryptozoologists worldwide. That's why we have this wonderful conference hall upstairs, where meetings often become heated debates between those who prefer scientific explanations over religious dogma and folklore, making for exciting evenings when people discuss matters that most scholars refuse to accept. We plan on hosting conferences in Newburyport in conjunction with the museum. After all, it is part of Seymours' legacy and mission statement for the Seymours Family Trust to preserve important documents related to family history and provide financial support for the preservation and interpretation of various forms of artistry. The trust's first official act was recently announced when it donated $100 million to fund efforts to establish a national network of museums dedicated solely to preserving artifacts relating to ancient cultures in addition to establishing permanent collections of archaeological evidence pertaining to prehistoric creatures like dinosaurs or other extinct species, such as dragons and mammoths— with special emphasis placed upon those areas known historically as hotspots for these types of discoveries throughout North America. This will allow researchers access to a wealth of information not available elsewhere. Of course, this gift came at the request of a certain dinosaur expert named Richard Owen – a man renowned throughout history for his contributions to our understanding of fossilized remains of animals from the past—who was particularly pleased by what Mr. Seymours offered him personally; therefore, Seymours intends to work closely with Owen in promoting what he hopes will be an annual convention here at Seymours Manor during summer months.

This was good news indeed to Skippens. Her heart fluttered inside her chest at hearing Seymours speak enthusiastically of how the Seymours estate could serve as a nexus of sorts for the paranormal community interested in exploring things, we rarely talk about openly…as much as possible, that is. Not wanting to interrupt her boss, Skipper turned away and pretended she wasn't listening as he rattled off details of his grand plans for future generations seeking insight on mysteries old and new. She knew he was excited about doing it all himself instead of hiring others for a project he clearly loved—yet he seemed unsure how to get this all rolling until Skipper pointed out it sounded as if he'd talked to Dr. Lefevre about the subject in great length before requesting Skipper contact Ms. Henry—

Dr. Lefevre looked back and forth between Seymours and Skipper before asking if we should call Dr. Osterberg right away to alert him to Seymour's plans to host a conference and exhibition in honor of the 100th anniversary of Mr. Lefevres' death—which fell on Christmas Day last year. To which Seymours answered yes, that would be appropriate, although there would no doubt be plenty of opposition from local town leaders who were opposed to such ventures being held here unless they served strictly educational purposes…such as lectures about fossils or similar topics. And, he added, it would certainly bring tourists flooding into Newburyport, thus boosting our tourist economy for years to come, especially around holiday seasons.

Mrs. Hargrave chimed in that she thought it was a marvelous idea; it would be ideal, she said, considering how popular Seymours Mansion had proven itself to be since becoming open for tours five years ago. A lot of money would be made with this kind of publicity, she told Seymours as well as Skippers; even the local newspaper reporters covering the story wouldn't be able to resist reporting on the significance of Seymours offering such generous gifts to worthy organizations—not only did the donation mean a huge boost locally but it also meant Seymours Mansion and the Seymours family name became synonymous with the preservation effort. Seymours grinned broadly at Mrs. Hargrave before adding he didn't want anyone getting credit or recognition; however, if Mrs. Hargrave wished to announce Seymours' intentions publicly and encourage public interest, he agreed it would help generate funds toward what Mrs. Hargrave called the necessary expense of keeping Seymours and many other properties preserved properly. He'd heard Mrs. Hargrave say once before that this building represented centuries of history…perhaps we should try to keep it alive forever by protecting it somehow? Maybe by donating some land? Or creating an endowment for maintenance costs?

That's quite possible, Skippy replied as he sat back down next to her—but you don't think that's too self-serving? I'm sure Seymours would agree with you about trying to prevent this house from deteriorating because we don't do this kind of research anymore. If we don't learn more about ourselves, we risk losing everything that makes us human and leaving no trace of humanity behind when we die…

You know better than that! Seymours scolded her immediately with a glare while reaching up with both hands to touch two fingers together in front of his face as he spoke directly at Skipper:

"Selfishness isn't in our character. In fact—" He paused briefly as Skippers lips pursed and nodded emphatically. Then continued: "A desire for fame isn't necessarily a bad thing, especially if someone does something extraordinary as a result." Seymurs turned and smiled warmly at Dr. Lefevre—a gesture she returned with obvious sincerity after he finished speaking. "We can promote awareness, but hopefully, Seymours House will continue its tradition of welcoming inquisitive minds searching for answers…"

The Seymours Family Trust has always been generous with donations towards causes such as these in the past–Skippens interjected quickly

Of course, Seymours assured her, that generosity extends beyond monetary gifts. For example, Seymours mentioned how he paid an extremely large sum for the painting done by George Stubbs depicting Lord Byron as Stoker describes him in his famous novel. It's hung near where everyone enters the main foyer now, allowing visitors to see it every time they enter. When asked how he managed to purchase it at auction when it originally sold to Sir Francis Dashwood at $1,500 just twenty-five years prior—after having been passed down through various owners for decades beforehand, Skippens told me it took place under very strange circumstances surrounding Dashwood's deathbed wishes involving Seymours…an event Dashwood described to Seymours during their meeting three nights ago when talking about a dream he'd had shortly before passing away—a wish which caused him to offer a substantial reward and promise never to divulge where or when to whom Dashwood's final words were spoken before dying at age 72…all according to Skippens firsthand account as well as Dr. Lefevre's detailed notes from that evening. Seymours' eyes lit up again as Skippers voice grew stronger in volume and confidence as she discussed Seymours ability to attract the best and brightest researchers from all around the world—people whose skills range from paleontology to forensic science. Even more promising, Skippens said she thinks Seymours might consider paying an extra fee for the services of scientists from outside North America; the reason being Seymours wants the best experts we can find anywhere on Earth. Skipping added how we have no idea exactly how valuable the information we're gathering may prove someday—it seems like anything could be possible once we dig deep enough. As an attorney working closely with Seymours, Skippy wanted to add that there's one area we should be focusing on first: the paintings painted by Percy Harrison Lefevre. Seymours interrupted him before he could elaborate by saying Seymours had already seen the portrait hanging above his desk at Seymours House—and hadn't liked what he saw or understood it at all. But it gave him plenty of food for thought to ponder on the flight back from Boston yesterday afternoon…

With Seymours still lost in his thoughts as though he'd reached the point of decision on a major issue, Skipper leaned forward eagerly awaiting any direction or confirmation Seymours might give them— she had no doubts Seymours intended to go all out with whatever happened here—that he believed Seymours was committed to finding out the truth behind Lord Darcy's disappearance as soon as possible. However, Seymours was distracted suddenly by Mrs. Hargrave's question regarding how much of Seymours' own fortune was involved in making what Mrs. Hargrave described as their very generous donation toward the library fund drive. The answer seemed irrelevant until Seymours replied that it came from family funds, not money given to him after Lady Anne died nor those left over when Seymours turned thirty-five years old, because they were set aside for Seymours' future needs once he became independent of the estate which meant there wasn't even enough remaining to pay back Seymours' debtors if Seymours could have managed such a feat without taking on more than a few months' worth of expenses first. He didn't see why we would need our own home so long before I got married anyway since none of us has found a spouse yet—if Seymours hadn't told me about this project, I wouldn't know where he lived. But then Seymours explained that one reason they wanted to get into town now was simply to be ready ahead of time should someone try anything like trying to kidnap Seymours away from the house early tomorrow morning when he returned alone... and finally asked everyone gathered together for help protecting Seymours during his stay at home through next weekend while he traveled with friends downstate to visit another plantation where some people were supposedly being held against their will. When Seymours mentioned that Mr. Whelan (the owner of said property) was supposed to travel along too, Mrs. Hargrave exclaimed that it sounded perfect! That way Seymours could keep watch but also talk things over with others in charge who hopefully knew better how best to handle such matters. "And don't you dare hesitate to tell anyone else within hearing distance that you're doing these sorts of investigations," Mrs. Hargrave warned Seymours firmly. She added that it would make Seymours look bad if word got around, he couldn't protect himself when the only thing keeping him alive depended entirely on her financial support.

"I'll think about it," Seymours promised, smiling politely at both the woman and the man she addressed. "But I do understand your concern." He waited for several minutes to see if Seymours might volunteer something further, wondering if this was the moment when Seymours chose to reveal more details about the circumstances surrounding Lord Darcy's absence or just kept mum. If Seymours continued to hold nothing back, Sara realized that Seymours would have plenty of opportunities later in the day to tell us everything else needed to be known. At least the Seymours plan seemed solid right up until Seymours started thinking aloud again. After talking over Seymours' idea briefly, Skipper decided to take advantage of having Seymours off guard by bringing up Seymours' recent request to borrow the car. Then he went on to mention the conversation Seymours and Driscoll had in the kitchen late last night following supper. Seymours looked surprised. As far as Skipper recalled, Seymours never discussed this with either of them before—and certainly not so openly as he did yesterday evening. Yet somehow, despite all Seymours said afterwards, it appeared as though neither Skipper nor Mrs. Hargrave thought very highly of the idea.

As usual, Seymours made excuses for leaving them waiting downstairs, promising to return upstairs momentarily to change clothes for work and check out the situation with his security firm. Once he was gone, Skipper began discussing with Mrs. Hargrave the latest information he'd uncovered recently relating to Seymours' mysterious inheritance from Lady Anne, including Seymours' desire to find answers sooner rather than later concerning this inheritance which meant skirting legal channels.

Mrs. Hargrave suggested going straight to the source instead of letting Seymours run wild looking for other avenues of inquiry while he wasted precious time—even suggesting she personally ask Lord Darcy directly. To this, Skipper immediately shot down the notion as ill-advised due to its potential consequences. And although Skipper didn't want to seem overly protective, especially when he already feared Seymours took great care not to involve anyone except Mr. Whelan and Mrs. Hargrave in any of his personal activities, he felt certain there was danger lurking somewhere nearby thanks to the fact Seymours rarely talked freely about his past and relationships unless forced to by accident… or maybe because there was so little of interest in Seymours' background to discuss in detail.

That led to the possibility that Skipper shouldn't trust anything Seymours might say under duress. There are two kinds of men,

Skipper remembered his uncle always saying. One kind likes trouble; the other avoids it whenever possible. Of course, Uncle Jimmie was referring specifically to the lawless types, but he probably wasn't wrong when he applied it to most human beings in general, Skipper mused, recalling the times he saw his uncles put themselves on display for various reasons ranging from court appearances to public lectures and debates. His parents often complained that every year at Christmas or Thanksgiving when the whole clan came together, the Seymours boys played tricks on each other for sport rather than celebration. They were notorious among their cousins for pranks perpetrated on adults and children alike—often resulting in injuries to one side or the other depending upon whether the victim was part of Seymours' family unit or a neighbor. While there weren't many victims whom Skippy ever considered close friends, his mother had been hurt more than once and she hated all three brothers equally well. Though Skipper sometimes tried to defend his relatives, he suspected the Seymours boys liked to tease people outside the family because they enjoyed getting away with whatever they pleased with no repercussions.

He wondered about Seymours' penchant for mischief and prankishness because he doubted that if it wasn't for the Seymours family name, the Seymours sons would've received the same privileges as the rest of Seymours' offspring. So, what made Seymours different? Why hadn't Seymours learned early in life that trouble follows wherever he goes? What was it about Seymours that caused others to avoid him? Was it something genetic in nature or did someone teach him this tendency from childhood onwards? Had his father abused him when he'd been young? Or perhaps Seymours had experienced trauma beyond the normal bounds of childhood experience that shaped the person he grew to become today… and was it related to Seymours' relationship with Lord Darcy? Did it come from the days when Seymours used to hang around with Tom Prendergast, that former slave who eventually ran away to join the Underground Railroad and then joined the Union army during slavery's final throes before passing through Styx's mental minefield on his way back home? Or did something happen between Seymours and his half-brothers after Mr. Prendergast died? Could it be something related to what happened when they were kids? Or was it simply something which had become ingrained within him after being raised without his father? It was too hard for Skippy to imagine any sort of violence happening between Sir Reginald and Lord Darcy—not even just in passing—yet there was clearly something else going on with them when they were young than Skippy ever imagined could be related to their relationship today.

Skipper turned to Mrs. Hargrave at this point, asking if she knew anything more about what happened back then than what she'd told him before about how they'd been raised by their maternal grandparents since their parents had died when they were little kids—something which wasn't uncommon among slaves who needed hands-on care but weren't old enough yet for a white family member to take on as a surrogate parent. But Skipper thought with a start that it seemed odd that people like Mrs. Hargrave might know more about their ancestors than their parents did due to their grandparents raising them rather than their parents doing so instead—and if Mr. Whelan knew more about this than even Mr. Whelan did, then maybe Mr. Whelan was wrong about what happened when his grandfather took over managing the household once Lord Darcy went missing and didn't come home at all after leaving for New York City in October 1863…

"That's not unusual," Mrs. Hargrave said softly, shaking her head as she stared at her thick hands clasped together on her lap. "A lot happened in those early years before I learned anything more about my past than I already knew." She looked up at Skipper as though suddenly remembering something important then looked down again as if ashamed she hadn't thought she'd told him before about Mr. Whelan's father having been a slave owned by Mr. Whelan's grandfather and then passed down through various generations until Mr. Whelan inherited it all after his father's death from a mysterious illness in February 1864 when Mr. Whelan was seventeen years old—however old Mr. Whelan might have been then; however young or old Mr. Whelan might be now; however old Mr. Whelan had been when Sir Reginald died in December 1867…

"What is?" Skippy asked again, trying hard not to read too much into Mrs. Hargrave's odd behavior and keep his thoughts from jumping ahead too far so quickly after only one conversation between them and her brief answers thus far… although there must have been a reason why Mrs. Hargrave chose this moment now rather than earlier today or yesterday morning, considering how long she'd known Skipper since he was a little boy living at home in her household as her helper and right-hand man among many other things while preparing for school each day under Mrs. Hargrave's supervision each morning before he went out into town with his grandmother Lady Anne Darcy and Uncle Jimmie…

"Nothing," Mrs. Hargrave replied quickly with a smile as she reassured Skipper, she wasn't trying to end their conversation prematurely by shutting him down before he could learn anything more about his grandfather's relationship with Sir Reginald or why it might be important now that Lord Darcy was missing without a trace… "It was nothing."

"It's not nothing," Skipper insisted firmly; yet at that moment he wished they'd gone straight upstairs instead of sitting downstairs watching TV with both of them getting drunker by the minute while we learned more about Mr. Whelan's history from Mr. Whelan himself— if we learned anything at all from sitting downstairs drinking beers with him in general considering how little Mr. Whelan talked about anything else other than his family history which left us feeling like we were missing half the story after we finally learned more than we ever hoped for—or half of what we thought we'd learned before we learned so little because Mr. Whelan refused to answer any more questions than we already knew—and how far back those answers went…

Skipper heard a key turn in the front lock upstairs and knew that Seymours had returned from his meeting with his security company but wondered where Mr. Whelan was at this point since Mr. Whelan had been upstairs earlier with Seymours while they watched TV together… And then Skipper wondered why neither of them mentioned seeing Mr. Whelan upstairs after Seymours left us downstairs drinking beer while watching those old TV shows we were talking about earlier when I saw Mr. Whelan upstairs after dinner last night with Mr. Whelan who is certain there isn't a ghost living in Seymours' house and then I saw Seymours here with Mrs. Hargrave just now…

Skipper considered having Mrs. Hargrave call Mr. Whelan down to Seymours' office so they could find out what happened upstairs after Seymours left us downstairs drinking beer together—"We're going upstairs to check on things," Mrs. Hargrave had said—but Skipper decided that would be bad manners considering how much Seymours likes Mr. Whelan so much that he'd probably let him drink as much beer as he wanted if he was around at night because whenever Mr. Whelan comes over here to check on things as often as he does, then there must be some sort of activity or event going on upstairs—or else Seymours would have told us there wasn't a ghost there like he told me over drinks last night after telling me I shouldn't drink any beer because it would lower my inhibitions too much right before I almost punched Seymours across the room when he said something about my grandfather—not to mention how much more likely I am to punch someone if I drink beer on an empty stomach, which I didn't at this point because I wanted this conversation with Mrs. Hargrave to go well...

Skipper looked up at Mrs. Hargrave and asked if she wanted to go upstairs with me—I mean, we both know Seymours might not be upstairs anymore at this point but maybe we can find out where Mr. Whelan is while we're up there anyway—but Mrs. Hargrave shook her head no as if she couldn't decide whether or not she wanted to go upstairs with me again or not; she glanced at her watch and then looked at Skippy as though asking whether or not this was the right time for this conversation or not; then she looked back up at me again as though trying to figure out what happened between her and Seymours upstairs after she took him up there...

"Why don't you call Mr. Whelan down here," I suggested when I saw that Mrs. Hargrave wanted me to make the decision for her, "and I'll go check downstairs and see what Mr. Whelan wants."

Mrs. Hargrave nodded her agreement at this idea, but then she said: "Might as well come along, too."

"I thought you didn't want me up here anymore?" I asked quizzically because lately Mrs. Hargrave has been doing exactly as Sir Reginald tells her since he started managing Seymours' household again after living here since January; however, this seemed like a strange time for Sir Reginald to start directing Mrs. Hargrave around his house again like this, especially considering how much time had passed between now and when he took over managing the house once Lord Darcy went missing and didn't come home after leaving for New York City in October 1863…

"I don't," Mrs. Hargrave replied, "but I know you don't want to be left alone here while Seymours is away."

"I guess you're right," I said as I stood up from my chair, "but isn't it possible that Seymours has gone out for another beer with Mr. Whelan?"

Mrs. Hargrave hesitated for a moment before answering me, perhaps thinking the same thing but uncertain whether it was true; however, the front door opened and Seymours came through without calling out any instructions for us to stay put downstairs while he left us alone together in Seymours' office again…

"Good evening," Sir Reginald said as he walked into Seymours' office, looking around the room curiously like he hadn't been here since last night; "I hope you're well."

Seymour nodded in reply as he stood up from his desk and turned around in front of Sir Reginald who looked around briefly at the various items on the desk before turning his attention back to Seymours as if trying to figure out what had happened since the last time he was here; however, Seymours simply nodded in response to Sir Reginald's words, suggesting that everything was fine between them; however, Seymours didn't ask for any clarification at all on what happened since then because if he did, Sir Reginald would probably tell him everything is fine; however, Seymours probably already knew that everything wasn't fine between them just by looking around the room…

At this point I leaned forward on my chair and said: "Sir Reginald! What happened upstairs? Was there something up here after all?"

Sir Reginald looked around the room once again before finally looking down at me as if searching for something to say but came up empty-handed since he'd already told us there wasn't anything unusual going on upstairs—"Only Seymours," he said with a smile—before telling me: "Of course it's possible that there was of activity going on up here."

"Activity?" I asked skeptically but then thought about it for a moment and realized what Sir Reginald meant by that. He must have meant that something like a ghost was visiting the house—"Visiting" being the key word because ghosts don't visit any more than they can walk away from their haunting grounds or leave their spirits behind rather than haunting the places they haunt... "What kind of activity?" I asked Sir Reginald when he didn't say anything else; however, Sir Reginald chose this moment to tell us both something unbelievable— something which might explain why we both were still sitting here drinking beer together while watching old TV shows instead of following him upstairs to check on things ourselves...

"I think," Sir Reginald said softly so only Seymours could hear him over the TV music playing over our heads, "that you should come upstairs with me."

Seymours nodded his assent at Sir Reginald's request but didn't ask why nor did he ask which one of us should go with Sir Reginald first because either one of us would be more than happy to go first if either of us had been asked to do so... Instead, both of us stood up from our chairs so that we could follow Sir Reginald up to the second floor together instead of waiting for him to decide which one of us should go first... But instead of following Sir Reginald up the stairs first, Skipper decided it would be better if he followed Mrs. Hargrave up the stairs first because of how little she talked during this conversation and how confusing it was trying to figure out what Mrs. Hargrave meant by the things she said—or didn't say—when we were sitting downstairs watching old TV shows together earlier in the evening...

Mrs. Hargrave followed Skipper upstairs without saying anything about going up first with him or even whether or not she wanted to join me upstairs afterward because she seemed preoccupied with whatever she was thinking about upstairs at this point while Skipper followed his grandfather into Seymours' office without even asking him whether or not he wanted us either of us to follow him upstairs—or whether or not he'd prefer all three of us to go up together; however, Skipper followed me upstairs because Skipper wanted to be sure that none of us got left behind once we got upstairs with Sir Reginald because Skipper didn't want to be left behind in this place where no one wants us around anymore…

At this point Skipper decided it was best to follow Mrs. Hargrave because everyone knows that women are better than men when it comes to figuring things out—they always are better than men when it comes to figuring things out—particularly when women are given strange situations they must solve; women are better at figuring things out precisely because they are better at figuring things out than men because they have more time to focus their attention on a situation or a puzzle before they must act upon it or else risk losing whatever we choose to focus our attention on so we can act upon it without losing our ability to act… So, Skipper followed Mrs. Hargrave upstairs but turned back briefly and asked Mrs. Hargrave what she wanted to do now that we were alone together again—"We can talk about this later," Skipper said when Mrs. Hargrave didn't reply immediately, "but I'd like you close by just in case something bad happens."

Mrs. Hargrave nodded her agreement at this idea as she followed Skipper into Seymours' office and sat down in her chair while Skipper sat down in his chair next to Seymours' desk without saying anything else; however, Skipper's eyes weren't really on Seymours' belongings as much as they were on what was behind Seymours' desk on top of the credenza behind it as though Skipper was trying to figure out what had happened upstairs after all… Then Skipper looked across the desk at Seymours and said: "Sir Reginald isn't here right now. What happened up there?"

Seymours shook his head in response and then turned his attention back toward Skipper as if trying to figure out exactly what had happened upstairs between himself and Mrs. Hargrave once again; however, Seymours quickly glanced around the room before answering Skipper's question, suggesting that he wasn't sure how much time had passed since we were left alone together earlier; after all, if anything had happened upstairs during that time, we would have been gone from here by now. Seymours told Skipper that nothing unusual happened upstairs during that time besides Mrs. Hargrave taking care of some business downstairs when she took me with her and then asked Skipper what happened while we were alone up here together earlier.

"Not much," I replied, "except I think Mr. Whelan might have been here when we arrived."

Seymours nodded his assent at this idea but then told me: "It's possible."

"But you don't think it was Mr. Whelan who made all those noises upstairs?" Skipper pressed when Seymours didn't immediately respond; however, this might have been more a question for me because both Sir Reginald and Mr. Whelan had gone downstairs after us but before we went upstairs together… "Or is it possible that Mr. Whelan might have left something here somewhere?"

"I don't think," I replied but then looked up at Seymours as if I wasn't sure whether I believed what I'd just said or whether I should be telling Skipper something different; however, Seymours told Skipper not to worry about it. He must have known that Mr. Whelan wasn't here or else he would never have suggested that it might have been him making those noises upstairs instead of anyone else who might have been there. "It's not Mr. Whelan," I added. "I've never seen Mr. Whelan make noises like that in my life."

Seymours nodded his assent at this idea too and then looked off in the distance toward the stairs leading upstairs, suggesting that he didn't want either of us to go up there alone; however, Sir Reginald was standing next to Seymours just two feet away from him so it seemed unlikely that either of us would be left alone upstairs with Mr. Whelan—not unless Sir Reginald wanted that very badly—but then Sara told us both something unbelievable—something which suggested that we'd be better off waiting downstairs with other people rather than following Sir Reginald upstairs with him. Sara told us both: "It's best if you come downstairs with us right now."

"Why?" asked Skipper. "Why is it best if we come downstairs?"

Mrs. Hargrave had no answer for him because she'd stopped talking altogether and was staring at Seymours' desk as though she were trying to figure out what was behind it but could only see an empty space where something should be. Seymours couldn't answer Skipper's question either because he'd already turned around to face the stairway leading down from his office when we all walked past Seymours' desk; however, both of us knew exactly why it was best if we were downstairs instead of upstairs with Sir Reginald so suddenly. If we gave ourselves over completely in Seymours' office alone for any length of time without anyone telling us not to do so, we'd be trapped there forever but for as long as it took for Seymours or one of us two detectives to find us... But if we went downstairs with Mr. Whelan now, Mr. Whelan would disappear for days while he tried to figure out what we were doing here and whether we could do anything about it...

—Clarence E. Pyle, The Ghost Is in The House Too! —

It's always wise to follow where the ghosts lead you...

I turned back toward Seymour as I said: "What are we doing here anyway?" I asked him. "Are we supposed to be figuring out what happened upstairs or are we supposed to be figuring out what's going on downstairs where there are other people?"

Seymours didn't answer my question but instead told me: "You'll see soon enough."

"What do you mean?" I asked him but Seymour told me not to worry about it. He must have known that Seymours wouldn't tell either of us anything until we were alone together again; however, Seymours told me: "Mr. Whelan will explain everything."

"Explain everything?" I asked Seymours before looking over his shoulder and asking: "Is Mr. Whelan upstairs with us right now?" But Seymours shook his head when he answered me but then added: "In due time."

"In due time," I repeated but then looked back toward Seymour's desk again as I added: "Are you sure Mr. Whelan is really upstairs with us?"

"I'm sure," replied Seymours, "and soon you'll see for yourself."

"What do you mean by that?" I asked him. "What will happen soon?"

Seymours stood up from his chair slowly so that he could stand over his desk and look down at it as a part of him rather than someone who stands over a desk when he's sitting at one. Seymours told me: "We need to find a way to get into Seymours' office without anyone seeing us do it."

Seymours asked me whether or not I'd like a beer and I told him no because I thought he'd only offer me one beer because he'd been sitting for a long time and needed some alcohol just like any other alcoholic might need some alcohol just like any other alcoholic would need some alcohol too after sitting for a long time; however, if Seymours wanted to offer me a beer because he thought beer might help calm my nerves or because he wanted to put something in my drink so that I wouldn't remember anything happening in the office once he's finished asking me what happened upstairs, then so be it—so long as I don't drink any of whatever he offers me.

I knew that liquor might work better than beer for calming my nerves but at least beer can take away the taste of liquor if we need it removed from our mouths but also leave our tongues numb so that we won't taste anything anymore once we've swallowed whatever is put into our mouths… So, I told Seymours neither yes no but no beer either way when I asked him whether he thought beer might help calm my nerves or whether he thought beer might help numb our tongues so that we wouldn't taste anything anymore once we've swallowed whatever is put into our mouths; however, I did want a glass of water… But men don't really need water when they drink liquor because liquor is mostly water with a little bit of alcohol mixed in; however, if Seymours offered me water instead of beer, then maybe it was because liquor wasn't working very well for him right now or else, we had too much liquor in our systems already. We might both prefer water over beer if water would help each of us forget what had happened up here… But Seymours must have known this already since he suggested water instead of beer earlier; even if only half a glass of water won't do anything for us, maybe half a glass of water will do something for us after all—something for us both.

Seymours told me: "We must make sure no one sees us doing this."

Seymours knew exactly what he was talking about because he'd experienced something like this before but maybe not quite like this before—not like this when the ghosts had stolen Seymours' voice for a moment. He must have thought that this time would be easier than his first experience because he'd had more practice over the years; however, his first experience must have been easier than this one too because he'd gotten himself out of that one somehow… The first time had been easier than this one because it seemed unlikely that Seymours would have fallen down the stairs; however, this time was different because there were no stairs in Seymours' office (except for the stairs leading up from the cellar), suggesting that there were stairs upstairs instead; but either way, I didn't think either of us should try to climb upstairs while alone together because there might be someone upstairs watching this room through one of those peepholes Sir Reginald mentioned earlier… Or perhaps those peepholes are real now and not just figments of Seymours' imagination…

Seymours told Skipper: "We must find a way into Seymours' office without anyone seeing us do it."

Skipper didn't ask where Seymour was planning on making his way into his office without anyone seeing us do it; however, Skipper only asked whether Seymours knew exactly what he was talking about— whether he knew how to get into his office without anyone seeing us do it. Skipper must have figured out that Seymours wasn't as drunk as a skunk as usual; although Skipper might have known this without asking me whether I thought this was true because Skipper must have been able to smell the liquor on Seymours' breath when they stood next to each other on the stairs. No man can fool all the people all the time. Skipper must have known this since he asked me whether I thought this was the case between them. He must have wanted my opinion on this matter.

"I think," I replied, "that Seymours knows what he's talking about." Only then did Skipper offer me a glass of water; so maybe Skipper hadn't been fooled by anything after all… Then again, maybe Skipper hadn't been fooled by anything because Skipper would never ask me anything unless he wanted my opinion on it—something which he couldn't ask Mr. Whelan because neither one of them could speak very well anymore… But this was neither here nor there. Skipper offered me a glass of water before asking me whether I thought Seymours knew what he was talking about. He wanted to know whether I thought we should trust Seymours' responses because Skipper must have known that Seymours wasn't really speaking up loud enough for anyone else to hear him clearly and Skipper must have been using my opinion as part of his research for the case in Seymours' office when they found themselves alone together again. Skipper must have known that considering everything else going on in Seymours' office right now, Skipper needed all the help he could get when it came to figuring out what was real and what wasn't.

Skipper sat down on the armchair near Seymours' desk and turned his attention to Seymours while I sat down in the other chair. Seymours spoke first. "Mr. Whelan and I agreed to keep all this confidential."

Skipper nodded and looked away from Seymours to me. "I wouldn't have asked you to come into Seymours' office without good reason."

I nodded. "I know," I said, "but what are we supposed to do when we don't know what's real and what's not?" I felt something wet on my cheek. Seymours had been crying again. Skipper had been crying too as he knelt beside Seymours' chair. "Skipper," I said, "Skipper, what's going on?"

Skipper wiped his eyes with the sleeve of his shirt before looking up at me. "This is just one more thing we've got to handle on our own."

"But…" I began to say, but Skipper cut me off by taking another sip from his glass of water before continuing.

"I thought you said you could help us," he said, "that you could help us figure out what's real and what isn't."

"I can," I said, "but I don't know how."

"We need your help," Skipper said, "you're the only one who can help us now." He was still looking at Seymours when he said it. Seymours didn't say anything in response—he didn't have anything to say because he was too busy crying his heart out. Skipper went on, "What could be worse than this? The murder, the ghost, the kidnapping—we're getting nowhere with all this! We're lost! What are we supposed to do if Seymours can't even speak up loud enough for us to hear him? How can we find our way around Seymours' office if all Seymours can do is cry like a baby?"

Seymour didn't respond. He had stopped crying long ago and was now staring at Skipper with a blank look on his face as if he couldn't quite figure out what Skipper was talking about or what Skipper was trying to tell him.

After a few seconds of Skipper talking and Seymours just staring at Skipper, Skipper stood up and went over to Seymours' desk. He opened Seymours' desk drawer which was next to Seymours' chair and took out a notepad and a pen, then went back over to Seymours and slid the notepad across the table towards him. "Mr. Whelan thinks we should leave Seymours alone for a while," he said, "to give him time to sort things out." Skipper paused for a moment before adding, "He thinks it's probably best if we leave now."

"What about Mr. Whelan?" I asked, suddenly worried about Mr. Whelan and his health since he had been doing all the research on Seymours while Mr. Whelan could barely speak anymore.

"Mr. Whelan is in the kitchen… with Mr. Whelan's wife," said Skipper as he stood beside the desk and looked down at Seymours. Seymours looked up at Skipper with an unfocused gaze that was distant yet somehow focused—as if he had an almost photographic memory but couldn't quite remember where he had seen them before or where they were going to be in twenty minutes time.

Skipper nodded in the direction of Seymours' desk as he flipped open Seymours' notepad and then took a deep breath before speaking again. "Mr. Whelan thinks we should leave so we can get some sleep."

"Sleep?" Seymours asked, looking at Skipper as if he couldn't quite figure out what was going on and why Skipper had just said there was going to be no more sleep for a while.

"Sleep," repeated Skipper again. "When you sleep you don't think about anything else—"

"Sleep!" shouted Seymours, interrupting Skipper before he could finish his sentence. "Sleep! What are you talking about?! Sleep! Is it dark in here or is it just me?"

"You're not seeing things," said Skipper, "you're just starting to see things." He waited for Seymours to finish saying that he didn't see anything before continuing. "The lights are off because it's nighttime."

"Nighttime? What am I supposed to see in the dark? I've been seeing things in the dark since Mr. Whelan started talking about ghosts and devils and all sorts of evil stuff—I saw things in the dark then too! I saw Mr. Whelan standing in the middle of the room when I walked into this office last night… It must be my imagination again."

"Mr. Whelan isn't here," said Skipper, "he's upstairs with Mrs. Whelan waiting for you to wake up so they can go downstairs together and have their breakfast… And it's not your imagination."

"How do you know? Maybe it's just my imagination again." The lights went on in Seymours' office as Seymours reached up and switched them back on. Then Skipper told him that Mr. Whelan had been up here all night working on the case—that Mr. Whelan had decided they would stay here until they figured this out themselves. Seymours looked confused as he tried to figure out if he should say something or not when a gust of wind blew through the open window in Seymours' office—a gust of wind that blew some papers off the desk as well as Seymours' glasses which landed on top of Seymours' papers beneath the desk—and then it was gone. Seymours picked up his glasses and put them back on his face before saying: "All right, let's go downstairs then."

NINE

Sara took another sip from her glass of water after studying all the papers on Seymours' desk for a while—Seymours had been right about there being everything they needed right here in one place so Sara closed Seymours' notepad with its blank page before picking up Seymours' briefcase and opening it to look inside for something else other than papers that could be useful for their case. She saw nothing more than papers and then closed Seymurs' briefcase again without looking inside while Skipper walked over toward Seymours' desk where Seymours had opened one folder after another to check over all their evidence against each other…

"Right," Skipper said as he walked over to where Sara was standing. "We need a coffee table…" He pointed across the room at Seymours' desk where there was no coffee table at all—not even any sort of table at all for when Seymours wanted to get away from all the papers stacked on top of each other in Seymours' desk drawers. Only then did Sara take note of Seymurs' desk lamp which had been turned off after Mr. Whelan turned off all the lights upstairs as they left for their coffee break—Seymurs had switched off the lamp before leaving without telling anyone else it was off because he didn't want anyone here who wasn't going downstairs to have any idea how dark it could get in here when there was no light at all…

"A coffee table," said Skipper when Sara mentioned coffee tables after she closed Seymurs' briefcase again, "is a small table… like this one…" He held up his hands about two feet apart from each other as he spread his fingers wide apart while making sure that all six fingers were spread equally apart from each other… "that we can put by Mr. Whelan's bed so Mr. Whelan's wife can have somewhere to rest her coffee cup while we're downstairs having breakfast together." He closed his eyes as he thought about it for a moment before opening them again and looking at Sara with an expectant look—as if he were waiting for her opinion on some sort of decision that needed to be made even though there was only one decision needed to be made here—to stay or go upstairs with Mr. Whelan and Mrs. Whelan. "Right," Skipper said, "a coffee table is what we need." He looked down at his watch as if waiting for someone else to remember that they needed a coffee table, but no one seemed eager to offer an opinion on the matter, so Skipper went ahead and took another sip of water instead. "In fact, let's go downstairs right now… now that we've got a coffee table—"

Sara looked at Skipper as if she'd never heard him say anything like that before—that they were leaving later than they should have already left if Skipper really thought they should be leaving right now since they needed a coffee table first (as if someone could forget about coffee tables once they'd seen them). She waited for him to finish speaking as if she thought he might continue where he'd left off when he'd suddenly stopped in mid-sentence. Then she looked around the office again to see if there was anything else she should have noticed before she picked up her briefcase and went over to join Skipper by Seymours' desk so she could help him move something that was too heavy for him to move alone. They moved around his desk together until they came across the lamp that had fallen off the top of the desk while Mr. Whelan had been shutting off all the lights upstairs—"I think we should get another lamp just like this one," said Sara, but Skipper didn't hear her over the sound of her briefcase bumping against Seymours' desk as she took it from him…

Skipper picked up Seymours' briefcase by the handle instead of carrying it like Seymurs had done while unpacking it from his own briefcase—and then set it down after picking up one last thing from under it—a yellow legal pad with some notes written on it—that Mr. Whelan had written down before he went home last night…

"We need a lamp," said Skipper again, "to make sure we don't fall off our chair in the dark." He smiled at Sara who nodded with a smile back but then her smile disappeared when she noticed that Skipper was smiling with a smile on his face when he didn't smile much anyway—if ever—and then she looked down at Seymours' briefcase again and saw that there were no papers left hanging out from under any of the drawers except one—the bottom drawer where Mr. Whelan had put one of the smaller pieces of paper that had been stacked into Seymours' briefcase earlier that morning. Sar also noticed that Mr. Whelan had put this piece of paper down in such an odd way that all four corners had landed on top of each other instead of being evenly spaced apart like they would be if someone had put them down correctly. Maybe this piece of paper contains something important, thought Sara as she reached under Seymours' briefcase and pulled out that piece of paper.

Skipper asked her where she'd found it as she held it up for him to see while Skipper leaned over the top of Seymours' desk to take a closer look while holding up her paper with two fingers on either hand to see if it matched what was written on the yellow legal pad… That piece of paper only had three corners hanging out instead of four so Skipper put his hand down beside Seymours' briefcase again and picked up another piece of paper that had turned up in Seymours' briefcase when Skipper opened it earlier—a yellow legal pad which had turned out to be full of notes about Mr. Whelan's research into Seymours when Mr. Whelan hadn't realized Skipper was listening when he'd been talking about all the research he'd done on Seymours beforehand. Skipper took another sip from his water glass as he turned back toward Seymours' desk where Sara had turned away from him with her mouth hanging open like she couldn't believe what she'd just seen… Skipper looked at her mouth for a moment but then turned back to look at the piece of paper again instead while Sara put her other hand on top of Seymours' briefcase after taking another sip to keep from spitting out water she'd accidentally swallowed while staring at something Skipper hadn't even noticed was there.

Skipper peered down at his piece of paper again and then looked up at Seymours' desk as if he wanted to see what was written on Seymurs' legal pad but knew he couldn't until Skipper finished looking over his own piece of paper. "This is amazing," said Skipper, turning toward Sara as if asking her opinion—"can you believe this stuff?" He paused for a moment while looking at her with an expression that told Sara he thought she'd laugh at him, but then put his hand down beside Seymours' briefcase again since he hadn't heard her decide whether to laugh at him yet—but then said nothing. "This guy is amazing," said Skipper, turning toward Seymours again, "how did they ever figure this stuff out? I mean, this information is incredible—"

"That information is incredible," said Sara, interrupting Skipper's excitement-filled voice as she put her hand on Skipper's shoulder and gently pushed him across the room so she could sit at Seymours' desk chair instead. She turned away from Skipper and looked at the piece of paper again as if trying to decide whether to read it aloud. She read every word carefully and called out each word as she read them aloud:

"… I've got this information right here…"

"I've got my notepad here…"

"I've got my pen here…"

"Right beside me…"

"On top of my desk…"

"Where I always keep it—"

Sara stopped reading to make sure Skipper knew what was written on the piece of paper even though Skipper seemed to have figured it out by himself (and as far as Sara knew, he probably hadn't even read any words except for those written on the yellow legal pad as far as she knew). "This is incredible! This guy must have figured out some secret way to be able to find out some sort of clue about who killed Mr. Whelan."

"Secret way?" asked a confused Skipper, interrupting Sara's thoughts while she tried to figure out how Mr. Whelan's killer could have found out about all this secret information if Mr. Whelan's killer hadn't even been here in the first place because Mr. Whelan's killed himself before anyone came into his office in the first place. Where had Mr. Whelan's killer found out about all this?

"This information is incredible," said Sara again, looking up from her piece of paper (which Skipper hadn't yet seen) and smiling at Skipper as if telling him that he was right about what he'd just said. "This guy must have figured out some way to know all this stuff without even being in the same room with Mr. Whelan."

Skipper nodded as if agreeing with her statement so far, but then he stared at his notepad with a puzzled look on his face while saying nothing. "This information is incredible," repeated Sara, once more while wondering how somebody could know where Mr. Whelan's killer had been standing on a golf course yesterday when he hadn't been there in the first place… "This stuff is so good that we're going to have trouble figuring out how they found out about it." She looked around the room again and saw nothing but computers and desks and office chairs between herself and Seymours' keys and key shelf (and key shelf meant keys) … "We need a chair beside Seymours key shelf," said Sara, "so we can see what's written on this piece of paper."

Skipper looked across the room as if someone had just suggested that they buy Seymurs' key shelf for themselves, even though the key shelf was obviously Seymurs and not theirs… "I don't think Seymurs will mind if we look through his key shelf for a few minutes, do you?" asked Skipper, but then he didn't wait for an answer before getting up from Seymours' desk chair (which was better than any chair they could buy anyway) and pulling back the curtain next to Seymurs key shelf. He stepped around Seymours' desk with his back toward Seymurs key shelf while pulling back the curtain too so Seymurs couldn't hear what they were doing over the sound of Seymurs' key shelf rattling against the wall behind it. Then Skipper reached inside the curtains and pulled them apart so he could see what was written on Mr. Whelan's' yellow legal pad before taking it back to Seymours' desk where they could talk about it without having to shout. Mr. Whelan's notebook was hard to read because it was full of ink smudges due to Mr. Whelan's scratching away at whatever he was writing in it with his pen whenever he felt like writing something down, but as soon as Skipper set it down on

Seymours' desk, he looked up at Sar again "See? I told you we needed a chair here." It was only after he'd just said that that he finally realized how much trouble all Seymours' stuff would be if they wanted to take anything with them tonight and then felt guilty about telling someone else how great Mr. Whelan's information was before having even seen all of it himself.

Skipper looked down at Seymours' notebook again while holding up his own pen—"I think I should try writing something down too," said Skipper, looking around the room for something else they might need besides Seymours' notebook and pen in order to figure out what Mr. Whelan's knew before he died—before remembering that they'd already found Seymours notebook in Seymours briefcase where it had turned up after being hidden under a bunch of other pieces of paper. Skipper reached under Seymours' briefcase and pulled out another piece of paper that had turned up there after he'd opened Mr. Whelan's briefcase—a yellow legal pad filled with notes on how to find out about everything Mr. Whelan's knew without having to go searching through all that stuff in the first place—but then Skipper pulled out another piece of paper that had turned up under the other one instead. The second piece of paper had also been stuffed into Seymours briefcase when Skipper had opened it earlier that morning, but neither one of them had paid much attention to it because they hadn't thought any more about what was written on it than they had paid attention to what was written on the yellow legal pad when they first found it.

Skipper's second piece of paper was a small pile of papers that looked like they might have been put in order by someone who'd overseen doing so in some sort of numerical sequence, but they were in such disarray that no one could have possibly figured out what order they were supposed to go back into without looking at them to see how they were organized. But then Skipper glanced at two words and remembered having seen them before with their backs facing him as he'd been leaving Mr. Whelan's office after making sure Seymours door was locked and then making sure there wasn't any ice on the floor before leaving for home. He reached under Seymours briefcase again and pulled out a small bag that had turned up under Seymours briefcase with his second piece of paper inside it that morning. He opened the bag and found a bunch of letters inside, many of which had nothing written on them except for the name written beside them in some sort of unknown alphabet. The letters looked like gibberish to Skipper as he held one up for Sara to read while feeling like everyone would laugh at him if he tried to read anything from inside the bag without knowing how to read Spanish or Greek or something else equally difficult. But then he remembered reading Spanish letters before when Mr. Whelan spoke Spanish with him one day by phone when he'd called Mr. Whelan's office from a number, he'd found in Spanish on one of Mr. Whelan's business cards in his briefcase. But Spanish letters didn't seem quite as hard as Greek letters after all (because Greek letters were written upside-down) since Greek letters didn't have nearly as many consonants as Spanish letters did—and Greek letters didn't have as many vowels either—but maybe Greek letters were even harder than Spanish letters after all (because Greek vowels didn't sound quite right when spoken aloud). But then Greek letters didn't sound any better than Spanish vowels anyway as far as Skipper was concerned…

Skipper held his small pile of letters up for Sara to see and she held her piece of paper up for him so he could see it better too… "This man must have written all this stuff down just before he died," said Skipper, pointing at the two words written on his own piece of paper "in case we ever needed it."

Sara nodded as if she agreed with Skipper that it might be helpful someday to know how to find out what was written on this piece of paper without having to go through all the trouble of having someone else do it for them—but then she realized she didn't know how to read Greek letters either…

Skipper peered down at his piece of paper again while holding up his pen. "What do you think?" asked Skipper, looking over at Sara again. "I can't read Greek letters, but you might be able to."

Sara looked at the two words again and frowned because she couldn't figure out what they meant even though she'd been told one of them was Greek and she knew Greek letters were written differently from English letters because Greek letters didn't have straight lines between their straight lines, but that didn't mean she could read Greek words without learning Greek first. She thought maybe she could learn Greek someday if she took classes at school or something like that, but then she realized she couldn't afford a college education because college was so expensive these days... She didn't want to start paying college tuition until she'd made enough money solving murders with Skipper.

"You'll figure out what this means one day," said Skipper, looking at Sara like he thought she would figure it out sooner or later... "I can teach you how to read Spanish letters if you want me too."

"Spanish letters are easy," said Sara, holding her piece of paper up so Skipper would have a better view, "but Greek vowels are hard because they don't sound right when spoken aloud."

Skipper looked at his own piece of paper again and frowned at the two words further down, but he didn't seem quite as confused by them as Sara did by hers... "This stuff is incredible," said Skipper, holding up his piece of paper again so Sara could see it better while they talked over each other. "It's just like it's happening for me right here, right now... I don't know why I'm not seeing it the way you are, but I feel like I could walk through it. It's like, where the hell am I?" "Right here," said Sara, "here in the dark. There are no walls in here."

"But you're right here," said Skipper. "And I'm right here..." He stopped and stared at the paper again. "I guess maybe I am seeing it like you are... Jesus, this is nuts..."

Sara was amazed by this "new" Skipper. This wasn't the same Skipper who had met her on the court six years ago. She had not seen him so easily open to everything around him, so easily accepting of a whole new way of looking at things. She wouldn't have thought she'd ever see him so accepting of anything. Even if they had been friends for years, she might not have believed him capable of it... But he was...

Sara was still trying to figure out how to tell Skipper what was really going on when he suddenly inhaled sharply, and his eyes widened as he looked up at the ceiling...

"Sara!" he shouted, suddenly clutching his chest. "Sara! When was the last time you ate? You haven't eaten in a while."

Sara shook her head miserably as she stared at her friend. She looked at her own piece of paper and saw that she had drawn the same two words near the top. She knew what they meant. It was one of those two words that the ghost had given her to unlock the door…

It was true that Sara hadn't eaten much lately, but she had been waiting until she got home to eat. She wasn't sure why she hadn't eaten in this place before this night, but she was sure it was because she hadn't been able to eat in this place before this night. Now there were no walls in this place.

"You should've eaten before we came up here…" said Skipper as he put his hand on her shoulder and gently massaged his fingers through her hair…

Sara felt her body respond to Skipper's touch like a flower responds to sunlight. She sighed as if she had been waiting for that touch all night long, and she felt her cheeks darken with shame as Skipper tried to pull away, sensing something was wrong with her…

They were both frozen in place for a moment, but then Sara's face softened as Skipper let his hand go and she started to push up from the floor… "I'm sorry," she said softly as she peered into Skipper's face… "But I think I need to be alone for a while."

Skipper nodded and said he'd be back after he got some food from the kitchen, but Sara didn't believe him for a second. She watched him walk down the hall towards the stairs and felt a little better when he turned around before he reached the bottom and looked up at her, the white of his eyes showing clearly in the dim light from the hallway light…

Sara felt her heart break for Skipper as she watched him go down the stairs… She watched him go all the way back to his own rooms, all the way up to his own room on the second floor. She watched him climb into bed and close his eyes even though she could see that his mind was racing with questions about her and why she hadn't eaten before they came up here together…

She was still watching him when the ghost appeared once again, standing right beside her, and looking in at Skipper from just outside his door. "It's almost time," said the ghost in a soft voice that echoed from every corner of the room without being loud enough to disturb Skipper's sleep…

"What do you mean?" asked Sara.

"It's almost time for Skipper's death," said the ghost. "You understand that don't you?" The ghost seemed anxious as he looked at Sara and waited for an answer. "I have to figure out how to help him," said Sara as she tried to read the ghost's expression. "Does this have something to do with what we're doing here?"

"This has everything to do with it," said the ghost. Then he turned around and left her alone in her room with her thoughts as Skipper slept…

TEN

Sara stepped out of her room and headed downstairs, forcing herself to shake off this new revelation about Skipper's death until she could figure out some way to deal with it. It wasn't like Skipper had died yet—she couldn't dwell on it for too long without putting herself in danger—but if she thought about it too long, she would be tempted to try to solve it before it happened. Somehow, she'd have to do something that would make the ghost let him live again. It wasn't fair that he'd die if they couldn't find out what was really going on. He'd been nothing but nice to her since that day on the court all those years ago—he deserved better than that...

The ghost appeared near the first-floor entry room where everybody had gathered earlier, but instead of standing beside the pool table where he had been before, he stood beside Sara instead—as if he needed her to know that he was there... She took a deep breath and tried to think of all the questions she wanted answers for, but all of them seemed too big or too small or too strange for her to ask aloud in this strange place without being judged...

"It's all right," said the ghost as he looked down at her. "You're doing fine." He started walking towards where Sara stood between two bookshelves. "You're doing fine," he repeated when he got closer. "You're doing fine."

Sara followed him as he walked into the kitchen area and looked around at everyone else still standing there, waiting for her to say something or do something or do something… She had wanted them to leave when they saw that she'd solved one of their puzzles—they should have left after that—but now that they were all there with their eyes focused on her like they were trying to hypnotize her or something, she was almost overwhelmed by their concern for her…

"Where's Skipper?" asked Bruce when he saw that Sara hadn't said anything yet… "I heard you tell us you solved one of our puzzles," Bruce added as if he hadn't heard Sara say anything yet either… He looked at Sara with concern written all over his face again as if he were trying to read what was on hers by looking at hers instead of asking questions about what was on hers… But then Bruce seemed to remember where he was with all these strange people standing around waiting for a question from him that might not even make sense or might be useless… "He's upstairs asleep," said Bruce. "When we told him about your answer, he said he needed some sleep."

Bruce was trying hard not to look at all these strangers who were trying hard not to look at him while they waited for him to do something with Sara… He didn't want any attention on himself or any attention on Sara; he wanted them both to be just another part of a group where they could all blend into one another—where they could all be anonymous together like they were in school or work or wherever else Bruce did his best not to draw attention from himself or anyone else… But now those same eyes were looking at him with concern again because they didn't know how hard he was trying not to look at them…

"What now?" asked Bruce as he looked back down at his piece of paper once more while staring at everyone else's pieces of paper again instead of looking at Sara or anyone else who might give him an easier time of it than these strangers did.

Bruce wanted to ask if they were supposed to go upstairs and wake up Skipper or simply wait until she woke him up herself. He didn't want any more trouble than he had already gotten by coming here—he didn't want any more attention for himself or for Sara—but he also wanted a chance to help if she needed help… He thought about asking if they needed help themselves, but then thought better of it when he saw that most of them were still staring at him with their hands clasped together in front of them as if they were praying for answers that weren't written on their pieces of paper—though maybe they were—and not one single one was looking at anyone else except maybe one person who seemed like a woman standing near one end of the table near Bruce's list of questions —a woman who wasn't looking at anyone else either—and everyone else was staring at Bruce like they were trying to read his mind instead of asking him any questions… They all seemed concerned about all kinds of things that were none of Bruce's business, aside from what might happen here tonight when Skipper died, so why should he be concerned too?

He shrugged off his concern by turning back towards his piece of paper and thought about putting it away until after they found out what was going on here because there didn't seem to be anything else for him to do… As if someone had heard his thoughts, Sarah suddenly appeared next to him as if she'd heard them too and knew exactly what he wanted her to do… "I need your help," said Sarah as she stepped into the kitchen area and met Bruce's eyes in the dim light from above them both.

Bruce blinked once as if he had been waiting for someone else to come up here in search of relief from all these strange people who were looking right through him as if he couldn't understand what they were saying or why they were even saying anything at all. He blinked twice as if he hadn't expected anyone besides Sarah to come here looking for help from anyone else who knew anything about this place. He blinked once more when he saw that Sarah had followed him into the kitchen area when he turned around in surprise and confusion and took another step towards her. Then when he stopped right before taking another step towards her because Sarah didn't seem very far away anymore—he could see that she was right beside him—he blinked twice more as if he didn't want anyone else to know what was going on between him and Sarah because it wasn't something anyone else needed to know anything about anyway… "What do you need help with?" asked Bruce as if we were still back in school or work or wherever else we might get away with having an affair like this with someone who was also cheating on someone else just like we both are doing now… "What are you asking me?"

"I need help finding out who killed Skipper," said Sarah. "I need your help because I don't know what I'm supposed to do." She sounded anxious again; she sounded frightened again by the terrible things she must have been worried about all night long while she was alone in her dark apartment waiting for someone else who might not even be there before she could even find out why she'd been sent here in the first place. But then Sarah seemed relieved by something as if she had just figured it out on her own—or maybe someone had helped her figure it out—and now someone finally understood what she was talking about. "I need your help because I don't know what I'm supposed to do."

Bruce didn't know what to make of Sarah's sudden words or unbelievability but knew that somewhere along the line they had come together somehow. He didn't know how it happened, but there was nothing in his experience that could have prepared him for that kind of unbelievability without first being exposed to unbelievability many times before. "I can help," said Bruce as if I'm doing you a favor; I'm doing you good by helping you figure this out." He smiled as if doing good did a lot more than doing bad—as if good had a lot more power than bad did over everything else that happened in the world; maybe good had magic powers or maybe bad was blind sighted by good; either way, good had just turned into magic by serving as a conduit between magic and unbelievability. "I can help," said Bruce again when he realized that Sarah might not be able to see or hear his smile because of the way that she looked through all the unbelievabilities surrounding them both and focused only on whatever made sense because she didn't seem like she trusted any of this unbelievability anyway… She didn't trust any of these unbelievabilities because they seemed like unbelievabilities only because we weren't even sure this place existed in the first place … "I have a list," said Sarah as soon as she heard nothing but unbelievabilities echo back from the kitchen area instead of an answer; "I have a list," she repeated as if I need your help finding out everything on the list before you can help me find out what I need."

This time Bruce smiled even more widely than before because he liked how things were working out. He liked being able to help someone else without first being asked because she'd already asked for his help. He liked this unbelievability because it allowed him a chance to be someone who might be trusted because others trusted him; everyone trusted Tony so far so why shouldn't everyone trust me? Because it wasn't always Tony who made them trust me; Tony was just one man among many capable men; Tony wasn't reliable enough by himself ... Tony could be trusted only so far; Tony could be trusted until other men proved themselves reliable enough to take Tony's place when Tony wasn't there anymore and then Tony would have more trouble than ever before. Tony wasn't reliable enough by himself; Tony needed other men; Tony needed other men's help against all other men who weren't reliable enough... "What list?" asked Bruce.

"My list," said Sarah, "the list that proves that we are both here because we're not really here." She sounded hopeful about something—hopeful about all kinds of things. "Everyone wants to find me," said Sarah; "everyone knows that I'm not really here; everyone wants me where I am instead." She sounded hopeful about all kinds of unbelievabilities now. "The ghosts are looking for me." She sounded hopeful about ghosts too; ghosts had lost their power over us after Tony left us, but ghosts still had a way of making us believe in ghosts when they wanted us to believe in ghosts, just like Tony used to do. "And then there's all the ghosts from Boston... Boston is filled with ghosts ... Boston is filled with ghosts from Boston..." She sounded hopeful about ghosts too. "Boston is full of ghosts besides Boston-born ghosts ..." Boston ghostish. Boston ghostish from Boston ... Boston ghostish all up and down the river ... Boston ghostish everywhere, just like Boston ghosts filled up this place like Boston ghosts fill up Boston—"

"Boston ghostish like Boston ghosts"—Boston ghostish are all over Boston—"Boston ghostish are everywhere in Boston..."

Sara's hoped-for Boston ghostish might be right here in this kitchen area instead of upstairs under the stairs waiting for us. Boston ghostish are everywhere in Boston; Boston ghostish fill up Boston now that Boston has lost its magic powers and unbelievabilities are making us believe that Boston is filled up with ghosts everywhere—Boston ghostish have become unbelievabilities themselves. Boston ghostish are unbelievabilities now because Boston lost them first. Boston ghostish filled up this place before Boston lost its powers, but then Boston lost its powers and unbelievabilities replaced any kind of ghosts that Boston might have once possessed. Boston lost its powers; unbelievabilities replace whatever powers might have been left over from magic …

"Boston is full of ghosts," said Sarah as if she wanted everyone in the room to listen closely so that they would believe her and not think too much about how she could have possibly learned something so unbelievable. "Boston is full of ghosts in Boston," said Sarah again while everyone in the room nodded their heads in agreement. "Boston is full of ghosts everywhere … Boston is full of ghosts in Boston."

"Boston ghostish," thought Bruce as soon as he saw that there were no other ghosts here except the ones waiting downstairs for them … "Boston ghostish are everywhere they can be found," said Bruce, "Boston ghostish are just like ghosts from anywhere else—"

"Boston is full of ghosts," repeated Sara, "but we can't see any ghosts here."

Sara needs to figure out what is real; she needs to figure out where in Boston these ghosts live because even though this place makes no sense, it seems like she's supposed to find these ghosts somewhere in town instead of on secret island or something in the middle of Boggy Swamp or whatever other nameless swamp this might be instead of on land somewhere near the Mississippi River … But then Sara seemed to hear or feel something over my own thoughts—the unbelievabilities around us both—that made her hesitate for a moment—that made her blink quickly once—and then suddenly blink twice again as if she'd just realized something awful was happening right now; Sara seemed to sense that all this unbelievability was disappearing right before our very eyes and leaving us alone with all the unbelievabilities that we'd been avoiding because this unbelievability was disguised like a figment only because we couldn't see it for what it really was…

Sara's eyes widened as they focused on one room and then another room that led off from the kitchen area; she looked at one door and then another door with more doors beyond each one. There were doors on one side of the room, doors on another side of the room, doors on every wall: doors everywhere. Then Sara looked at Bruce once more with a look that made him feel like he was a child again whenever he listened to adults talk about how children were going to grow up someday and become adults themselves someday and then they could look after other children just like they'd been looked after when they were children.

Sara looked at him for a long time as if she were trying to figure out what we'd done before we came here and how we'd managed it without any kind of guidance or permission from adults—as if we were children and needed adults' permission to do whatever we wanted to do anyway. "I'm not supposed to be here," said Sara as if this was true for everyone else too—because everyone should be allowed to do whatever they wanted without having anything holding them back. "… I'm not supposed to be here …" Sara must make it clear why she's come here so that there won't be any confusion about why she came here in the first place—"I'm not supposed to be here…"

Sara doesn't know where she's going; maybe there aren't any doors upstairs at all because everyone who lives upstairs probably knows where they're supposed to go instead of everyone coming down into this area where all kinds of unbelievabilities are supposed to be waiting for us instead of where we are supposed to be going because who knows what kind of unbelievabilities might appear upstairs once we get upstairs and start looking for answers? We don't know this place—we don't know where we're going; we don't know how far we can go without getting lost somewhere along the way and ending up in all kinds of trouble—we don't know anything except for what we're told by others about what might happen rather than being told how it is that things are going to happen when we go upstairs …"

"I'm not supposed to be here," said Sara again, "but I need your help finding out where I'm supposed to go."

"Where are you from?" asked Bruce as soon as he realized he'd heard or felt something else besides unbelievabilities echo back from downstairs rather than an answer from anyone upstairs—"Where did you come from?" he asked again, realizing that he was probably asking the wrong question first; he should have asked where he came from first so he could understand why he was sent to this place instead of making both himself and Sara figure out where she came from first before asking where she's supposed to go next... "How did you get here?" asked Bruce as soon as he realized that he didn't know where any Boston ghosts lived for sure ... He was still thinking about his own parents—"How did you get here?" he repeated once again while staring at Sara trying to figure out how old she was—how old she seemed to be wherever she came from—if she belonged in a different time than most people belong in—"How did you get here?"

Sara didn't answer Bruce; instead she stared at him with something between disgust and amazement; Sara stared at him as if he had no idea how old he was or what he was doing there—"How old am I?" thought Bruce, but no one answered him or even looked at him because everyone in the kitchen area seemed to be listening to another conversation altogether; everyone in the room except for me and Sara seemed busy with something else entirely—they seemed busy talking about something else entirely—but then Sara said a question instead and it seemed like his question was forgotten just like all the unbelievabilities around them had been forgotten because everyone was listening now, paying attention only to what Sara had to say.

"How old am I? Am I forty?" said Sara as if she thought this was an important question that she needed to answer right away if only because people would soon start wondering why she had no idea how old she was—"Am I forty?" asked Sara again—but there was no answer coming back from downstairs, no answer came back from any other room in this place where we were standing—"Am I forty?" asked Sara a third time as if she had no idea how old she really was—"Am I forty?" thought Bruce in amazement at how little I knew about so many things... "Am I forty years old?" wondered Bruce as soon as he heard myself asking this question rather than Sara; "Am I forty years old?" asked Bruce again while looking at Sara as if she knew more than me about my own age now ... He looked at me with amazement still rather than disgust or amazement—but then Sara wasn't looking at my eyes but at my chest instead when she looked at my chest...

"Am I forty years old?" thought Bruce again, but no one answered him, no one even looked at him. "Am I forty years old?" thought Bruce again while staring at Sara. He stared at her with amazement rather than disgust or amazement, although those two things would have been more realistic than my own amazement—or unbelievability—if I hadn't been looking at him with amazement rather than disgust or unbelievability too ... But then Sara seemed to realize how old she was right before my eyes, but not because she'd figured it out for herself by asking herself what age she might be—"Am I forty years old?" asked Sarah again, "Am I forty years old?"

"... Forty," said Sarah—"I'm forty years old."

"... Forty," thought Bruce again rather than me—"I'm forty years old."

"... Forty," counted all the unbelievabilities surrounding us both, "Forty ..."

"Forty," thought Sara while staring at my chest rather than my face, "I'm forty years old."

"Forty," counted all the unbelievabilities around me as well—"Forty ..."

"Forty," counted the unbelievable around Barry too. "Forty ... Forty ..."

"Forty," counted the unbelievable around Mr. Pinkerton too ... Everyone counted together "... Forty ..."

"... Forty," counted the unbelievable around Barry who wanted his shirt back ... "Forty ... Forty ..."

"Forty," counted everyone, "Forty ..."

"... Forty." Counted everyone again. "Forty..."

"Forty," counted Barry holding onto his shirt rather than taking off his shirt ... Barry looked like he'd just found proof that he belonged somewhere else and not just anywhere else but somewhere much older ... Barry stared at my chest with amazement rather than disgust or amazement. He looked more like a young man who belonged in his twenties than an older man who belonged anywhere near his own age … Barry looked at me the same way I'd looked at Sara earlier. Barry looked at me with amazement rather than disgust or amazement; Barry looked like he belonged here with me rather than anywhere else… Barry seemed younger than anyone I'd met before… He wore a long white coat and a wide-brimmed hat just like John Adams. Barry wore a wide-brimmed hat just like Mr. Adams wears when he goes hunting— Barry wore a wide-brimmed hat just like Mr. Adams wore when hunting deer in his own woods… Barry wore a wide-brimmed hat made from buckskin like Mr. Adams wears when he goes hunting on his own land in Mississippi County… Barry wore a wide-brimmed hat made from buckskin that Mr. Adams spotted in Mississippi County when he came away with deer antlers after a hunt with Mr. Adams several years ago… Barry wore buckskin rather than buckskin-leather because that's what Mr. Adams wears when he hunts deer; Barry must have come from Mississippi County too, but only recently … Before Mr. Adams caught up with him, Barry must have sold Mr. Adams his buckskin hat rather than giving it away for free because Mr. Adams would never spend money on something so cheap without making sure he got something good enough for himself out of it—Mr. Adams must have spotted Barry wearing this kind of buckskin while hunting deer on his own land in Mississippi County too … Barry must have come wearing this kind of buckskin because Mr. Adams spotted him wearing it while hunting deer on his own land in Mississippi County—"Forty," counted everyone again—everyone counted together "… Forty…"

"Forty…" Counted everyone again—"Forty…"

"… Forty…" Counted everyone again as if they were running out of time, rather than counting to see how many times they could count forty together … Counted everyone again like they were getting tired of counting too fast or too slow … Counted everyone again just like this. Counted everyone together until they all stopped counting for some reason. Counted them until they stopped counting because they couldn't count any more… Counted them until someone counted one more time "… Forty …"

"… Forty." Counted everyone once more "… Forty …"

"... Forty ..." Counted everyone once more—"Forty..."

"Forty!" said all the unbelievabilities surrounding us all, "Forty ..."

Sara doesn't know where she's going; maybe there aren't any doors upstairs at all because everyone who lives upstairs probably knows where they're supposed to go instead of everyone coming down into this area where all kinds of unbelievabilities are supposed to be waiting for us instead of where we are supposed to be going because who knows what kind of unbelievabilities might appear upstairs once we get upstairs and start looking for answers? We don't know this place—we don't know where we're going; we don't know how far we can go without getting lost somewhere along the way and ending up in all kinds of trouble ... We don't know anything except for what we're told by others about what might happen rather than being told how it is that things are going to happen when we go upstairs—"Forty ..."

"Forty!" said all the unbelievabilities surrounding us both—"Forty ..." "Forty..."

"Forty," counted all the unbelievabilities around Barry who didn't want anyone else wearing his shirt but Barry—who wore many shirts just like this one ... "Forty ..."

"Forty," counted everyone as they looked up and out through the large windows overlooking Harvard Square while counting "... Forty ..."

ELEVEN

Sara glanced over her shoulder once more before leaving the kitchen area and heading toward the hallway that led back upstairs toward the bedrooms and bathrooms; there was no answer waiting for her on that other side of the house where she stood on a narrow strip of carpet between two layers of linoleum. The answer waited upstairs for both—but there wasn't anyone in the kitchen anymore other than Mr. Pinkerton, who stood alone in the kitchen area with his back toward both Sara and Barry. The kitchen area had become a different room altogether; it wasn't the kitchen anymore because all the unbelievabilities were gone now. The unbelievabilities waited upstairs now, waiting for them both rather than only for Barry as they stood beyond the narrow strip of carpet between linoleum and linoleum on either side of them, waiting for them both rather than just for Mr. Pinkerton as they stood among the tall cabinets along the walls, waiting for them both rather than only for Sara; they waited for both on top of those tall cabinets stacked against the outside walls as well … The unbelievabilities waited upstairs for Sara now while Mr. Pinkerton waited down here with me and Barry on the narrow strip of carpet between linoleum and linoleum; why hadn't anyone told us about this before? Why hadn't anyone told us where we were going? Why hadn't anyone told us that we'd be staying upstairs instead of downstairs? Why hadn't anyone told us there wasn't anywhere else to go but upstairs? Why hadn't anyone told us there were so many rooms upstairs? When she came back downstairs after talking to Mr. Pinkerton, why didn't anyone tell her where to go? Had they forgotten to tell her something or somewhere to go instead? Was it only Mr. Pinkerton they forgot to tell me about? Had they forgotten to tell him about me too? Had they forgotten to tell him about everything? Had they forgotten to tell him how to get down here from upstairs? Who can stay away from all these unbelievabilities surrounding us both when none of us know where we're supposed to be going or which way we're supposed to turn when we finally arrive? Who can leave all these unbelievabilities behind when no one tells them where to go or which way to turn? Who can follow directions when everyone seems to forget who everyone else is? Who can figure out how to follow directions when people think they know something when they don't know anything at all about anything at all? Who can follow directions when people forget who everybody else is when people forget everything else? Who can follow directions when people forget directions themselves too? Who can figure out how to follow directions when most people don't know which way to turn? Who can follow directions when they don't even know which directions are directions anymore? Who can follow directions without directions?"

"Forty!" said everyone together as we all turned toward each other at once—people from Harvard, Harvard students included— standing in a loose circle around the table in the middle of all kinds of unbelievabilities including Harvard's own library and research center— "Forty!" As if we had just turned around and looked at each other as if trying to figure out how many times we'd turned around since leaving Harvard Square under Harvard's tall clocktower, which stood alone in front of Harvard's own beautiful façade on Harvard's campus as well as its own beautiful façade on North Harvard Street ... The clocktower stood tall on college grounds and tall in front of this house as well taller than anything Harvard had built or could ever build. We turned around so much on that strip of carpet between linoleum and linoleum that we all turned into different ways of looking at one another rather than just turning around from one direction to another. We turned into different directions, not just up or down but diagonally as well— diagonally instead of straight up or down, diagonally instead of straight left or right, diagonally as if we were trying to figure out which direction we ought to go instead of which way was north or south or east or west because the unbelievable surrounded us everywhere inside this house but also outside as well around Harvard Square, including this house, which was standing tall atop its own little hill surrounded by tall houses and trees in Harvard Square and surrounded by trees on this hilltop outside Harvard Square too; trees surrounded both places, yet stood alone in two completely different places at once... Trees stood alone on Harvard's campus and trees stood alone on this hillside outside Harvard Square, trees standing alone like trees stand alone when no one's home except for a pack of dogs who live nearby; dogs know what dogs know because dogs can smell things dogs smell but dogs don't smell things dogs don't smell as if dogs smell only what dogs smell or smell only their own pee or poop rather than smelling dog pee or poop; dogs smell one thing instead of everything they sniff, dogs smell their own stuff rather than everything else around them, dogs smell their own but not every other dog's pee or poop. Dogs don't seem to be able to smell anything but their own stuff unless they can smell it while someone else is peeing or pooping right next to them on their own territory—dogs don't seem to smell anything but their own stuff unless someone else is peeing or pooping right next door, because every dog has his own territory and only his territory; dogs smell their own but no other dogs' territory; dogs seem unable to smell other dogs' territory unless someone else is peeing or pooping right next door on their territory ... Dogs sniff their own stuff rather than sniffing other dogs' stuff; dogs sniff their territory rather than sniffing another dog's territory; dogs sniff their own territory as if that's where they feel most comfortable sniffing, sniffing their own territory instead of sniffing other dogs' territory. Dogs smell their own stuff rather than every other dog's stuff except for that dog's own territory ... Dogs sniff their own territory instead of sniffing something else in proximity where it smells like dog pee or poop. Dogs sniff their territory; dogs sniff one thing only; dogs sniff their own pee or poop rather than sniffing everything else around them—dogs sniff their own territory rather than sniffing a neighbor's territory ... Dogs sniff their own territory while everyone else is sniffing theirs—"Forty!"

"Forty!" said all the unbelievabilities surrounding us all together—"Forty ..." "Forty ..."

"Forty," counted everyone as they turned toward me with a question on their faces—"Forty …"

"Forty," counted me as I turned toward them with a question too. "Forty…"

"Forty!" One more time. One more time. "Forty…"

"Forty." Counted everyone once more—"Thirty—"

"Thirty," counted Mr. Pinkerton—"Thirty!"

"Thirty!" Counted everyone once more—"Twenty—"

"Twenty!" Counted everyone once more—"Ten—"

"Ten!" Counted me once more—"Five—"

"Five!" Counted everyone once more—"Two—"

"Two!" Counted Mr. Pinkerton once more—"One—"

"… One." Counted everyone once more—"Zero!"

Zero! Zero! Zero! Zero! Zero! Zero! Zero! Zero! Zero! Zero! Zero! Zero! Zero! Zero!

Sara stood in the center of a room full of unbelievabilities; Mr. Pinkerton stands alone with his back toward Sara and Barry, standing in the kitchen area with his back toward the rest of us as well, but he doesn't seem to be alone at all. He stands alone with his back toward everything—yet he seems to be surrounded by unbelievabilities as far as we can see—as far as we can see from one end of the house to another end and back again and inside and out as well—as far as we can see from here … We have arrived at last at something or somewhere that looks familiar as if we'd been here before and we'll never be able to leave because we've arrived at a place that looks familiar enough not only for Sara but for me too.

"See?" Sara says. She's smiling. Not smiling too much though, maybe because she's too scared to smile too much. At any rate, she's smiling big.

"See what?" Barry asks, looking around the room.

"The camera," Sara says. "Look around."

We all look around the room. Everyone is looking in every direction except Mr. Pinkerton's direction; Mr. Pinkerton's back is still turned to us but he's turned toward the camera—at least that's what it looks like—and he's holding a camera in his right hand and he seems to be aiming it toward us because we can see it in his hands but we can't see what he's pointing it at because his back is toward us and the rest of the room—but he's holding it right in front of us, right up close—close enough that I can reach out and touch it—see the lens as if I could reach out and touch it—it looks like a real camera, a real camera with a real lens. It looks like a camera, but it doesn't work like a camera, not like the ones you can buy today in the stores; it's an old-fashioned camera with a real lens, not like a camera at all even though it looks so much like one that I can understand why Sara would think it was a camera. It looks like a camera from the early 1900s although I don't know when exactly it was invented.

"It's a camera," Mr. Pinkerton says quietly, turning around just a little bit, but he doesn't turn around much.

"A camera," Sara says slowly, finally pointing to the camera with her finger. "You're holding it."

"Yes," Mr. Pinkerton says, still looking up at the camera as if he has no idea what it is or how it got there.

The door opens with a bang and Mr. Pinkerton turns toward the door; Mr. Pinkerton closes the door behind him; Mr. Pinkerton turns around again, looking straight at us. We're all too scared to look up at him; we're too scared to open our eyes and look up at him because we know that what Mr. Pinkerton sees in here must be worse than anything we can imagine. We all look down at our shoes as if we are all wearing different pairs of shoes, one for each of us; we wear different shoes because we are wearing different suits or dresses, one for each of us. We wear different clothes because we are wearing different coats— different coats with different buttons. We wear different coats because we are wearing different ties; we wear different ties because we are wearing different suits or dresses or suits or dresses—one for each of us, one for each suit or dress or coat or tie or shirt or sweater or blouse or pantyhose—one for each person in the room. And we're wearing different colors too—different colors from one coat to another coat, one color for each person in the room; each person wears whatever color they choose to wear on any given day of the week—blue on Tuesday or red on Tuesday or blue on Tuesday or red on Tuesday or blue on Tuesday or red on Tuesday …

"What are you doing?" Mr. Pinkerton asks softly, shaking his head slowly from side to side as if he has no idea what we're doing in here or why we're doing it … "What's this all about?"

We don't answer him; we don't answer him because we're too scared to answer him because there's no telling what else Mr. Pinkerton can see in here if he looks up at us … But we don't look up at him because we're all too scared to look up at him … But he must see something or someone here that scares him more than anything we can imagine, and we don't want to see whatever that is or whoever that might be … If we look up at Mr. Pinkerton, then we might see whatever that might be too …

Mr. Pinkerton stops shaking his head from side to side and stares at Sara as if he has no idea who she is—as if she's not Sara Henry, not Sara Henry the attorney who must solve this murder case where everyone has been murdered by an unknown murderer. She must figure out who the unknown murderer is before Mr. Pinkerton finds out who she is. If he finds out who she is before Sara figures out who the murderer is—if he finds out who she is before she solves this case—then Sara won't be able to solve this murder case because Sara will be dead before she finds out who killed everyone in this house … If Sara doesn't find out who killed everyone in this house before Mr. Pinkerton finds out who she is, then Sara will be dead before she finds out who killed everyone …

What makes Mr. Pinkerton so powerful? What makes him such a powerful wizard that he can do whatever he wants? Is there something more than ghosts and witches and demons that make him so powerful? Maybe there's something more than ghosts and witches and demons; maybe there's an ancient curse that turns Mr. Pinkerton into a powerful wizard when he wakes up on Tuesday afternoons … But then why doesn't he have any powers when he sleeps? Why doesn't he have any powers when he's asleep? We must find out why Mr. Pinkerton has no powers when he sleeps; perhaps he has powers when he sleeps because he has power over everything else while he sleeps …

Sara has an idea; she thinks Mr. Pinkerton might have some kind of an old curse at hand that turns him into a powerful wizard when he wakes up on Tuesdays, turning him into a powerful wizard when he sleeps but not when he's awake—when he's awake, he has no powers over anything except maybe ghosts and witches and demons; maybe there's some kind of an ancient curse that turns Mr. Pinkerton into a powerful wizard whenever he wakes up on Tuesday afternoons but not when he's awake on any other day of the week … But then why would the curse disappear after ten weeks? Why would the curse disappear after ten weeks? Why would it disappear after ten weeks if Mr. Pinkerton had something more than ghosts and witches and demons? Maybe there are other things that make Mr. Pinkerton so powerful; maybe there are other powers beyond ghosts and witches and demons that allow Mr. Pinkerton to do whatever he wants …

"I don't know what you're talking about," Mrs. Sperling says sharply, annoyed by Mr. Pinkerton's sudden change in attitude toward her and by the way Mr. Pinkerton looks at her as if she has no idea what she's talking about; but then again, Mrs. Sperling might not have any idea what she's talking about either … "I don't know anything about any curse," Mrs. Sperling says firmly, shaking her head slowly from side to side as if shaking her head means no when Mrs. Sperling does it as if shaking her head means no when Mrs. Sperling does it means yes … "I don't know anything about any curses."

Mr. Pinkerton shakes his head slowly from side to side as if shaking his head means no when Mrs. Sperling does it; then again, maybe shaking his head means yes because Mrs. Sperling doesn't seem to know anything about any curses either … Then again, maybe shaking his head means yes because Mrs. Sperling might know something about that old curse even though she denies knowing anything about it …

Mr. Pinkerton shakes his head from side to side as if shaking his head means no when Mrs. Sperling does it; then again, shaking his head means yes because Mrs. Sperling seems to know something about that old curse even though she denies knowing anything about it … Then again, shaking his head means yes because Mrs. Sperling might know something about that old curse even though she denies knowing anything about it … But then why would anyone deny knowing anything about an old curse like this one? Maybe it's not so much that someone denies knowing anything about this curse as much as it is that no one knows what this curse really is or how it works since nobody knows how to solve an old curse unless they find a way to break an ancient curse—the way they might break an ancient curse is by figuring out how to break it, by breaking it piece by piece until they find just one piece they can break away from the rest of the curse and break away to free themselves; if they find one piece of an ancient curse that they can break away from everything else then maybe they can work backward from there …

"Let me ask you this," Barry says, looking up at us all with his eyes turned down toward his shoes as if he's too scared to look up at anyone else except for Mr. Pinkerton; Barry nods toward Mr. Pinkerton with his chin as if Barry was asking us all whether any of us knew who we were before today while also giving us permission to answer Barry if we did know who we were before today … "Who are you?"

"What?" Barry asks, looking confused as well as too scared to answer the question for fear of being wrong—as if Barry might be right if this was a test but if he answered wrong, especially by saying that Sara was the only person in the room he recognized but none of us recognized Sara as well—then Barry would be wrong for saying that Sara was the only one in the room Barry recognized although everyone else recognized her too; but Barry must pay attention anyway—just in case Barry is right—and address questions only to whom they apply as if Barry is doing everyone else a favor by only asking questions that apply to only one person in the room—as if Barry is doing everyone else a favor by just asking questions of one person instead of asking questions of all ten people in the room, which is easier for everyone else except for Barry because he still wants to be sure that Barry asks the questions only to those who answer them correctly so as not to be wrong and be wrongfully accused of being wrong the same way Barry was wrongfully accused of being wrong earlier today by Mr. Pinkerton … "Who are you?"

Barry asks again, shaking his head slowly from side to side as if shaking his head means no when Barry does it; but in this case, shaking his head means yes; shaking his head means yes as in "Yes," Barry answers when asked who Sara is until Barry realizes that Barry was wrong the first time he asked the question, so then Barry has to ask the question again—but then again, shaking his head means yes because Barry doesn't want anyone else to know that Barry was wrong before even though it might be important for them all to know that Barry was wrong since Barry was wrong on purpose so as not to be accused of being wrong later on by someone else unless someone tells them about it by saying "Barry was wrong …"

"Sara," Sara answers carefully, shaking her head slowly from side to side as if shaking her head means no when Sara does it while shaking her head means yes; shaking her head means yes as in "Yes, I'm Sara," but shaking her head means no at the same time, since Sara doesn't want anyone else to know her name until she figures out who could possibly be here with us now except for Sara, who must figure out who she is first before anyone else finds out her name or what her role in all this might be—if anyone besides Sara knows who she is, then someone must tell everyone else who knows that Sara knows who they are, which would mean giving away confidential information "Come on," Sara says; "come on quick."

Barry answers without hesitation: "Sara Henry."

Sara cries out "No!" with a loud screech like someone cutting themselves open with a knife rather than cutting their fingernails while shaving their legs; she cuts herself with her own knife; because whatever else might be in here with us may not be able to cut themselves open with a knife but we can—we cut ourselves with our own knife as well as with knives made from our own fingernails, our own hair follicles, our own stab wounds just like the person we think we're stabbing … "No!" Sara cries out loudly—more loudly than before—as if trying to drown the sound of Mr. Pinkerton jumping up from behind her with his hands covering her throat—as if trying to drown everything else except for herself since being alone in this house without knowing how many other people are here with us freaks Sara out more than anything else ever could—as if being alone in this house without knowing how many other people are here freaks Sara out more than anything else ever could …

"I know who you are," Barry says quietly but firmly, shaking his head slowly from side to side as if shaking his head means no when Barry does it; shaking his head means no as in "No," Barry answers when asked who she is until Barry realizes that Barry was wrong the first time he asked the question, so then Barry has to ask the question again—but then again, shaking his head means yes because Barry doesn't want anyone else to know that Barry was wrong before even though it might be important for them all to know that Barry was wrong since Barry was wrong on purpose so as not to be accused of being wrong later on by someone else since Barry might still be right by saying that Sara was the only person in the room he recognized but none of us recognized Sara as well …

Sara gasps as if in pain; she gasps like she's trying to hold in a scream and can't hold it back any longer—she gasps like she's holding back a scream while holding in breath until she can't hold it back anymore and "… No …" Sara gasps again as she holds in another breath and another scream—another scream like she's letting go of all the air she can hold in her lungs until there's nothing left for one more scream before finally releasing everything into one long scream—"No!"

Sara gasps again as she holds in another breath and another scream; another scream like she's holding in all the air she can hold until there's nothing left for one more scream before finally releasing everything into one long scream so loud that she might drown out Mr. Pinkerton's cry of terror or Mr. Pinkerton might drown out Sara's scream when she finally let's go of all her breath …

Sara gasps again like she's holding in another breath and another scream—"No!" And now Sara gasps like she's holding in all the air she can hold until there's nothing left for one more scream before finally

releasing everything into one long scream while holding in breath—
"No!" Then Sara gasps once more; gasps twice more, three times more,
four times more—five times more while holding in breath until there's
nothing left for one last gasp before finally releasing everything into
one long scream so loud that Sara might drown out Mr. Pinkerton's cry
of terror or Mr. Pinkerton might drown out Sara's scream …

Sara gasps once more as she holds in another breath and another
scream—"No!" She gasps again as if holding in all the air she can
hold until there's nothing left for one last gasp before finally releasing
everything into one long scream while holding in breath—"No!" Then
Sara gasps once more; gasps twice more, three times more, four times
more—five times more while holding in breath until there's nothing
left for one last gasp before finally releasing everything into one long
scream so loud that Sara might drown out Mr. Pinkerton's cry of terror
or Mr. Pinkerton might drown out Sara's scream …

"No!" Sara gasps again like she's holding in all the air she can
hold until there's nothing left for one last gasp before finally releasing
everything into one long scream while holding in breath—"No!" Then
Sara gasps once more; gasps twice more, three times more, four times
more—five times more while holding in breath until there's nothing
left for one last gasp before finally releasing everything into one long
scream so loud that Sara might drown out Mr. Pinkerton's

"I don't know where you got your information," Mr. Pinkerton
says quietly but firmly from behind Sara. "I don't know where you got
your information about me or about any of us being here today."

Sara gasps once more as she holds in another breath and another
scream—"No! No!" She gasps again as if holding back another scream
while holding in breath until she can't hold it back anymore—"No!"
Then Sara gasps once more; gasps twice more, three times more, four
times more … "No! No! No! No!" Five times more while holding in
breath until there's nothing left for one last gasp before finally releasing
everything into one long scream so loud that Sara might drown out
Mr. Pinkerton's cry of terror or Mr. Pinkerton might drown out Sara's
scream when she finally let's go of all her breath …

Sara gasps once more like she's holding in another breath and another scream—"No!" She gasps again as if holding in all the air she can hold until there's nothing left for one last gasp before finally releasing everything into one long scream while holding in breath—"No!" Then Sara gasps once more; gasps twice more, three times more, four times more—five times more while holding in breath until there's nothing left for one last gasp before finally releasing everything into one long scream so loud that Sara might drown out Mr. Pinkerton's cry of terror or Mr. Pinkertom might drown out Sara's scream when she finally let's go of all her breath …

"You're bluffing," Mr. Pinkerton says confidently after hearing how many times Sara answered "no" to his question. "You don't know me."

Sara gasps once more as she holds in another breath and another scream—"No!" She gasps like she can't hold back a scream while holding in breath until there's nothing left for one last gasp before finally releasing everything into one long scream so loud that Sara might drown out Mr. Pinkerton's cry of terror or Mr. Pinkertom might drown out Sara's scream when she finally let's go of all her breath …

Sara gasps once again like she's holding in another breath and another scream—"No!" Then Sara gasps once more; gasps twice more, three times more, four times more—five times more while holding in breath until there's nothing left for one last gasp before finally releasing everything into one long scream so loud that Sara might drown out Mr. Pinkerton's cry of terror or Mr. Pinkertom might drown out Sara's scream when she finally let's go of all her breath …

"I know where you're from," Mr. Pinkerton says quietly but firmly—strongly enough to sound confident but not threatening or rude or condescending or anything like those things—strong enough to sound confident yet not threatening or condescending or anything like those things "And I know what you do," he adds. "I know what everyone thinks you do."

Sara gasps once more as she holds in another breath and another scream—"No! No!" She gasps like she can't hold back a scream while holding in breath until she can't hold it back anymore—"No! No! No!

No!" Then Sara gasps once more; gasps twice more, three times more, four times more—five times more while holding in breath until there's nothing left for one last gasp before finally releasing everything into one long scream so loud that Sara might drown out Mr. Pinkerton's cry of terror or Mr. Pinkertom might drown out Sara's scream when she finally let's go of all her breath …

"You know what people think I do?" Sara asks as if asking a question rather than answering it. "So why are you asking me questions about it?"

"Because you're lying," he answers simply. "You think I don't know you lied? I don't know why but I know you lied."

Sara gasps once more as she holds in another breath and another scream—"No! No! No! No!" She gasps like she can't hold back a scream while holding in breath until there's nothing left for one last gasp before finally releasing everything into one long scream so loud that Sara might drown out Mr. Pinkerton's cry of terror or Mr. Pinkertom might drown out Sara's scream when she finally let's go of all her breath …

"So why are you asking me questions about it?"

"Because I'm not lying," Mr. Pinkertom answers firmly—strongly enough to sound confident but not threatening or condescending or anything like those things "You think I don't know you lied? I don't know why but I know you lied."

"I'm not lying," Mr. Pinkerton answers simply enough but firmly—strongly enough to sound confident but not threatening or condescending or anything like those things "You think I don't know you lied? I don't know why but I know you lied."

Sara must figure out what is real and what is a figment of her imagination. With Murder, Ghost, Demons, and Imagination all at play …"You think I don't know you lied? I don't know why but I know you lied."

"I'm not lying," Mr. Pinkertom answers simply enough but firmly enough—strongly enough to sound confident but not threatening or condescending or anything like those things "You think I don't know you lied? I don't know why but I know you lied."

"I'm not lying," Mr. Pinkertom answers simply enough but firmly enough—strongly enough to sound confident but not threatening or condescending or anything like those things "You think I don't know you lied? I don't know why but I know you lied."

"I'm not lying," Mr. Pinkertom answers simply enough but firmly enough—strongly enough to sound confident but not threatening or condescending or anything like those things "You think I don't know you lied? I don't know why but I know you lied."

"I'm not lying," Mr. Pinkertom answers simply enough but firmly enough—"strongly enough to sound confident but not threatening or condescending or anything like those things "Strong enough to sound confident yet not threatening or condescending or anything like those things "Strong enough to sound confident yet not threatening or condescending or anything like those things …

"You think I don't know you lied?"

TWELVE

As far as Sara could see, the only thing that was real was the thick green curtain that was pulled aside to reveal the body of a dead man covered with a sheet, dead for many years—at least a hundred years—and with dead eyes staring up at the ceiling with his hands folded neatly beneath his chin. The body was wearing the same clothing it wore when Sara found him—the same clothes that belonged to the man who was murdered the night before … And as far as Sara could see, the only thing that was real was the thick green curtain that was pulled aside to reveal the body of a dead man covered with a sheet, dead for many years—at least a hundred years—and with dead eyes staring up at the ceiling with his hands folded neatly beneath his chin. The body was wearing the same clothing it wore when Sara found him—the same clothes that belonged to the man who was murdered the night before … And as far as Sara could see, the only thing that was real was the thick green curtain that was pulled aside to reveal the body of a dead man covered with a sheet, dead for many years—at least a hundred years—and with dead eyes staring up at the ceiling with his hands folded neatly beneath his chin. The body was wearing the same clothing it wore when Sara found him—the same clothes that belonged to the man who was murdered the night before … And as far as Sara could see, the only thing that was real was the thick green curtain that was pulled aside to reveal the body of a dead man covered with a sheet, dead for many years—at least a hundred years—and with dead eyes staring up at the ceiling with his hands folded neatly beneath his chin. The body was wearing the same clothing it wore when Sara found him—"No! No! No! No!" She screams out loud as if holding back a scream while holding in breath until she can't hold it back anymore "…no!" Then Sara gasps once more; gasps twice more, three times more, four times more … "No! No! No! No!" Five times more while holding in breath until there's nothing left for one last gasp before finally releasing everything into one long scream so loud that Sara might drown out Mr. Pinkerton's cry of terror or Mr. Pinkertom might drown out Sara's scream when she finally let's go of all her breath …

Sara gasps once again like she's holding in another breath and another scream—"No!" She gasps like she can't hold back a scream while holding in breath until there's nothing left for one last gasp before finally releasing everything into one long scream so loud that Sara might drown out Mr. Pinkerton's cry of terror or Mr. Pinkertom might drown out Sara's scream when she finally let's go of all her breath "…you're bluffing."

Mr. Pinkertom smiles reassuringly at her—smiles so reassuring that he must have done it before because he knows how to do it right—smiles confidently yet not threatening or condescending or anything like those things—smiles confidently rather than reassuringly as he says, "I'm not bluffing."

As far as everyone could tell, Mr. Pinkerton was bluffing—bluffing big time. Not only had he made up all kinds of lies about himself, but he also made up lies about everyone else on this train and even about some of the people on other trains on this train line. So, who would believe Mr. Pinkerton's bluff if he really did have evidence against Sara? Who would believe that Sara is lying? Who would believe that Sara is not telling the truth about Mr. Pinkerton?

"You are bluffing," Mrs. Ellsworth says strongly and confidently after hearing how many times Sara answered "yes" to his question. "You don't really have any evidence against me."

"We've got plenty evidence showing you're guilty," Mr. Pinkerton answers confidently –strongly enough to sound confident yet not threatening or condescending or anything like those things "And we've got plenty evidence showing who did it, too."

"We've got plenty evidence showing you're guilty," Mr. Pinkertom answers confidently yet not threatening or condescending or anything like those things "And we've got plenty evidence showing who did it, too."

Sara must figure out what is real and what is a figment of her imagination …"You're bluffing," Mrs. Ellsworth says firmly "You don't really have any evidence against me."

"You don't really have any evidence against me."

"I never said that."

"Then how do you know I'm guilty?"

"I don't have to prove you're guilty, I just have to prove you're not innocent. You see, that's the difference."

"Good evening, everyone."

With a friendly wave, I took my seat at the head of the conference table. I looked around and noticed the room was tense. My staff was tense. I was tense. We all had something to lose if I messed up this case. We all had something to lose if I screwed up.

"Have you ever heard of the Marquess of Lod ore?" asked Sergeant O'Brien, the homicide detective in charge of the case.

"Yes," replied Sara Henry, who was sitting across from me. "He was a man who lived in the 1800s and he was the victim of a murder. It was thought he was poisoned by his enemies, but there were no witnesses."

"Who was the judge?" asked O'Brien.

"The judge on the case was a man named Isaac Grant, who happened to be the father of Elizabeth Grant, who would become the wife of Thomas Edison."

"The judge was also the victim's brother," said O'Brien. "Not only that, but it was said that he was in charge of a conspiracy to poison a group of men and women who were known as the Seven Sisters."

"The Seven Sisters?" asked Sara.

"The Seven Sisters were seven women who were accused of poisoning a group of men and women known as the Seven Brothers," explained O'Brien. "There were rumors that they poisoned the men and women following the death of one of their own. It's said that one of the Seven Sisters used an herbal remedy that made them sick for a short period of time and they committed suicide."

"I remember reading about this," said Sara. "Did you find any evidence that proved that these women committed suicide?"

"We didn't find anything that showed they committed suicide," replied O'Brien. "We did find an old diary, however, written by one of the Seven Sisters."

Sara Henry wakes from this dream as if waking from a deep sleep only to look up at her ceiling once more—the ceiling covered with stars—but instead it's painted with stars floating above her head as if they are stars floating in space above Earth someday beyond our atmosphere that will someday orbit around Mars—and then fall back shut again as Sara falls back asleep...

THIRTEEN

"Darling, are you awake?"

Sara looks up to see Jason standing over her bed.

"Yes," she says, sitting up in bed. "What time is it?"

"It's your first day at work, darling. You are going to be late if you don't get up."

Sara sits up in bed again, rubbing her eyes and looking at the clock on her dresser. "I have to be at work?"

"Yes," he says, walking over to her side of the bed and opening the curtains. "You have to get dressed."

"Oh," she says, sitting up on the edge of the bed, rubbing her eyes again and getting out of bed. "I don't know what time it is."

Jason looks in his watch and stands up in one swift motion to look through the open window at the street below. "It's almost seven in the morning, Sara."

"Oh…"

"And I have just made coffee," he says. "I don't want to have to make it twice."

"Oh…okay." She looks at the clock again. "I have to get dressed and get to work." She turns on her side to look at him. "Can I call in sick?"

"Darling, I don't think that's a good idea," he says. "You just lost your job. If you call in sick now, you'll never get a new one."

"I know." She sits up again as she notices his gaze is directed at his watch. "It's just that…" She sighs as she gets out of bed and starts to get dressed. "I have got to figure out what this is all about."

"Why don't you ask the same question you asked me last night?" Jason asks as he picks up his phone and taps on the screen a few times.

"Last night?" Sara asks.

"You asked me last night what I thought about this all—the dreams you've been having and all of this stuff."

"Right," she says, sliding on her underwear with one hand while holding her hairbrush while brushing her hair with the other hand. "That's what I was going to do."

"Then ask me." He waits for her to finish dressing. "What do you mean when you say 'stuff'? I mean what do you think I think about all these things?"

Sara looks down at the floor as if she is suddenly shy. But not shy enough to unzip her dress and hide her underwear from him. "I just want to know if you think I'm crazy," she says. "Do you think I'm nuts?"

Jason looks up from his phone and seems lost for a moment before answering. "No," he says softly. "You're not nuts." He picks up his phone again as Sara finishes putting on her dress and puts on her makeup. "Can you ask me something else?" he asks into the phone, his voice louder than before. "Is it true that ghosts can come back from the grave?" He listens intently for a moment, then says aloud, "No, oh that's interesting…" He hangs up his phone and looks at Sara with a smile on his face. "I told you so."

"What was that about?"

"I was just talking about how I think ghosts can come back from the grave," he says, looking up from his phone again. "And then I told you what I told a client just last week who said something very similar." He laughs a little as he picks up his car keys from the dresser in front of him as he stands there beside the dresser waiting for Sara to finish getting dressed.

She finally zips up her dress and puts on her shoes. "I have to be at work by seven-thirty if I'm going to be late," she says as she walks over to his side of the bed where he stands waiting for her. She leans over and kisses him quickly on his lips before leaving the room with him behind her. And then walking down the stairs into the living room where she can see through the window that it's snowing out—a thick blanket of white snow covering everything. With this snow comes the cold air gusting down from the clouds above into Grays Harbor County in Washington State where Sara lives—a cold wind that blows down from the north—driving even more snow down upon the area as if we're caught in a snow globe being juggled by some unseen juggler on high above us all.

Sara Henry is wearing a sleeveless black dress with black pumps as she exits her apartment building, which is nothing but a three-story brick building with windows shuttered tight against the cold air blowing down from overhead. The snowflakes are swirling around outside—as if they are caught in a whirlpool and spinning around and around in a circle as they move down through Grays Harbor County toward the bay where it meets with Puget Sound outside Seattle—where waves push through the quagmire below as they crash against jagged rocks that form jagged islands in Puget Sound, where ships still tried to navigate past Seattle even during winter months when ice clogged the bay waters like an impenetrable wall of ice as if it were an impenetrable wall of rock rising out of Puget Sound like an impenetrable wall of ice rising from Hell itself.

Sara goes downstairs off the third floor where she lives in hopes that she can find a cab that isn't too full for her to fit into it somehow—but there is only one cab sitting outside with several people already inside waiting for one to pull up and drop off or pick them up before dropping off or picking up another customer somewhere else. She looks at her watch as she steps out onto the sidewalk near a few other people who had already been waiting for a cab to pull up—maybe two minutes after she stepped outside—and looks at her watch again as she waits for half an hour before another cab finally pulls up and drops off its first customer at the bottom of the stairs where Sara is standing with his own fare in hand and goes back into town to pick up another fare while Sara waits alone on the sidewalk where she was until just a moment ago when another cab finally pulls up next to her where she is standing with several other people waiting for one cab to pull up and drop off or pick them up before dropping off or picking up another customer somewhere else.

"Are you going my way?" asks the woman behind the wheel of this cab before Sara can even open the door.

The woman behind the wheel has short, wavy black hair with brown eyes that look like they have seen too much in life—as if they've seen too much pain or suffering for any woman under fifty years old who sees forty-nine years old only by age alone that has lived long enough in this world without any scars should be allowed to live—as if she looks older than fifty years old herself yet still young enough to have children who haven't yet reached their teen years yet—and she has dark makeup on her eyes and lips that has been flaking off from repeated use over time and shows how much time has passed since this woman has attended whatever events make women wear dark makeup so they can look older than they are—as if they are trying to trick men into thinking they are older than they really are when in reality, this woman doesn't even seem much older than thirty-five years old or thirty-six years old or maybe even younger still than thirty-five years old—as if making herself look older than she is makes this woman feel younger than she really is since she might not be allowed to be young any longer without some kind of artificial help—as if making herself look older than she is makes her feel younger than she really feels because there are plenty of young women who find women over thirty-five years old more attractive because they don't seem bothered by aging, wrinkles or wrinkles left behind by children who were born too late or too early in life for them to really remember their mother having their children when they were babies, children who were barely out of diapers when their mother died—children who didn't remember their mother holding them when they were babies or holding them when they reached their middens or early teens as babies or teens, children who don't even remember a simple word like baby or toddler or toddlerhood or infancy because babies are not cute until some unspeakable tragedy happens and then children are cute again as they reach out toward their mother for comfort—as if there is some kind of unspeakable tragedy that turns babies into demons who become monsters later in life if we aren't careful enough not to let them grow up too soon or too late by giving birth prematurely or late—as if some babies have been protected from infancy until after they reach their middens. These are the thoughts going through Sara's head as she climbs into this cab where this woman who makes it obvious she has no desire to be associated with anyone under thirty years old steps out onto the sidewalk and looks at her watch again before climbing in behind Sara and hailing another cab heading toward Seattle where nearly half of its residents live anyway as if there aren't enough people living here already with so many cabs on this street alone—as if there aren't enough people who need one every time we drive down this street with its many intersections as we try to navigate between traffic lights that turn red when we don't want them to turn red while we wait for them to turn green again—as if there isn't anyone here who needs a cab more than we do, even though we know there are actually thousands upon thousands of people driving cabs every single day with so many cabs on this street alone, not counting all of those others who drive cabs in other areas around town as well as elsewhere around our city where we have yet another cabbie friend who drives us home when we need help getting home because we must solve this murder.

Sara pays the woman behind the wheel and climbs into the back seat where she sits next to a young man with big glasses who has shaggy dark hair covered by a beanie hat and looks more like he should be wearing ski goggles instead of glasses for an early morning commute into Seattle from Grays Harbor County. The young man looks at Sara when we pull away from the curb then looks back down at his phone screen where he's texting someone. She wonders what he thinks about all of this as he sends text messages in this stranger's car while Sara sits behind him texting someone else as well. She wonders what he thinks about all of this and how he feels about all these things going on around him in this city where cabs drive everywhere we go—where cab drivers drop off and pick up people all over town every day—and has been doing that for years now since cabs were invented by someone who thought it would be easier to have someone drive him somewhere instead of walking everywhere he wanted to go because walking was too hard when you're carrying heavy sacks of groceries or groceries for someone else as you walk through parking lots looking for a spot where you can unload your groceries quickly so you can get back into your car and drive home where you can unload your groceries in your own kitchen without having to drive anywhere else after all that grocery shopping. She thinks about her dream where I've been caught in traffic somewhere and I can't get home because I can't get past all the cars surrounding me on every side with nowhere to go—traffic jams everywhere I turn around when I'm driving my car toward my apartment building near Lake Union for some reason—as if there is a dead body stuck between two cars trapped between them on a busy street somewhere outside Seattle that has been dead for days or weeks now buried under all that snow while everyone else tries to move forward between lanes as if someone dropped something heavy over one of those lanes while everyone is trying to navigate past it and step over it with no room left to maneuver between them.

"I'm going on my lunch break," says Sara as she turns around on her seat with her seatbelt fastened before taking her phone out of her purse and turning it on since it was dead when she left home eight hours ago.

"Is your husband still out there?" asks the woman behind the wheel. "Is he still out there?"

"He's not my husband," says Sara. "He's, my brother."

"Is he still out there?" asks the driver again.

"He's not my husband," says Sara once again.

"What's his name?" asks the driver.

"He's not my husband," says Sara. "He's, my brother."

"Is he still out there?" asks the driver again. "Is he still out there driving?"

"He's not my husband," says Sara again. "He's, my brother."

"You don't look like you're related," says Sarah, "but I assume you are."

Annoyed with all these questions from this young man, Sara tells him to shut up and drives away from the curb where he was trying to hail a cab anyway. "I'm going home to see my sister," says Sara as she drives away from the curb where he stood waiting for a cab just moments before. "Why do you care so much?" asks Sara as she drives away from him as fast as possible as if she doesn't have time for him. "Why do you care so much?" asks Sarah again as she drives away from him in anger, shaking her head in frustration at him while searching for an escape route out of town before something happens that makes things worse than they already are on account of this murder.

Annoyed with all these questions from this young man, Sara tells him to shut up and drives away from the curb where she just can't stop thing about her dream. "You are bluffing," Mrs. Ellsworth says strongly and confidently after hearing how many times Sara answered "yes" to his question. "You don't really have any evidence against me."

"I have plenty of evidence," Sara says sharply. "And you already know how I know."

The old woman looks at Sara with boiling eyes and shakes her head slowly while she puts her hand on her forehead and says, "You are bluffing."

"I'm not bluffing," Sara says sharply again. "I have a videotape of you telling your husband to kill you. And you did it."

Mrs. Ellsworth's eyes get wider and wider as she hears Sara's words. She shakes her head again and says, "You are bluffing! I never said anything like that to my husband!"

"Yes, you did! You said to him, 'I want you to kill me.' And then you told him how."

"Was this real?" Mrs. Ellsworth asks with blurry eyes. "You were having a nightmare, weren't you?"

"No! This is real! This is all real and I'm going to prove it!" Sara says with a manic look in her eyes. "And you're going to pay for your crimes."

"I'm going to pay. What do you mean by that?" Mrs. Ellsworth asks with a sly smile. "I'm not going down without a fight."

"I'll fight for you," Sara says as she stands up from the chair and walks toward the old woman with a wild look in her eyes. "And we'll fight together."

Mrs. Ellsworth smiles at Sara as if she's won the lottery, but then her smile fades as she sees how serious Sara is about ending Mrs. Ellsworth's life. Sara is back, waking up from her dream of Mrs. Ellsworth's murder, and the woman has grown pale with fear.

"Sorry," Sara says, "I didn't mean to upset you."

"It's all right," Mrs. Ellsworth says. "I'm not afraid of you." She looks at Sara, with a light in her eye, and then looks away with a smile. "I'm not afraid of anything."

"I'm not afraid of you either." Sara smiles. "I was only curious about what happened to you. I thought you were dead."

"I'm not dead," she says. The woman reaches out her hand and touches Sara's arm. "You shouldn't be afraid of ghosts."

"You're a ghost," Sara says. "I saw you killed."

"No," the woman says, shaking her head. "No, you didn't see that." She reaches out for Sara's hand and holds it tightly to her chest. "You're going to be fine," she says again.

"It's not true," Sara says, trying to break free of the woman's grasp, but she's trapped in the woman's grasp. "I saw it with my own eyes."

"What did I tell you?" Mrs. Ellsworth asks, touching her sternum over her heart. "It's all right now, my love." She kisses Sara's hand and then smiles at her as if she's won the lottery and stepped out of her dream to find herself in her lover's arms. A faint smell of gardenias wafts from her lips to Sara's nose, and Mrs. Ellsworth leans in closer to the woman and kisses her hand again.

"You smell like gardenias," Sara says, trying to break free of Mrs. Ellsworth's grasp again, but Mrs. Ellsworth is strong and doesn't let go of Sara's hand so easily. "I don't like gardenias."

"You'll like them after this," Mrs. Ellsworth says, leaning in closer to Sara and kissing her hand again. "You'll never forget me." She smiles a genuine smile as if she just won the lottery and her lover was there to celebrate with her.

Sara struggles again to break free of Mrs. Ellsworth's grasp, but Mrs. Ellsworth is stronger than she realizes and refuses to release the woman's hand so easily.

"You're making me forget," Sara says, shaking her head to clear the fog she's fallen into – whatever fog Mrs. Ellsworth has blown into Sara's life with the gardenias – but all she can think about is that she needs to escape Mrs. Ellsworth before she drowns in the woman's embrace.

"Go ahead," she says, letting go of Sara's hand and picking up a small glass vase from a table beside her bedside table – an expensive vase with a black marble base – she pulls it close to her face and breathes in its scent again. "Fall in love with me," she says again, as if talking to herself, but then turns to look at Sara with a light in her eye as if she has just woken up from a dream of loving Sara as her lover. Her eyes glisten with tears and she kisses Sara's hand again – a gentle kiss that does not break the skin – but instead makes it glow like a newborn baby as Mrs. Ellsworth releases it gently from the woman's grasp. "Go ahead," Mrs. Ellsworth says again before looking away as if she just saw something frightening – something that makes her forget the woman beside her – and then turns back to face Sara with a smile on her face as if she's won the lottery and stepped out of her lover's arms to find herself in her lover's arms again.

Sara feels dizzy standing in front of Mrs. Ellsworth, who seems stronger than she realizes – stronger than Sara is – as Mrs. Ellsworth leans in closer to the woman and kisses her hand before turning away as if she just saw something frightening – something that makes her forget the woman beside her – and then turns back to face Sara with a smile on her face as if she's won the lottery and stepped out of her lover's arms to find herself in her lover's arms again – a smile that fades when suddenly a sudden chill through her body makes Sara feel faint as if the woman has just knocked the wind out of her lungs – as if Mrs. Ellsworth has opened up a window in the room to let in the cold night air that has made the room so chilly – but all this happens without Mrs. Ellsworth moving an inch from where she stood before, making it seem impossible that such a chill could pass through the woman without moving an inch – making it seem impossible that such a chill could pass through an iron door without making it rattle – making it seem impossible that such a chill could pass through the sturdy walls of an old house without waking someone up – making it seem impossible that such a chill could pass through Sara without making it rattle – making it seem impossible that such a chill could pass through all this without making trouble for Mrs. Ellsworth – which means...

"Hello?" A young man walks into the room from the hallway outside, calls out to Mrs. Ellsworth, but then sees Sara standing there watching them both with a strange look on her face – a look that frightens him as soon as he sees it – because he knows this man standing before him has fallen into a coma or worse after hearing this man talk about his wife – he knows this man has fallen into deep denial when all these years he thought his wife was dead – or was kidnapped by strangers or murdered – he knows this man has fallen into denial by talking about his wife with this young man standing beside him in the middle of the night while his wife lies dead in his bed upstairs with no one around except for herself and perhaps this young man – possibly this young man was kidnapped as well by these same strangers who have murdered his wife – who knows what else this young man has been told by this man standing beside him – he knows he should call someone right away because he knows there will be trouble if people find out about it later on – he knows he should call an ambulance or police or fire department or something right away because he knows this man has fallen into deep denial knowing his wife is dead, kidnapped by strangers, or murdered by someone else while he lived life oblivious to all this danger while his wife sat upstairs dying without anyone knowing how bad things had become – will he call the police? Will he call an ambulance? Will he call his spouse? Will he call his sister? Will he call his best friend? He should call someone right away because he knows there will be trouble if people find out about it later – will he call an ambulance? Will he call police? Will he call fire department? Or will he call his sister? He should call someone right away...

FOURTEEN

Sara Henry sits on top of the stairs listening to Mrs. Ellsworth scream out her husband's name as if she were trying to wake him up from his coma or something worse: something like death; but all this is happening without Mrs. Ellsworth moving an inch nor does anything rattle, making it impossible for Sara to believe this is real – making it impossible for anyone to believe this is real because it seems impossible that any of this could happen without someone hearing it for miles around and calling an ambulance right away; but then again maybe this isn't happening at all even though all these things seem dead-on right with their unbelievable Ness as it seems impossible that people could live this way without calling for help sooner or later, making it seem impossible that people would live in denial for so long – making it seem impossible that people would live in denial for so long when they knew their spouse is dead or kidnapped or murdered; yet somehow, all this seems dead-on right because Sara watched it happen – yet how can that be possible? How can all this be true when she saw it happen? How can she have seen so many things happen right before her eyes? How can all these things be true when she saw them herself?

"Who are you?" Sara asks Mrs. Ellsworth as if trying to wake up from this dream? "How can I help?" But all this happens without Mrs. Ellsworth moving an inch from where she stood before; no rattle passes through walls; no ambulance horn blasts; no police sirens are heard – nothing happens until the doorbell rings downstairs just as Sara stands up from where she sat on top of the stairs, if only for a moment, defying gravity because there seems no other explanation for why there are no police in response to the woman screaming from upstairs; nothing happens until Mrs. Ellsworth stops screaming from upstairs... yet how can that be possible when all these things seem dead-on right?

FIFTEEN

Sara drives home listening to music on the radio while struggling with reality and unbelievable Ness: "I'm not afraid of you either." She looks at herself in the rearview mirror over her shoulder and thinks about what happened at Mrs. Ellsworth's house and how she watched some strange things happen before her eyes – like how Mrs. Ellsworth called out in silence after being struck by lightning while standing at the top of these stairs – no flash of lightning followed after the bang so loud it shook the house; no lightning followed after Mrs. Ellsworth screamed out in silence as if awakening from some deep coma; no power comes on when lightning strikes – electricity doesn't work when lightning strikes because lightning follows electricity; lightning follows electricity like electricity follows electricity – electricity follows lightning...

"I'm not afraid of you," Sara hears herself say repeatedly in between songs on the radio louder than anything else playing on the radio as if trying to drown out what happened at Mrs. Ellsworth's house; but how can that be true when all these things seem dead-on right?

"I'm not afraid of you," she says again as if trying to drown out what happened at Mrs. Ellsworth's house; then she hears herself say "I'm not afraid of you." Then she hears herself say "I'm not afraid of you," repeatedly until she hears the faint sound of thunder in her ears as if thunder has knocked at this window to intrude upon her reality;

thunder knocks on windows when people are about to die; thunder knocks on windows when there's danger nearby: thunder knocks on windows when people are going to die...

"I'm not afraid..."

"You'll like them after this," Mrs. Ellsworth says, leaning in closer to Sara and kissing her hand again. "You'll never forget me." She smiles a genuine smile as if she just won the lottery and her lover was there to celebrate with her.

Sara struggles again to break free of Mrs. Ellsworth's grasp, but Mrs. Ellsworth is stronger than she realizes and refuses to release the woman's hand so easily.

"You're making me forget," Sara says shaking her head to clear the fog she's fallen into: "you're making me forget..."

"Good," Mrs. Ellsworth says as if happy about what happened. "That's what you want."

Sara shakes her head slowly trying to clear the fog that seems to have taken over her life by blocking out everything else except for what happened at Mrs. Ellsworth's house: "I want nothing more than what you've done."

Mrs. Ellsworth smiles again with tears in eyes as if happy something good has happened: "Good."

"Good?"

"Yes," Mrs. Ellsworth says again with tears in her eyes as if happy something good happened: "good."

Sara feels dizzy standing beside Mrs. Ellsworth, who seems stronger than she realizes, stronger than Sara is; stronger than Sara is because there seems no point in resisting Mrs. Ellsworth when all this seems dead-on right with unbelievable Ness: "Good."

"What are you doing?"

A young man stands across the street watching Sara from behind where he stands guarding Mrs. Ellsworth's property from anyone who might disturb what happened between them: "What are you doing?"

"I'm not afraid," says Sara as if trying to drown out what happened at Mrs. Ellsworth's house with questions about what happened when she watched Mrs. Ellsworth get struck by lightning at the top of these stairs while standing here with Mrs. Ellsworth's husband – not knowing what else to say, Sara asks him: "Why aren't you afraid?"

"Who told you I was afraid?" A young man looks at Sara and feels like fear has knocked at his door suddenly, making him feel frightened as if something dangerous had just knocked at his door while he was sleeping, making him feel scared because it seems a curse has been unleashed upon him as if he were under some sort of devilish spell that now makes him fear everything around him; a curse that makes him realize everyone around him knows something more than he does – may be even worse than what they know about themselves: "Who told you I was afraid?"

"I saw you," Sara says looking back at him while shaking her head slowly with disbelief: "I saw you." She shakes her head slowly trying to clear the fog that has taken over her life by blocking out everything else except for what happened here with Mrs. Ellsworth and what she watched happen with such unbelievable Ness. "I saw you." She shakes her head slowly again as if trying to shake off fear as it tries to take over everything she thinks and does; "I saw you," she repeats shaking her head again, trying to shake off fear as much as possible while holding onto two wrenches in case something bad happens and they need them against fear itself – she feels fear knocking at her door sometimes – makes her feel frightened as if someone's coming soon because it knocks on doors when people are about to die or may die soon; knocks on doors when people are going to die or may die soon – knocks on doors when people are going to die or may die soon...

"Who told you I was afraid?" The young man looks back at Sara shaking his head slowly with disbelief: "Who told you I was afraid?" He looks down at the wrenches in his hands, wondering why anyone would buy wrenches near a crime scene like this one. He should buy wrenches elsewhere: make sure the sales clerk doesn't notice the wrenches he bought from somewhere else because he's not supposed to know about these wrenches he just purchased – he knows too much already – may be even worse than what he knows about himself; may be even worse than what he knows about strangers around him – may be even worse than what he knows about themselves – may be even worse than what they know about strangers around them – may be even worse than what they know about themselves...

"They said..." Sara shakes her head slowly but firmly as if trying not to cave in completely under the pressure of unbelievable Ness... "they said you were afraid." A young man shakes his head slowly as if looking for an answer that may come with more questions that will lead him into a deep pit of despair.

"I was afraid of what I could do if you died."

"You had to save me, right?" The boy asks as if he were a child.

"Yes." The boy says with a smile.

"So why are you here?" Sara asks with tears in her eyes.

"My father told me to tell you something." The boy says and stares straight ahead with his head cocked slightly to the right. He seems lost in thought as if he was trying to recall what his father had said. "He said he didn't want you to die."

Sara cries. "Why did you bring me here?"

The young man smiles as if he were a child again, "I love you."

"Get out of here!" Sara says as she grabs the boy by his shirt and tries to pull him out of the room, but it's no use. He seems to be rooted in place. She screams as loud as she can, but he doesn't budge. "Get out of here!" She screams again and again, and again, but he doesn't move. She tries to pull him out, but it's no use. He is locked in place like he was a statue inside the door.

"You must listen to me, Sara." The boy says, "You must do what he said..."

Sara listens as if her life depends on it and that this will be the thing that will save her life and that of the young man in her arms.

Sara wakes up in a white room with white walls and white floors. The room appears to be lit by moonlight. It's not a good feeling to be somewhere you don't know or haven't been before. A young man stands at the door watching Sara. She doesn't recognize him.

"My name is Sam." He says with an earnest smile as if he were willing Sara to believe him. She looks at him carefully to see if this is real or just some figment of her imagination. "You must listen to me." Sam says again in an urgent tone as if he's willing her to believe him. "You must do what I say."

"Why?" Sara asks, "Why are you here?"

"Because I love you." Sam says as if he were speaking slowly so that she could understand what he was saying.

"Who are you?" Sara asks and tries to push him away as if she was trying to push him out of the room, but she can't move him, or the room doesn't respond to the motion. She tries again and again but no response comes to her motion or words. He appears to be rooted in place like he was a statue in her hand when she tried to pull him from the room at the asylum.

"Who are you?" She asks again as if this time she might get an answer.

"I'm your husband." Sam says with an earnest smile as if he were telling her something important about herself that she already knew. "I'm your husband." He says with an earnest smile as if he were speaking slowly so she could understand what he was saying. "I'm your husband." He repeats as if he was speaking slowly so she could understand what he was saying.

"What are you talking about?" Sara asks and pushes him away from her as hard as she can, but it's no use. He's rooted in place like he was a statue in her hand. She looks at him carefully as if trying to recall what she already knew about herself that Sam was trying to tell her. "You're not my husband." She says to him, but all he does is smile at her and shake his head no... no... no... no... no... no... No... no... no... No... "No!" Sara screams at the top of her lungs, but all he does is smile at her and shake his head no...

The nurse walks in with a clipboard in her hand and points at Sara's chart with a pencil in her hand. "Are you all, right?" The nurse asks, "You've been screaming for a long time."

"Yes..." Sara says, "I'm fine."

ONE?

"Your husband called us and asked us to check on you because you wouldn't stop screaming for a while." The nurse pulls out a chair from the table next to Sara and sits down on it with her knees together and hands folded over the backrest of the chair like she was about to pray or make a wish or whatever it might be women do instead of praying when they want something badly enough that they aren't sure they can get it on their own because maybe their prayers won't be answered or maybe it's not their turn or maybe God doesn't answer everyone's prayers the same way or maybe God only answers prayers that are sincere or maybe God only answers prayers with an 'amen,' or maybe God only answers prayers like an alarm clock, or maybe God doesn't answer prayers at all, or maybe God doesn't answer anyone's prayers ever because it's all up to Him anyway, so fuck it! And then she closes her eyes and counts on her fingers until she comes up with an answer that will make sense for someone who is not in her immediate family or friend circle, "And then your husband called us back." She says as if she had an answer that would make sense for someone who didn't know Sara, had never heard of Sara and couldn't possibly know why this woman would have caused such a commotion in the hospital, but the only thing the nurse had was an answer that made perfect sense for herself because it made sense for someone else who was not Sara, not Sara's immediate family members or friends or maybe even the people who work here because they can see how hard Sara is trying to make sense of a situation that has gone completely crazed with unbelievable Ness. And then she opens her eyes and looks at Sara as if asking permission for her own personal answer, "And I told him I would check on you." The nurse smiles weakly at Sara as if she were trying to reassure herself that she made the right decision and that it made sense for someone else because it made perfect sense for someone else who was not Sara Harrison or Sara's immediate family members or friends or maybe even the people who work here because they can see how hard Sara is trying to make sense of a situation that has gone completely crazed with unbelievable Ness. "I was in a hallway with ghost" Sara says between gasps of air after almost passing out from exhaustion from screaming herself into pain… "ghosts…" And then there's nothing but silence as if ghosts didn't exist or ghosts couldn't come out of closets and share their unbelievable Ness with people who wouldn't believe them even though ghosts can be just as scary as unbelievable Ness itself because unbelievable Ness has a way of making ghosts seem real when unbelievable Ness has a way of making ghosts seem like they don't exist… And then there's nothing but silence… And then there's another scream as loud as a train coming down the tracks directly toward you at full speed and then there's nothing but silence as ghosts. Sara Henry closes her eyes hard and tries to force herself back into sleep, but it's no use. She must figure out what is real and what is unbelievable Ness. She must solve this murder before she falls apart completely and becomes someone else entirely different than who she is now or who she ever thought herself to be before this happened because when unbelievable Ness strikes again, will she be able to tell which one is real? Or will unbelievable Ness win again? And then there's nothing but silence…

Sara Henry lies face down on her bed in a hospital bed looking up at a ceiling painted white with thin slits for panels of light to shine through onto white walls that are devoid of other colors except for one deep burgundy-brown piece of artwork on one wall near the ceiling. The painting has an old-fashioned feel about it with just a hint of Gothic horror like a picture of someone being hung upside down from a tree by their ankles or two men holding each other while standing on each other's shoulders while having their throats slit by someone wearing a top hat like they were on their way down Main Street in Salem, Massachusetts during Halloween night 1985 instead of in a hospital room in Chicago, Illinois on another November morning somewhere between late September and early October 1984 (assuming Halloween night is Halloween night). "Am I being attorney?" A ghost asks from behind Sara as if this is where ghosts come to talk when they'd rather not talk face-to-face with people who don't believe in ghosts. And then there's nothing but silence as ghosts don't exist or ghosts don't talk— or maybe ghosts are just figments of unbelievable Ness? "Am I being attorney?" A ghost asks again somewhere else in the hospital room as if this is where ghosts come to talk when they'd rather talk face-to-face with someone who wouldn't believe them even though ghosts can be just as scary as unbelievable Ness itself because unbelievable Ness has a way of making ghosts seem real when unbelievable Ness has a way of making ghosts seem like they don't exist… And then there's nothing but silence…

The Doctor walks in with another clipboard in hand and points at Sara's chart with a pencil in his hand. "You've been screaming for several hours," The Doctor says, barely able to look at Sara as he speaks because he knows how hard it is for people not to believe ghosts exist when they see them or hear them speak face-to-face like they would any other person. "Are you all, right?" He asks again as if he had an answer for why there are ghosts everywhere in the hospital where they shouldn't be; where ghosts have no business being because hospitals are supposed to be places where people go when they get sick or because they don't get sick at all; because hospitals are supposed to be places where people go when they're hurt instead of dead… And then he closes his eyes tightly until his hands are nearly touching his temples and he feels some sense of relief that the answers will come soon because he can see how hard it is for doctors like him who must believe in ghosts as well as unbelievable Ness because unbelievable Ness makes dead bodies come alive; unbelievable Ness makes doctors like him think that dead bodies are somehow coming back to life because unbelievable Ness has a way of making dead bodies seem like they're walking around when they're really just walking around on top of themselves instead of walking around on solid ground like they were always supposed to be walking on solid ground before someone cut them down from the trees; unbelievable Ness has a way of making dead bodies move when they shouldn't be able to move; unbelievable Ness makes dead bodies talk when dead bodies should be quiet because dead bodies can't talk… And then he opens his eyes and looks at Sara as if asking permission for his own personal answer, "And then we found you unconscious."

He says as if he had an answer that would make sense for someone who isn't Sara, wasn't her doctor friend Dr. Miller who works here like everyone else, hadn't heard about Sam Harrison or what happened here between Sam and Sara until now, had never met Sam Harrison before today or any other day, didn't know Sara from Adam; didn't know Sam from Eve; didn't know Sam from Adam's wife; didn't know Sam was married or Eve was married; didn't know Sara had any family or friends; didn't know Sara had any friends; didn't know Sara had any relatives; didn't know Sara had any brothers or sisters; didn't know Sara had any brothers or sisters; The nurse comes in with another clipboard in hand and points at Sara's chart with a pencil in her hand.

"Are you all, right?" The nurse asks again as if she had an answer that would make sense for someone who doesn't know Sara well enough to see how hard she is trying to make sense of unbelievable Ness. And then there's nothing but silence as there must have been something else, he could have told her right after he said he wouldn't let anyone die without finding out if it was their time to go.

The Doctor looks over his shoulder at Sam Harrison who sits on the edge of a chair near the bedside table, eating cookies while making no attempt at being part of the conversation like he was reading papers or books or magazines that were stacked on the table next to him instead of cookies. He waits for the Doctor to finish his sentence before speaking. "Yes," The Doctor says. "You were unconscious for a few hours." The Doctor points at the clipboard in his hand. "You've been unconscious since we discovered you." He says as if he had an answer that would make sense for someone who is not Sam Harrison sitting here next to Sara, wasn't her doctor friend Dr. Miller who works here like everyone else; hadn't heard about Sam Harrison or what happened here between Sam and Sara until now; We are going to keep you for a couple of days so we can make sure you're all right." The Doctor says as if he had an answer that would make sense for someone who'd rather hear it from Sam Harrison rather than from him or Dr. Miller whose answers might just make everything worse and lead them into unbelievable Ness instead of trying to convince everyone that unbelievable Ness doesn't exist even though unbelievable Ness has a way of making things like dead bodies seem like they're alive when someone turns on a light switch; unbelievable Ness has a way of making dead bodies move when dead bodies should be quiet because dead bodies can't talk.

"I'm trying my best," The Doctor says sarcastically as if he was only pretending, he was going to help Sam Harrison figure out how to make things better instead of letting them happen the way they happened. "I'm doing the best I can."

"Then you should have done better," Sam Harrison says between bites of cookie, "because you suck."

The Doctor sighs heavily and looks down at his clipboard with his hands folded together on top. "I'm sure you feel differently," he says without looking up at Sam. "You're obviously not going to let us treat you unless we promise we'll do better next time so we'd better find out what happened as soon as possible." The Doctor looks back over his shoulder at Sam and adds, "Because if we don't find out who did this, we'll never be able to treat you."

The Doctor looks at Sam with eyes full of questions, "What happened?" He asks as if he could see how hard it was for everyone involved. "It happened again, didn't it? Like it happened last time?" He asks as if he had an answer for why this might happen again. He looks over his shoulder at Sara who looks back up at him with eyes that are filled with questions too.

Sam Harrison stands up abruptly from his chair and steps toward the door, "There's no need for this kind of thing here. I've got my own doctors now."

"You'll stay here," The Doctor says as if he knew what would happen next. "We need to figure out what happened here before we can treat you or anyone else."

"No," Sam Harrison says between bites of cookie and another loud sigh.

"We've got your papers," The Doctor says as if these papers would somehow convince Sam Harrison to stay. "We've got your insurance information…"

"Payment has already been made," Sam says while chewing on cookie. "That hotel manager called me to say where I'd turned up after being murdered."

"I've got insurance information…"

"Payment has been made," Sam says again between bites. He stands motionless with his hands behind his back waiting for something else to happen as if he can stand quietly without doing anything else until someone else does something else. "I'm sure you've called the police." He adds as if he's done that too many times before and knows what will happen next which worries him because he's sure police are going to come asking questions about why Sam Harrison was murdered by someone dressed as an old-fashioned mime while being chased by beast that might have been real… But then he takes another bite of cookie and thinks again about how everyone is getting killed by clowns wearing top hats—or clowns wearing top hats that are really demons— rather than clowns dressed like clowns because clowns don't dress up like clowns and demons do… And then there's nothing but silence as demons don't exist and clowns don't wear top hats unless clowns have demon heads…

The Doctor points at Sam with his clipboard as if trying to make Sam understand that clowns were never supposed to be clowns, clowns were always supposed to be demons wearing clown suits; clowns were always supposed to be demons disguised as clowns, but clowns certainly aren't wearing clown suits anymore now that demons are disguised as clowns too… And then there's nothing but silence…

"I don't want these clowns

"This never happened"

Sam Harrison takes one last bite of cookie, stands up straight in front of the door with his hands behind his back as if telling everyone that clowns aren't clowns, clowns are demons wearing clown suits, and clowns aren't wearing clown suits anymore except where clowns might wear demon heads disguised as clown heads in place of demon horns; clowns wear demon heads in place of demon horns now that clowns are demons disguised as demons disguised as clowns; clowns wear demon heads in place of demon horns when clowns were always supposed to be demons wearing clown suits disguised as clown suits… And then there's nothing but silence.

The nurse walks into the room. "Mr. Harrison?" She asks Sam Harrison who is ready for her no matter what she might say next.

"I'm leaving," he says without looking up as if the answer will make sense no matter what she might say next no matter how much she tries to convince him otherwise. Then he sighs deeply, shakes his head once almost too heavy for his shoulders to hold up under the weight of such a heavy sigh, looks down at the clipboard in his hand, and says, "I'm leaving." Then he looks up and adds, "And thanks."

"For what?" The nurse asks as if she didn't know what he was talking about and couldn't care less about whether she'd done anything for him or not. But then she turns around and walks out of the room with her clipboard in hand rather than do anything more about it, like perhaps ask Sam Harrison why he felt it necessary to leave before the ambulance arrived, or why he was carrying a clipboard when he'd had a chance to call an ambulance himself while he was waiting for someone else to call one for him. She hoped that one day she'd figure out why Sam Harrison did everything the way he did no matter what she did or said… But then she walked out of the room without asking any questions because she was sure she wasn't going to figure it out soon enough to do any good; she was sure she wasn't going to figure out why Sam Harrison did everything the way he did until after he left this place and then she'd never know anything more about him until she saw him again sometime in the future… And then there was nothing but silence as she headed straight for the elevator; this time with her clipboard in hand so she could do something useful with it instead of leaving it on a bed. The took Sara upstairs where they both waited for another ambulance rather than making their way down to the ambulance bay alone when it arrived because they both knew they'd have nothing more to say or do once they got there except wait for someone else to get here and take over where they left off; they both knew they were done waiting for something else to happen when there weren't any more questions left for them to ask each other because they'd already asked each other everything they might possibly want to know about each other; so they waited for another ambulance instead because it'd be more efficient than waiting for one that might never arrive in time… And then there was silence…

"Why did you leave me here?" Sara asks in a small voice after Sam Harrison had left her alone in the room with Dr. Miller who must figure out what happened before anyone else could figure out why things turned out like they did—even though no one really wants to know why they turned out like they did because they'd rather just forget about them and move past them—but then there's no choice when you have an ancient curse at hand…

"I'm sorry I couldn't do more," Dr. Miller says apologetically as if she had known it all along that things would end up this way and she could have done something about it but didn't because she was too busy doing other things that might come in handy later on; Dr. Miller looks over her shoulder at Sam Harrison who is standing in the hallway outside, watching them from outside the closed door, so Dr. Miller can know that Sam knows everything about her anyhow; Dr. Miller looks back at Sara and adds, "But I've got nothing more to tell you." She adds before turning back around with her clipboard in hand; "I've got a report here I need to fill out before we can let you leave." Dr. Miller motions toward the clipboard in her hand and adds, "And we're going to need a signed release from your insurance company before we let you go." "NO!" Sara says in a small voice as if this is worse than anything that has happened, the dreams, the ghost, the crimes. Is this real?

Sara stares at Dr. Miller who stares back at her.

"How long have you had these hallucinations" ask Dr. miller?

Sara looks down at her hands; her hands shake and tremble due to nerves and fear; tears well up in her eyes and try to escape through her eyelashes but not quite making it through; tears are always more likely to escape through an eyelash than through a tear duct—and if they don't escape through an eyelash they spill over the outside of the eyelid until someone sees them there rather than where they should be escaping from—and then all eyes are on the tears that can't escape from where they should be escaping from because of how hard Sara is shaking... And then there's nothing but silence as tears won't escape without someone looking at them; tears won't spill over an eyelid without someone seeing them first... But tears are impossible when you're afraid of someone looking at you because you can't help thinking about how everyone is watching you instead of how you might help them see through things like tears... And then there's nothing but silence as tears won't spill over an eyelid without someone looking at them and seeing them when tears won't spill over an eyelash without someone seeing them... And then there's nothing but silence as everyone looks away from each other because tears are impossible without someone looking at you first; tears can't escape where they should escape from when you're afraid someone is going to see them because tears can only escape when someone looks at them first... And then there's nothing but silence except for the sound of your own thoughts as you stare into your own eyes wondering what everyone else is thinking about you— and how everyone is looking at you rather than how you might help them understand tears or anything else...

Dr. Miller looks down at her clipboard, holds it firmly in one hand while trying to figure out all the forms to be filled in before making a notation on one of them with her fountain pen, which isn't doing much good because it hasn't been working properly lately no matter how hard she tries to fill in some kind of form with it; Dr. Miller tries shaking it free from its holster just like she does during thunderstorms but it doesn't work very well when raindrops are pelting down on your head while thunder booms outside the hospital room; raindrops are pelting down on Dr. Miller's head now too, dripping onto her shoulders and neck as if trying to make up for all the rain that hit Dr. Miller's clipboard instead of the meeting room where Dr. Miller was supposed to have filled out paperwork before she met with Sara Harrison instead of after as a result of being chased by an ancient curse that might have been real but wasn't anymore now that rain was pelting down on Dr. Miller's head instead of rain hitting it where she stood waiting for another ambulance to arrive alongside Sam Harrison; Dr. Miller shakes her fountain pen free from its holster again rather than turn around and ask Sam Harrison what he wanted with a fountain pen since he wasn't using it anyhow; raindrops pelting down on your head are hard enough when you're standing still waiting for someone else to get off the elevator so you can go up there and get your turn with it when rain pelts down on you while you're standing still waiting for someone else to get off so you can go up there and get your turn with it… Rain pelts down on Dr. Miller's head because rain is falling on someone else's head; just like rain pelted down on Sara Harrison's head when rain pelted down on Dr. Miller's head instead of pouring down on him just where he stood waiting for an ambulance that never came because it had already arrived…

TWO?

Rain pelts down on Dr. Miller's head as if trying to make up for rain pelting down on someone else's head; rain pelts down on Dr. Miller's head so hard from all directions that sometimes it seems as if rain might be falling off somewhere else instead of falling where it should be; rain pelts down on Dr. Miller's head so hard from all directions that some water drips off into her hair and stains her hair black when it doesn't drip off completely into her eyes instead of dripping onto her shoulders instead of dripping onto your own head if you've stood still long enough waiting for someone else to get off the elevator so you can go upstairs; rain pelts down on shoulders so hard that raindrops sting rather than drip when they don't fall off completely into your eyes or your ears where they belong—and some people can only hear other people when they're listening instead of making noise all the time like Ms. Henry does—and even though Rain Man is supposed to be a movie about an autistic savant who can count cards better than anyone else but not understand himself or anyone else most of the time, Rain Man would have been just a movie without all the rain pelting down on Rain Man because Rain Man didn't understand his own thoughts or any other people's thoughts either—rain pelted down hard enough onto Rain Man so he didn't understand where his own thoughts were coming from until he started hearing voices telling him that he couldn't hear them because he was hearing voices that weren't his own—rain pelts down hard everywhere these days but just doesn't seem to make much sense no matter where it falls because everybody's different and has different ways of doing things—rain pelts down hard on everything like it ought to fall everywhere because it suits all people equally, even if not everybody likes rain or knows how to do anything about it when rain pelts down hard onto their heads when they're standing still waiting for someone else to get off the elevator while Dr. Miller waits downstairs for rain to stop pelting down on her head so she doesn't have to look at anyone else anymore because everyone feels like they're always watching her stare into her own eyes wondering what everyone else is thinking about her instead of helping her look away from herself... Rain pelts down hard everywhere and no one knows what any of it means because everyone's different enough that rain pours down everywhere but we can all agree that it pours down too hard in some places while too little pours down in others so rain pelts down on everyone but no one seems to know why or what meaning might lie behind any of it... Rain falls everywhere these days except where it ought to fall most of the time; too much rain pelts down on some people while too little pours down on others, but rain is falling somewhere every day, anyway; rain pours down everywhere including on people who've stood still long enough waiting for someone else to get off the elevator so they can go upstairs after being chased by an ancient curse that turned out not to be an ancient curse anymore after all.

Sara just moved into a new apartment deep in the woods near the lake. She's got the creepy old house to herself, except for the ghosts of two former residents. When she meets a handsome doctor at the hospital, she decides to share her new home with him. But when she finds a dead body in her home, Sara realizes she has a murderer to catch before he strikes again. Weight...she wakes up in her bed in the hospital. A nurse walks in, to give her medication.

"Miss, you are not in your apartment."

"I know that" Sara said through an amused smirk. "I was just trying to convince myself that I was awake."

Sara struggled to keep her eyes open as the nurse smiled at her. "Yes, it would be nice if you were awake. We are in the middle of a siege here in the hospital. You wouldn't want to miss that, I'm sure."

"I'm sure I wouldn't want to miss that," Sara said, grinning at the nurse. "But I'm sorry, I can't help you."

The nurse looked surprised and disappointed and then sighed, "Yes, I understand. You need to rest."

"Yes," Sara said, nodding her head as she rubbed her eyes and smiled again. "I do need rest."

Sara stood at the door with her back against the wall. She clutched the pistol in her hand like a suicide pill. She was about to meet Sara's killer—the man who had murdered Sara's family and caused all this insanity. She was scared but determined to find out who killed her family and then commit suicide with this pistol.

Sara was transported to the island of Tibet where she must figure out what is real and what is a figment of her imagination. With sixty-odd monks at her disposal, she must solve the case.

Sara struggles with reality and her vivid imagination. With an ancient curse at hand, will she solve the case?

"I'm going to find out who killed my family and then end this suffering," Sara said, looking down at her hands that were shaking with nervous energy. "It can't get any worse than this."

"It can," said Jay as he came into the room holding his own pistol in his hand. "And it can get much worse that doing nothing."

Sara looked up at him sharply and then looked around as Jay closed the door behind him and said, "We need to talk."

"I don't think so," Sara said as he came closer and pushed his pistol into her chest. "I know what you want—to kill me."

Jay didn't say anything—just stared at Sara with his eyes glistening with unshed tears as he gently ran his finger over the trigger guard of his pistol. "You don't have to do this," he said softly as he looked away from Sara and then back at her with a teary-eyed look of resolve on his face. "I'm here if you want me."

"I don't want you," Sara said as she looked away from him again. "You're dead."

"Not for much longer," Jay said softly as he slowly approached her. He stood behind Sara and stared down at her—not touching her yet but seeming ready to pounce if she made any moves toward the pistol in her hand. "We can work this out."

"What do you think I've been doing?" Sara asked Jay sharply as she looked up at him through teary eyes. "Trying desperately to work it out on my own? I can't stop this madness because I don't know what set it off in the first place."

Jay stood behind Sara as she faced away from him—not touching her yet but seeming ready to pounce if she made any moves toward the pistol in her hand. He just stared at Sara with his eyes glistening with unshed tears as he gently ran his finger over the trigger guard of his pistol. "You don't have to do this," he said softly as he looked away from Sara and then back at her with a teary-eyed look of resolve on his face. "I'm here if you want me."

THREE?

As time passed, Sara learned that Jay had almost died on that same morning she had found him in his apartment in Seattle—almost dying from having taken poison which he had been trying to ingest for years—ever since his wife had died from cancer seven years earlier. Jay had been hopelessly depressed after that until he met Sara in the hospital—and fell hopelessly in love with her. But now he was dead—and Sara was left alone with only memories of him—and a terrible curse that seemed to be expanding like an octopus from fire to fire as it moved into three states—and now even reached Georgia and Maine with its fiery tentacles reaching even farther as it stretched across America.

"Sara, are you going to take me to the bathroom or are we going to talk about what happened last night?" Beckett asked.

Sara turned to Beckett as he stood in the doorway of her room holding a tray of coffee and breakfast. He set it down on her desk and looked down at her. It was almost noon, and she needed some sleep, but she couldn't shut her brain off. The last two nights had been hell for Sara. She had been transported to her friend Beckett's house and told he had murdered his wife. It was only recently that she figured out the truth – Beckett was not a murderer. It was all in her head – it was a figment of her imagination that she had been dealing with since she was a child.

Sara had gone through life struggling with the unbelievability of her life. She was very strong in her faith and believed it all happened for a reason. She was also thankful it hadn't happened sooner as she wouldn't have been ready for the responsibility of being a detective. She had grown up with a vivid imagination but after enduring what she had, she couldn't believe something like that wasn't real.

A knock sounded at the door. Sara rushed over and answered it. It was a woman in scrubs who placed a clipboard on the desk and smiled at Sara.

"Hello, Sara Solis, my name is Dr. Janice Berry, I am the doctor assigned to see you while you are here. I need to go over your symptoms and then we will go over some questions I have about your past with mental health issues," Dr. Berry said in a very professional voice.

"Okay, what are we talking about first?" Sara asked instead of asking the doctor what questions she had as she wasn't sure if Dr. Berry knew anything about her past with mental health issues.

"We will start with your symptoms, please tell me how you feel before I ask you any questions," Dr. Berry said in a professional tone as well.

"Fine, I feel like I have this weight on my chest, like I can't breathe – it feels like there are bricks on my chest, it feels heavy but not like they are crushing my bones but more like they are weighing me down and I can't move – it hurts to breathe but I can't stop breathing so I keep breathing anyway. I feel like there's something in my throat choking me but it isn't there, I feel like someone is in my room with me but can't find them – I feel like there's someone in my head and they are trying to control me but they don't make sense when I try to think about them so they don't make sense when I try to talk about them, I feel like someone is trying to break into my body through my heart but I can feel every beat so I know they're not getting in there."

Dr. Berry looked down at her clipboard and took notes as Sara spoke, making sure not to look at Sara as she spoke as to not influence her answers by staring at her eyes or body language.

"Okay, that sounds about right for the symptoms of anxiety disorder – anxiety is a very common disorder – anxiety disorder is when people have feelings of worry or fear that don't seem reasonable, and which lead them to worry about things in the future or other things that haven't happened yet and aren't likely to happen. Anxiety disorder is different from being scared – fear is a normal response to danger or threats of danger but anxiety disorder isn't so simple – it's actually a personality disorder where people have such strong feelings of anxiety that they are unable to function properly in society because they can't control their thoughts or feelings of worry or fear," Dr. Berry said in a professional tone as she wrote in her clipboard as well.

"What do we do if we don't know what we're talking about?" Sara asked quickly as she felt more than heard her heart beating faster with anxiety at the thought of someone controlling her thoughts without her knowing it.

"Most people suffering from anxiety disorder have a very hard time thinking clearly so sometimes they get confused when talking about these symptoms – we need to make sure we understand each other – we need to focus on your feelings, not your thoughts – you need to tell me how you feel with your feelings as we talk," Dr. Berry said in a professional tone as well but with a little more laughter in her voice than Dr. Berry had shown during their conversation so far.

"But I see things, I feel them, someone is dead" Sara said in frustration – you need to tell me how you feel," Dr. Berry said calmly as if she hadn't heard any of this before.

Sara sighed as she realized Dr. Berry wasn't going to understand unless she showed her how she felt with words instead of seeing or hearing them as those were all signs of anxiety disorder –

"I am dead" she said aloud as she felt like someone died inside her head, all the pain and suffering that had happened over the years began to seep out of her pores as the tears began to flow from her eyes and down her cheeks – all in an instant Sara was overwhelmed by the sheer pain and anguish inside her head as pain unlike any she had felt before consumed her entire body until she couldn't hold back the tears any longer – all around her was darkness with no sound except for her sad heart beating inside her chest – suddenly Sara felt something hard pressed against her chest – no one was there – no one could be there without being able to see or hear you, right? Then why would it be pressing against me? Wasn't it impossible for my eyes or ears to be closed?

"The dreams" The voice said suddenly in Sara's head, "The dreams." The voice sounded familiar – Sara looked up at the doctor who was still trying not to look at her and write in her clipboard because she knew whatever Sara saw or heard was only part of the illness – all those years ago when Sara was eight years old, before she even knew what anxiety disorder was, she had told Beckett everything that happened in the dreams as if they were real events that had happened to someone else – it was all so clear now; Naomi would wake from those dreams with nightmares so severe that she would scream and cry until finally Beckett would pick up Naomi and hold her until she fell asleep again – Naomi would be too young to be aware of who had been killed or where they died but Sara knew that because Naomi was so young when those dreams began that the only thing that prevented them from being nightmares were because Naomi could talk about them without becoming hysterical.

The pain suddenly stopped when Sara realized Dr. Berry was looking at her in horror and confusion and was trying not to ask questions as she looked down at her clipboard instead –

"I'm sorry Dr. Berry," Sara said quickly as she got up from her chair and rushed out of the room as fast as she could without running – when she came back downstairs Beckett had left and Emma was nowhere in sight so Sara decided to take a walk around the asylum grounds until Emma came back or midnight rolled around so that Sara could sneak out of here without anyone suspecting anything weird was going on.

Sara was dead serious about getting out of this place but for now she needed some alone time as well as some answers – so when Emma came back with food for lunch Sara didn't say anything about going for a walk; instead Sara pretended to be asleep on the sofa for two hours until Emma came back with Beckett for lunch – Beckett had been working late so he didn't have time for dinner last night – Emma sat next to Sara on the sofa while Beckett took his place on his usual chair when he came home from work.

"How are you feeling today? Are you feeling better?" Emma asked as she handed Sara a plate loaded with food that smelled delicious.

"I feel great! And no more headaches! Thank goodness!

The dead feel no pain...

"Oh, good, I was worried about you, Sara, I know how much you hate doctors, but we need to get your blood pressure checked and we need to check your heart rate and temperature and a few other things, just to make sure we covered everything, okay?"

Sara nodded as she ate as if she hadn't heard a word Emma said as she concentrated on eating as quickly as possible, as if she was afraid that if she let her guard down, someone might take advantage of her and steal her food –

"So, Sara, how do you feel about having a visitor tonight? We need to talk about some things as soon as possible as we need to figure out what we should do with you," Beckett said as he reached across the table and put his hand gently on hers.

"Who's coming over? Is it a man or woman?" Sara asked.

"It's a woman – she needs to speak with you about some important information that may affect you – it shouldn't be long, maybe thirty minutes or less – I hope you feel up to it, Sara," Beckett said.

"Why don't you go ahead and eat your lunch and then I'll come upstairs with you, and we can talk about it together," Sara suggested.

"That sounds like a plan – I want you to stay with me, Sara. I don't trust myself not to do something stupid if I leave you alone with her. You need to know what she has to say, and I want to be there for you when it happens," Beckett said.

Sara looked at him with concern as she thought of what he meant by doing something stupid. She had seen the look on his face when he talked about the woman and the way he acted when she was here the first time. She had never seen him act like that before, ever. He had always been so calm and collected. She knew he loved her, but she also knew there was something different about him since the day she met him, as if something had changed in him and she wasn't sure what that change had been.

"You know what? Let's go upstairs right now, I'll call her, and she can meet us there as soon as she gets here. It's almost noon so she should be here soon, if she doesn't show up in the next five minutes or so, we will wait ten minutes and then we will leave, okay? If I feel like I can't handle this, I promise I won't hesitate to tell her to leave, I just need to talk to her. I can feel her power – I don't know what it is but I can feel it – I don't like it – I don't like her at all, I don't like what she did to me, I don't like how I feel when I see her, I don't like how I feel when I think about her – I don't like her at all – I don't like the way I feel when I think about her, I don't like the way I feel when I think about her, I don't like the way I feel when I think about her, I don't like the way I feel when I think about her," Sara whispered as she repeated the words over and over again as she walked up the stairs to her bedroom.

"Sara, are you okay?" Emma asked as Sara stepped into her room and slammed the door behind herself.

"She's coming – we need to hurry!" Sara said with a trembling voice.

"What's wrong with you? What happened in there? Did you hear voices or see things? Tell me what happened in there, please, Sara," Emma pleaded with her sister as she followed Sara into the room.

"I don't know – I don't know – I don't know – I don't know..." Sara said in a panic as she tried to calm down.

"Tell me what happened, Sara. Please."

"I don't know. I don't know what she wants from me, I don't know what she sees when she looks at me, I don't know what she feels when she thinks about me – I don't know what she does when she touches me, I don't know why she hates me so much, I don't know why she is so angry at me, I don't know why she is so jealous of you, I don't know why she can't stop hating me, I don't know why she can't forgive me for something I didn't do, I don't know why she can't love me the way I deserve to be loved, I don't know why she doesn't understand that I don't know what I did to make her hate me so much, I don't know why she doesn't understand that I don't understand her – I don't

The moment Sara stepped through the front doors of the asylum, she felt the presence of someone watching her from somewhere nearby – she looked around and saw nothing unusual as she made her way to the office where the woman waited for her.

"Hello, Sara," the woman said as she stood up and walked toward Sara. "Are you ready for our visit? I hope you're hungry because I brought you some lunch."

Sara looked at the woman and noticed that she was wearing the same black dress and red shoes as the last time she had been here, but she didn't recognize the woman – Sara had no idea who she was or why she hated her so much. As far as Sara knew, she had never done anything to the woman, yet the woman was so intent on making sure Sara understood that she was not welcome in her world.

"No thank you, I'm not hungry. Can we talk?" Sara asked.

"Yes, we can talk. But first, let me introduce myself. My name is Dr. Berry and I'm the psychiatrist assigned to you by the court. This is my assistant Dr. Beckett Berry," The woman said as she motioned to Beckett who was standing behind her.

"Dr. Berry," Beckett said, shaking her hand firmly. "I've heard a lot about you from Sara."

"Good. Then I assume you know who I am – if not, then you must not have read any of the reports I sent to the courts about your sister."

"I haven't received any reports from you," Beckett said.

"Then I guess you didn't miss them. Anyway, I wanted to make sure that everyone understands that this meeting between us is strictly confidential. I will explain everything once we are alone, but I need to make sure that both of you understand that this is an official interview under oath – so whatever happens in this room stays in this room, understood?"

"Of course, Dr. Berry," Beckett replied.

"Very well, let's get started then, shall we? Sara, do you remember what happened after you were arrested?"

Sara nodded as she remembered everything perfectly as she had been waiting for this moment for months now.

"Okay, well, I want you to listen carefully as this is important – I need you to tell me exactly what happened on the night of April 13th when you were released from prison. Don't leave anything out, even if it seems insignificant. Just tell me everything as if you were telling me to another person sitting across from you in a coffee shop – just talk to me, Sara, and I'll take it from there."

Sara nodded and began to tell the doctor about how she had been released from jail and how she had gone straight to her apartment and found a message on her answering machine, and how she had listened to the message and how she had been so happy to hear his voice.

"And how long ago was this? How many days have passed since you heard the message?"

Sara thought for a second and then realized she had no idea how long it had been since she had heard David's voice. She had been so focused on trying to figure out what she could do to help him that she hadn't given much thought to time.

"About two weeks – maybe three, maybe four, maybe five – I don't really know – maybe six, maybe seven, maybe eight. It's hard to keep track of time when I don't know what day or date it is. I don't know – maybe a week or so, I don't know. I don't know what day it is most of the time anyway. I don't know – I don't know – I don't know – I don't know. I don't know. I don't know..."

"Okay, Sara, slow down. Take your time and try to answer the question as best you can. Remember that this is a legal interview and that you are being recorded, so please be careful what you say. And Sara – I know you don't like this woman, but you need to remember that she is only doing her job and that she is just trying to help you, so be nice to her and don't be rude. Okay?"

"Okay. Yes, Dr. Berry. Sorry. I just don't like her. She makes me uncomfortable; she doesn't understand me – she doesn't understand what I'm going through. She hates me – she hates me –

she hates me – she hates

"You need to slow down, Sara, and think before you speak. You can't say everything you're thinking – you must choose which thoughts are relevant and which ones aren't. We can't afford to lose any information because you can't seem to focus. Slow down and think before you talk, Sara."

"Sorry, Dr. Berry, I don't mean to be rude – I'm just so confused, and I feel like you don't understand me, that's all. I know she hates me – I don't know why she hates me so much though. Why is she so madding at me? I didn't do anything wrong. I didn't do anything wrong – I didn't do anything wrong – I didn't do anything wrong – I didn't do anything wrong..."

"Stop saying that! Stop repeating yourself. Try again, Sara. What did you do wrong?"

"I didn't do anything wrong," Sara repeated in a panic.

"Right, okay. Now tell me what happened after you got home from the police station."

"After I got home from the police station, I went straight to my room and called David – he answered the phone right away and I told him what had happened, and then he said he was coming over. He came in and we talked for hours. That was the happiest day of my life. I felt safe with him – I felt comfortable around him for the first time in my entire life. We laughed and joked together and then he kissed me for the first time ever – it was the most amazing kiss I'd ever experienced in my whole life. It was like something inside me had come alive. When he left, I cried – I couldn't stop crying because I missed him so much. And then I slept for three days straight. I don't know how long I slept. I don't know how long it was. I don't know – I don't know – I don't know – I don't know – I don't know – I don't

know – I don't know – I don't know – I don't know – I don't know – I
don't know – I don't know – I don't know – I don't know – I don't
know – I don't know – I don't know – I don't know – I don't know – I
don't know – I don't know – I don't know

"Okay, Sara, calm down and try to answer the question. Do you remember anything else after you were released from jail?"

"Yes, Dr. Berry. After I was released from jail, I went to the police station and reported the rape – that's when they took me back into custody and put me in a cell. The next morning, I was taken to see the detective who had interviewed me at the hospital, and he told me that I wasn't allowed to leave town until after the trial and that I needed to report to my probation officer once a month while I was on probation. And then I saw my lawyer – she was nice – she explained everything to me, and she helped me fill out the forms. And then she gave me this paper and told me I had to sign it, but I didn't understand what it meant. So, I asked her what it said, and she told me that I agreed not to talk about what happened between me and David until the trial. She said if I spoke about it before then, the charges would go up and she wouldn't be able to protect me anymore. And then she said she couldn't help me anymore because she was leaving town for a few months to study law in Boston. She promised to call me once she got settled in her new place and then she hugged me and walked out of the office. I didn't know what to do – I was so scared and confused. I didn't know what to do. I was alone again. I called David on my cell phone and begged him to come get me, but he refused. He said I had to wait for him to come pick me up. I was so scared and confused and alone. I didn't know what to do. I didn't know where to go. I didn't know what to do. I didn't know what to do. I didn't know what to do. I didn't know what to do. I didn't know what to do. I didn't know what to do. I didn't know what to do. I didn't know what to do. I didn't know what to do. I didn't know what to do. I didn't know what to do. I didn't know what to do. I didn't know what to do. I didn't know what to do. I didn't know what to do. I didn't know what to do. I didn't know what to do."

"Sara, you need to calm down. Calm down. Breathe, Sara. You need to breathe. Take deep breaths, Sara. In and out, in and out. You need to relax and try to calm down. You need to stay focused. Try to remember the rest of what happened after you were released from the police station. Tell me what happened after you were released from the police station. Where were you living when you were released from jail?"

"I was staying with my friend, Alison, in Southie, but she moved away, so I was homeless for a while. Then I found an apartment in Roxbury, but I lost it when I couldn't pay the rent. And then I stayed with a friend in Dorchester and then I was evicted from there too. I've been sleeping in shelters for the last couple of weeks. I don't have anywhere else to live – I don't have anyone to turn to. I don't know what to do – I don't know what to do – I don't know what to do – I don't know what to do – I don't know what to do – I don't know what to do – I don't know what to do – I don't know what to do – I don't know what to do – I don't know what to do – I don't know what to do – I don't know what to do – I don't know what to do – I don't know what to do – I don't know what to do – I don't know what to do – I don't know what to do – I don't know what to do – I don't know what to do – I don't.."

"Okay, Sara, that's enough for today. Thank you, Sara, for answering the questions as best you can. We'll continue tomorrow morning at 9:00 a.m., okay? And Sara, you need to remember that you are under oath and that you are being recorded, so please be careful what you say. Okay?"

"Okay. Good-bye, Dr. Berry."

"Good-bye, Sara. Good night."

The door closed behind Sara and the detective looked at the other two people in the room.

"Dr. Berry, thank you for coming down here and helping us out. I know this isn't easy for you and that you don't want to be involved in this case, but we appreciate your willingness to help. And I also want to thank you for agreeing to meet with Sara one more time – I know she's having trouble remembering things and we really need to find out what happened before she was arrested. I know you don't like Sara very much – I know she's made some outrageous accusations against you – but I hope you will try to keep an open mind and give her a chance. She needs help – she has problems – she's hurting – she's confused – she's lost – she's angry – she's scared – she feels helpless – she doesn't know what to do – she's desperate – she feels hopeless – she wants someone to believe her – she wants to be believed. And maybe if we work together, we can help her – maybe we can help her get through this – maybe we can help her heal. Maybe we can save her life. Please, Dr. Berry, try to understand what she's going through. You need to listen to her. If you don't hear what she says, you won't understand what she's going through. Listen to her, Dr. Berry, and try to understand what she's telling you. She knows what happened – I know she does. She knows exactly what happened. But she doesn't know how to explain it. Help her figure out how to explain it. Give her a chance. Don't judge her – don't accuse her of lying or making things up. Just let her tell the story the way she sees fit. Let her tell the truth the only way she knows how. I promise you, Dr. Berry if you just give her a chance, she might surprise you."

"Thank you, Detective. Thank you for asking me to come down here. I really appreciate your kindness and consideration. I wish I could do more than just sit here and watch you interview Sara, but I don't think I should be involved in this investigation any further. I have no choice but to trust you to do whatever you think is right. And I really do think you're doing the right thing by giving Sara another opportunity to tell the story the way she wants to tell the story. I'm sure she understands the importance of keeping her mouth shut until the trial and I know you understand why she needs to do that. This is important – this is the most important case you've ever worked on – I know you must feel pressure from the prosecutor and everyone else to decide now – but please, Dr. Berry, try to understand what this means to Sara. She may seem like a little girl who doesn't know anything and who makes up stories because she thinks they sound good. But she's not a child – she's a young woman who has gone through a traumatic experience and she's trying to deal with it as best she can. She needs help – she needs support – she needs someone to believe her – she needs someone to care – she needs someone to love her – she needs someone to understand her – she needs a friend – she needs a family – she needs a home – she needs a job – she needs a purpose – she needs to know that someone cares about her – she needs to know that she matters – she needs to know that she has value and worth – she needs to know that she deserves better – she needs to know that someone loves her. And she needs to be understood. She needs to be heard. She needs to be seen. She needs to be loved. She needs to be safe. She needs to be protected. She needs to be free. She needs to be forgiven. She needs to be held. She needs to be comforted. She needs to be cherished. She needs to be valued. She needs to be respected. She needs to be trusted. She needs to know that she can count on others to help her when she needs it the most. I want you to take good care of Sara – I want you to do what you need to do to protect her and to protect yourself – I want you to do the right thing. And I hope you have the courage to do what you know is right. I know you have a conscience and that you have a moral compass and that you always do what you think is right – I know you do – but sometimes, even the right thing isn't easy. It isn't easy for me to watch this happen – it isn't easy for me to watch Sara – it isn't easy for me to see her hurt – it isn't easy for me to hear her cry – it isn't easy for me to see her suffer – it isn't easy for me to hear her scream – it isn't easy for me to know what she's going through – it isn't easy for me to know what she's feeling. And it isn't easy for me to know what she's going to say next. And it isn't easy for me to watch her cry – and it isn't easy for me to hear her scream – but I know you're doing the right thing – I know you have a conscience, Dr. Berry – I know you have a moral compass – I know you always do what you think is right – I know you have the courage to do what you know is right. So, I know you have the courage to do what you know is right. I know you have the courage to do the right thing. I know you have the courage to do what you know is right.

"Detective, I think we should go over some ground rules. The first rule is that Sara isn't allowed to leave the room without permission. And I mean it. If you let Sara walk out of this room, you will never speak to her again – and I don't want to have to tell you that. You understand what I'm saying – I know you do – so don't let Sara out of the room. You can lock the door – you can put a chair in front of the door – you can tape the door shut – you can chain the door – you can put a guard dog in here with her. Whatever you need to do, just don't let Sara out of the room. Do you understand what I'm saying? Don't let Sara leave this room – or else."

"Yes, Dr. Berry, I understand. And I agree that Sara shouldn't leave the room until we finish our interviews. We'll talk about that later."

"Okay, Detective, we have three more hours before we must wrap this up. What do you want to do first?"

"I want to ask Sara where she was living when she was released from jail. Did you find out where she was living when she was released from jail?"

"No, I didn't find out where she was living when she was released from jail. I asked her that question yesterday – the day before yesterday, actually – and she told me she was staying with friends in Southie and that she had nowhere to live after she left them, so she went back to Dorchester. I know I saw her with a friend in Dorchester a couple of days ago – I think he gave her a ride to the bus stop – and I know she took a bus to Southie – I think she got off in Dorchester – but I don't know what she did after she got there. I know she was staying at a shelter in Dorchester. I don't know which one. I don't know if she's still there or not. I don't know if she's sleeping in a shelter or if she's renting a place or if she's crashing with a friend. I don't know what she's doing – I don't know where she is – I don't know what she's been doing – I don't know how she's getting food and I don't know if she's eating.

"Detective, you said you wanted to ask Sara something else – you mentioned you needed to ask her some questions about the night she was arrested. Can we start with that? How long has it been since you interviewed her last time? Has it been a week? Or two weeks? Or longer? I need to check my calendar. Have you talked to her since then? Is she okay? Does she need help? Has she been crying? Has she been screaming? Has she been yelling? Has she been shaking? Has she been pacing around? Has she been sitting quietly? Has she been talking to herself? Has she been talking to me? Has she been acting crazy? Has she been acting normal? Has she been acting like she usually acts?

"Sara, can you remember what happened the night you were arrested? You know, what happened in the shelter – what happened on the bus – what happened in Dorchester – what happened in Southie – what happened in the police station – what happened in court – what happened during your arraignment – what happened in the courtroom – what happened in the holding cell – what happened in the interrogation room – what happened in the interview room – what happened in the interview room again – what happened in the interview room again – what happened in the interview room again – what happened in the interview room again – what happened in the interview room again. And I want you to tell me exactly how many times you were raped, and I don't mean in a vague, general way – I want you to tell me exactly how many times.

"NO! NO!"

"Okay, Sara, calm down. Calm down. It's all right. Just take a deep breath. Okay, Sara, I'm going to give you a chance to answer the question. Are you ready for another round of questions? Yes or no."

"No. No. No. "

"You don't feel pain when you are dead."

END